10 THINGS
I CAN SEE
FROM HERE

ALSO BY CARRIE MAC

Wildfire

10 THINGS I CAN SEE FROM HERE

CARRIE MAC

EMBER

Text copyright © 2017 by Carrie Mac
Cover art copyright © 2020 by Sar Duvall

All rights reserved. Published in the United States by Ember, an imprint of
Random House Children's Books, a division of Penguin Random House LLC,
New York. Originally published in hardcover in the United States by Alfred
A. Knopf Books for Young Readers, an imprint of Random House Children's
Books, a division of Penguin Random House LLC, New York, in 2017.

Ember and the E colophon are registered trademarks of
Penguin Random House LLC.

Visit us on the Web! GetUnderlined.com

Educators and librarians, for a variety of teaching tools, visit us at
RHTeachersLibrarians.com

The Library of Congress has cataloged the hardcover edition
of this work as follows:
Names: Mac, Carrie, author.
Title: 10 things I can see from here / Carrie Mac.
Other titles: Ten things I can see from here
Description: First edition. | New York : Alfred A. Knopf, [2017] | Summary:
Maeve, a sufferer of severe anxiety, moves in with her recovering alcoholic
father and her very pregnant stepmother and falls for a girl who
is not afraid of anything.
Identifiers: LCCN 2015046690 (print) | LCCN 2016024868 (ebook) |
ISBN 978-0-399-55625-8 (trade) | ISBN 978-0-399-55626-5 (lib. bdg.) |
ISBN 978-0-399-55627-2 (ebook) | Subjects: | CYAC: Anxiety disorders—
Fiction. | Fathers and daughters—Fiction. | Love—Fiction. | Lesbians—Fiction.
Classification: LCC PZ7.M111845 Aam 2017 (print) | LCC PZ7.M111845 (ebook) |
DDC [Fic]—dc23

ISBN 978-0-399-55628-9 (pbk.)

Printed in the United States of America

First Ember Edition 2020

For Esmé, with love and love and love

Oh you delicate heart.
Sometimes it feels hard to live.
— Hawksley Workman

Stupid Things People Say

You are not your anxiety.
Don't worry your pretty little head.
It doesn't matter.
Don't exaggerate.
Why get upset about something so small?
Just put it out of your mind.
All good things. All good things.
Ignore it.
Let go and let God.
Think positive.
Move on.
Get back on the horse.
What's the matter, honey?
If you visualize good things, good things will happen.
Manifest destiny, Maeve. Make it happen.
You be the master of your life. Take charge!

Don't underestimate the power of positive thinking.
Keep calm and carry on.
Don't worry; be happy.
What is there to worry about?

All the things.

Being Hit by a Train

I could easily admit that it was nicer and faster to take the train from Seattle to Vancouver. But the last time I took the train, a woman threw herself in front of it just outside Everett. None of us had any idea what was happening while the train dragged the woman along until it finally screeched to a stop, spreading out her brains and entrails on the tracks. Which I knew because I researched these things. Her name was Carol Epperly. Thirty-six years old. Mother of two. Struggled with depression. No kidding. I read her obituary (of course), and it sounded like someone really angry wrote it. I'm guessing it was her husband, and if so, he was pissed. His name was Doug. He had a lawn-mower repair shop in Everett. *She struggled against the depression, but clearly not hard enough.* That's what it said. And at the end: *Never mind a charity; please consider donating to a fund for the boys, who will only know life without their mother from now on.*

I would not be taking the train again anytime soon. That

one moment was all I talked about with my therapist for almost three months straight. Nancy actually told me that it was time to move on. She had never said that before. That was like admitting defeat. That was like saying I had stumped her. She had never once offered a platitude before that.

So I took the bus, which I'd taken often enough to admit that it wasn't the worst thing, even if it was slower. Mom drove me from Port Townsend to Seattle. I started crying before the stop sign at the bottom of our road.

"Oh, Maeve, sweetheart." She drove with her hand on my knee. "It will be okay. I know it."

There wasn't anything for me to say. I'd already said everything. So I cried. The mountain of tissues in my lap grew tall and teetering. I was still crying as Mom looked for a parking spot at the bus station.

I cried while she bought my ticket. I cried and cried and cried when it was time to go.

"I love you," Mom said.

"I love you." But I didn't say goodbye, and neither did she. We never said goodbye when I went to Dad's. It was our superstition. Or mine, and she just played along. No goodbyes. Especially this time.

Nancy had told me that I should take the train again so that I would realize that people don't throw themselves in front of trains all that often. This is your horse, Nancy said. Get back on it, Maeve. Besides, Nancy told me, it was far more likely that my bus would get into a terrible crash than that another person would commit suicide by train. Which was not helpful in the least. But I just couldn't do it. I just could not get back on the train. Not yet. Not after Carol Epperly.

You could always walk, Dad had said. Which would be

4

kind of epic. It could be a whole coming-of-age spiritual experience happening right along the I-5. Imagine that.

I didn't want to do the train, or the bus, or walk. And there was no excuse to fly, considering how close it was, for one thing, and the litany of possible air disasters, for another. I just wanted to stay home. But that was not an option either. You're too nervous, Mom said. Imagine being alone at night. You'd just sit there trembling and anxious, which you do even when I'm home. And it was true. I worried and worried and worried until I was sick. But she was going to Haiti, so I was going to Dad's. For six months.

The wait at the border took extra long because some guy didn't have the right papers, and they took him into a room and questioned him for half an hour while the rest of the passengers just stood around wondering what the hell was going on and I chewed my nails and thought too hard. Were they interrogating him? Was he a terrorist? Or wanted by the FBI?

He looked pretty sheepish when he came out. Everybody else looked royally annoyed. Not me, though. I'd made the mistake of surfing the internet to distract myself from the potential serial killer in the little room, and because I couldn't help myself, I'd looked up *Greyhound bus deaths*.

Decapitation

Decapitation!

On a Greyhound bus!

July 30, 2008. Vince Li sat down beside Tim McLean, who barely noticed him before he fell back to sleep. A little while later, Li pulled out a knife and stabbed him. Screaming, blood everywhere, the other passengers scrambling over each other to get out. While everybody else fled for safety, Li sawed off Tim's head. Then he paraded the severed head up and down the aisle, and when he was done, he went back to his seat and sliced off some of Tim's flesh and ate it.

And so that was what I worried about all the way from the border to the bus station in Vancouver. I watched my fellow passengers very carefully. Especially the guy who'd been held at the border for so long. He had shifty eyes. And he kept his suitcase with him, instead of putting it under the bus. He could've had a hunting knife in there. There were no laws against crossing the border with a hunting knife. Or a box cutter. Or a blowtorch. Or a hammer. A person could do a lot of damage with a hammer. There have been an inordinate number of murders involving hammers.

Finally the bus wheezed into the station, and everyone filed out with their heads still attached to their bodies, including me. When I stepped off the bus, I heard violin music playing. It sounded familiar, and while I waited for my suitcase, I listened carefully, trying to ignore all the other city noise. Focus on the music, Maeve. Focus on the music.

Which worked for about a minute.

Because who was to say that I hadn't escaped decapitation only to fall victim to some other gruesome death? Awful things happened all the time in big cities. The statistics backed me up on this one. Big crimes happened in cities. People got away with things in big cities. So many people, and so much busyness, and everyone bustling around doing their own thing, and no one knew each other and nobody cared. That was how people got killed. That was how people got *murdered*.

To further boost the likelihood of catastrophe, Vancouver's bus station was located smack-dab in *the worst* neighborhood. Vancouver actually had a task force to deal with the amount of human excrement that ended up on the sidewalks and in the alleys around there. There were more hookers than kids in the neighborhood. At the Ivanhoe Pub across the street, a person could buy a drink, or sex, or stolen cheese or stolen jeans or a stolen car or a stolen child.

I wished that Dad lived in a nice little town like Port Townsend. Actually, I wished he lived in Port Townsend in particular. Not in Vancouver, where fifty-two women had disappeared from this very neighborhood, with the DNA of half of them ending up in the mud and pig shit at a farm just outside the city. The murderer had gone to prison in 2002, but he still scared the crap out of me. Also, I didn't think he'd worked alone. I thought his brother was just as guilty. He was still out there.

This was what happened when I had to wait. My mind raced. It got ugly. Fast.

In about the time it took me to eat a bag of chips, I could go from thinking about what song to listen to next to imagining what it would be like to have my head sawed off by a madman.

Tim McLean had no idea it was coming. He was just sitting there, asleep, and then one slice, and then pain and blood and screaming—

I stopped in my tracks so abruptly that my suitcase bumped me from behind. My heart galloped in place. I had to find Dad before it got worse.

Inside the bus station were two rows of wooden benches where Dad usually waited for me. He wasn't there. I checked the coffee shop. The newsstand. The little kiosk that sold international phone cards. I checked the parking lot.

It was getting dark, and the lights of the city sparkled. The air was warm. It stank of piss and exhaust and hot city garbage. And the music again. A girl at the edge of the park, her eyes closed as she played. She slid the bow across the strings as if the violin weren't there at all. I recognized the song. Coldplay. "Clocks." She was good. And she was cute. Very

8

cute. A man cut in front of her, hunched over, his face twisted as he argued with someone who no one else could see. The girl didn't even look up. She just kept playing.

If I had been a different person—say, a normal one—I'd have gone over there and listened and put some money in her violin case and asked an interesting question. Make an observation, Nancy would say. And then ask a specific question. But there was too much out there. Cars and buses and taxis. Horns honking. A siren. The SkyTrain slicing along overhead. A one-legged bum begging for change, two girls in stilettos arguing, a guy puking against the wall, and an old woman organizing her shopping cart. And the small, grassy park where that girl had just barely escaped being shoved into a cargo van the week before.

The music stopped. I looked across to the park. She was having a drink of water, her head tipped back. Flip-flops, tan legs, cargo shorts, a leather belt with stars stamped into it, a black T-shirt tight around muscular, tanned arms, a silver necklace with a ruby pendant, a jumble of cuffs and friendship bracelets on one wrist, short auburn hair.

Dad's truck wasn't out there.

How about some more dead women? In that same park there were fourteen pink granite benches arranged in a circle. A memorial to the girls who'd been murdered in their college classroom by a wacko with a gun and a manifesto. One bench for each girl.

The girl started playing again, and I thought, If I were her, I'd pick a better place. A safer place.

Murder happens.

The panic attack slammed into me from the front, as if I were being gored by a bull. I backed against the wall and

9

put my hands on my knees. I took ten deep breaths. Ten really good ones, Nancy said. Nice and deep and even.

I was drenched with sweat. My hands were clammy. It felt like the bull was sitting on my chest. I couldn't breathe. I wanted to go back inside. I wanted to be where it was safer. Inside, with air conditioning and shops and people wearing clean clothes and talking to other real people.

Honking horns. Screeching tires. Sirens coming from all directions. The air thinned and got hotter and the lights were too bright and the dark was too heavy and I still couldn't breathe. I couldn't be out there for one more second, but I couldn't move, either. Focus on the violin music. Soft and sweet and totally out of place amongst the grime and the crazies. The girl with the violin. Look at the girl.

She was playing with her eyes closed *again*. Totally oblivious. Stupid and naive. How many times had someone stolen her busking money right out of her violin case? How many times had she avoided something much worse?

Move, Maeve.

Move.

One foot. The other foot. Through the door. Back inside.

I shivered in the cool air and parked myself on the closest bench. I took out my sketchbook and pencils. Art as therapy, Nancy said. But it wasn't. It was art as survival. It was one of the only things that could calm me down. I sketched the big old clock high up on the wall. I sketched a woman walking by, holding a toddler by the hand.

Dad knew better.

It never went well when I had to wait. Never, ever.

I sketched the garbage can. A fire extinguisher. The guy

behind the counter at the newsstand, until he saw me studying him and gave me the finger.

I called Dad, hoping that maybe for once he would pick up. But no, his phone went straight to voice mail. Maybe he was at an AA or NA meeting. He always turned his phone off at those. I called his house. No answer. I tried Claire. No answer.

I had to pee, but I wasn't going to go. One time I found a pool of blood congealing on the bathroom floor. Another time I found two security guards and six firefighters standing over a woman who was splayed on her back on the floor, and two paramedics on their knees at her side. Just step around, honey, a fireman said. Go ahead.

I tried Dad again. Straight to voice mail.

I texted. *Where are you? Where are you? Where are you?*

And Claire. *Where is Dad?!?!?!*

And Mom, too.

Dad is late. If I disappear into the murky depths of the Downtown Eastside, know that I never wanted to come here and it will be all your fault. Enjoy the guilt.

I started a text to Ruthie. *I'm waiting for my dad at the bus station, and I*

Wait. What was I supposed to say to her?

I was thinking about how fucked up that day was

Delete, delete, delete.

I sent Mom another text instead, but she was on a plane to meet Raymond before leaving for Haiti.

Sorry. I love you. I'm fine. Really. I love you. I miss you. I won't disappear.

No one texted back. Dad had sent about three texts, ever,

in his whole life. Claire always had her phone on vibrate because she couldn't stand any ringtone out of the billion available, which was fine so long as she had her phone in her pocket or could hear it scuttling across a table. Mom was on a plane somewhere over the Rockies, and Ruthie was up in Alaska at a summer camp for science geeks, miles and miles from any cell reception at all, and about as far away from me as she could possibly get.

I could feel my pulse throbbing all the way to my fingertips. Stop it, Maeve. Breathe.

Maybe he would finally come and *I'd* be passed out on the floor. He'd see the security guards and the firefighters and the paramedics standing over *me*.

I needed to go home.

Coming to Vancouver had been a terrible idea.

Gut churning. Heart pounding and pounding and pounding. Fingers tingling as I dug in my backpack for the stupid paper bag that actually worked. I pulled it out and breathed into it, the top bunched in my fist. Three boys strode past in matching jerseys, laughing and pointing. I pulled the bag away.

"It's glue." I held it out, already feeling better. "Want some?"

They shook their heads, laughing.

I checked my phone with trembling fingers. No messages.

My throat was so dry that it hurt to swallow. I dug for some change to go buy a drink and felt something bunched up at the bottom of my bag. I pulled it out. It was the silk scarf Mom always wore. It was tied into a loose knot, with something inside. I brought it to my face and inhaled. Roses and geraniums and Mom. Now I could slow my breathing down. Inhale. Exhale. Now I could try to calm down.

I could be home by lunchtime the next day. And Mom would be there, even if she wasn't. Her clothes in the closet, the way the furniture was arranged, the quilt she'd made me, with the stars in all colors and sizes, the garden and all the vegetables that we'd planted, growing and growing, as if they were ignoring the fact that she was gone. As if that were possible.

Being Home Alone

Dan offered to keep an eye on me while Mom inoculated babies and swooned over her new geriatric boyfriend at his clinic in Haiti. He said he'd love to, in fact, and other than his shifts at the hospital, he was a homebody just like me. Sometimes he spent the entire day in his fuzzy one-piece rainbow-unicorn pajamas playing the guitar and drinking coffee. His house was only five minutes through the woods, or ten minutes along the road. He'd even offered to have me over for dinner every night. He was a really good cook. Plus he was a nurse. So he could handle things.

"Maeve, no." Was that pity in her eyes? Disappointment? I couldn't tell. It was *no*, that much was for sure. "Not this time."

And I knew why. Because the first and last time I had been left alone had been a complete disaster.

"What if I stayed at Dan's place the whole time?"

"And you'd crawl into his bed in the middle of the night instead of mine?"

We both laughed. This was not as weird as it sounded. Dan liked big hairy men who looked about as gay as your stereotypical hockey player. And I liked girls.

Or, one girl so far. For not quite a month.

I untied Mom's scarf and a card fell out. On the front was a picture of us that Dan had taken the fall before. We were sitting on the porch with our pumpkin harvest all around us. Seventeen pumpkins, lined up on the steps.

I love you, pumpkin. Don't worry. Xoxoxo, Mom.

It was like she had texted me back. Sort of.

I wound the scarf around my wrist and then unwound it. Wound it around again. Unwound it. I would not cry in the bus station. I would not.

I should've taken out my sketchbook again. I should've drawn the old woman eating a sandwich all by herself, or the man mopping the floor, his sleeves rolled up, his back stooped. I should've drawn one line and then another and another until it built something apart from my worries. But instead I just wound and unwound the scarf until my wrist felt hot.

Distracted Drivers

I didn't want to call Dad again. If he was on his way, he shouldn't pick up. He knew better, but he still talked on his cell while he drove, even though I told him not to. Every year over three thousand people died because of distracted driving. And that was just in the States. Not as bad as the one death every forty-eight minutes from drunk driving, but bad enough. Dad had already been lucky in that category once. Once that I knew of, anyway.

Or what if he was looking for his phone when I called and it was in his bag and he leaned over too far and lost control? What if he was in the hospital on life support and they couldn't find a number to call because his cell phone had been destroyed in the crash and he'd forgotten his wallet at home again? What if he was all alone, with a tube down his throat and machines keeping him alive? Or maybe not. It could be even worse than that. What if he was dead? *Dead.*

What if he was *dead* and I was sitting there waiting for a dead person who would never be coming?

An accident at work. He'd fallen off a catwalk on set and broken his neck and they just hadn't called Claire yet.

William "Billy" Glover, aged 41, died tragically in a workplace accident. He leaves behind his wife, Claire; his daughter, Maeve; his two young sons, Corbin and Owen; and his unborn child due in September. After a successful career as a musician with the Railway Kings, Billy became a scenic artist in the film industry, working on major films such as—

Would it mention Mom? That would require a rewrite:

William "Billy" Glover, aged 41, died tragically—

Stop it, stop it, stop it.

He was not dead. He was late. People were late all the time; it didn't mean that they were dead.

And then, as if to prove it, he hollered my name from the door.

"Maeve! Let's go!" He had no idea that I was composing his obituary. "I'm double-parked, kiddo." I barely had time to stand before he grabbed me in a bear hug and crushed the breath out of me. He stood back and took my wrists. The one I'd twisted the scarf around so much still throbbed, hot in his grip. "Look at you, all adult and shit. I just saw you a few months ago. You were, what, three years old?"

"Funny."

"Come on, I don't want to get a ticket." He lugged my suitcase toward the exit. "Want to drive?"

"No. I do not want to drive," I said. "It has wheels."

"What?" he said. "The truck? Of course it does."

"The suitcase," I said, fuming. "It has wheels. You can pull it."

"It's not that heavy."

His truck was parked with two wheels on the sidewalk in a no-stopping zone, right in front of the girl with the violin. She was playing something classical now, and as I came around the front of the truck, she smiled at me.

She smiled at me. But why? What kind of smile was that?

Your dad is an asshole?

Nice parking job?

Serves him right?

"Hey, buddy, hang on," Dad said to the security guard who was writing down his plate number. "There was nowhere else to park."

Or was she just smiling at me in a nice way?

"You're obstructing the pedestrian walkway."

"Come on, man. Don't write me a ticket." He threw my suitcase into the back of the truck. He rooted in the glove box until he found an old five-dollar bill. "Here, take it." The security guard just shook his head and kept writing. "Asshole," Dad muttered when the guard tucked the ticket under his windshield wiper.

"I've been waiting over an hour, Dad."

"Shit." He grabbed the ticket, crumpled it up, and threw it in the general direction of the security guard.

"I thought you were dead."

"Seriously? An hour?" He opened the driver's-side door. "I thought your bus pulled in five minutes ago. Sure you don't want to drive?"

"The last time I drove, I almost hit a deer."

"But you didn't, right? Deena said you handled it like a pro."

"She didn't say that."

"Okay, no, she didn't." He shrugged. "Still, why not give it another try? Horse, fall, remount."

"I have never ridden a horse in my entire life," I said. "Did you know that almost eighty thousand people end up at the hospital every single year because of horse accidents?"

"It's just an expression."

"Still," I said, "it's not helpful. My bus pulled in an hour ago, Dad. An hour that I have spent worried sick." I got in on the passenger side. I did up my seat belt and crossed my arms. "And just so we're clear, I absolutely do not want to drive in the city. Ever."

He started the truck and bumped off the sidewalk, joining the traffic waiting to get out of the tiny parking lot.

"You didn't answer your phone. A bunch of times."

"No, I didn't."

"How come?" He'd grown a goatee since I'd visited at spring break. It looked good on him. He was wearing sunglasses, even though it was completely dark now. His black hair was artfully shaggy and had a blue streak at the front. He looked like a rock star, except for the paint-splattered jeans and hoodie and boots. "I thought you were lying unconscious in a hospital bed, Dad. Or dead."

"None of the above. All good." He turned up the music.

19

"Jimmie Vaughan. I love this one. Keith Ferguson on the bass. Sure you don't want to drive? Last chance. We can switch places while we wait for these taxis to get out of the way."

"I do not want to drive! I want to know why you—"

"You still a lesbian?"

"What?" I was caught off guard. "As far as I know. Why? Why the hell are you even asking? I want to know why you were so late. AA? NA? Got caught up with a painting and totally zoned out?"

"Easy, beast. Oh, hey, some guy at work asked me if you had a boyfriend, because his kid just moved in with him too and he wondered about setting you up on a blind date. And I told him that you liked girls. But then I figured you might've changed your mind after, you know, after what's-her-name moved away."

Jessica.

Jessica Elena Elliston-Haywood.

"Which is totally okay, by the way—keep us posted. I just thought that chick might've been a one-time thing, you know?"

"Not *chick*. Jessica."

"Jessica, right."

"I still like girls," I said. "It wasn't Jessica-specific. As far as I know."

"Duly noted." He patted my knee. "And how's Ruthie? Still awkward and smart?"

Oh, Ruthie. Of course she was still awkward and smart. And so stupid, too.

"She's fine. Stop changing the subject." I glared at him. "What was so important that you were an hour late?"

"Look, here I am now. Not dead." He rolled down his window, pulled a cigarette from a pack of American Spirits on the dash, and lit it. "It's all good, kiddo."

"You said you were going to quit smoking before the baby comes."

"Go figure, no baby yet. You'll be the first to know."

"Smoking kills almost half a million people every year. And secondhand smoke kills fifty thousand people a year. Dad, that's almost *five times* the population of Port Townsend."

"The baby is due in September." He took two deep pulls on the cigarette before flicking it out the window. He honked as a taxi driver in front of us got out to help with his customer's luggage. "I'll quit by then, boss."

His ears were turning red, which always happened just before he lost his temper. I figured that out when he was driving me to a friend's sixth birthday party. I wouldn't stop pestering him for driving the ten blocks without his seat belt on. I just would not shut up. I kept begging and he kept not doing up his seat belt until we were both screaming at each other, and then he hauled off and slapped me across the face.

His ears were that same color now. Which was why I was not going to tell him about the risk of fires started by tossed cigarettes.

"In the meantime," he said, "don't nag me about it. I get that enough from the twins."

"September isn't that far away." I did the math. "You have eighty-one days."

His ears were fiery red now.

"I know the due date, kiddo. Even if I'm not the one who's pregnant." He turned up the music. Conversation over.

21

"Babies come early all the time," I murmured, but he didn't hear me. Or he was ignoring me.

The last time I'd visited, Corbin had flushed Dad's cigarettes down the toilet. I'd thought it was hilarious, but Dad did not find it funny at all. He yelled at both boys and took eight bucks out of their piggy banks and stormed out in a huff to buy another pack. His ears were pretty red that time too.

"I can hear you thinking." One more taxi in front of us and then we could finally turn out of the lot. "I'm a big boy, Maeve. I'll handle it. Now leave it alone." He pushed his shades up and grinned at me. "It's good to see you. I missed you, kiddo." He pulled me into a headlock and planted a noisy kiss on my forehead. When he let go, I saw her again. The girl with the violin. She was looking at me, her violin in one hand, the bow in her other. She was looking right at me. I smiled, and she smiled back. And then we were driving away. She got smaller and smaller, until I couldn't see her anymore and she was just another girl I would never get to know.

Apartment Buildings

Dad and Claire and my six-year-old brothers lived in a three-story U-shaped complex with a landscaped courtyard in the middle. There were some smaller apartments, but mostly there were apartments with two or three floors with very small footprints, so it was like little blocks stacked on top of one another. Each home—however many bedrooms—had a front door that opened out into the courtyard. There were long, snaking cracks running down the length of the building. The whole complex leaned a little to the west, like it might slide all the way downtown in an earthquake. Dad insisted that it did not lean at all, but whenever I visited, I tried not to look at those cracks.

Dan and I had had an earthquake-kit competition back home. Mine included everything on all the lists, plus things like tampons and antibiotics, layered in a big garbage bin on wheels, but Dan trumped me by putting his kit in a giant rolling toolbox with everything meticulously organized and labeled. I'd had to buy him a dozen doughnuts.

Dad and Claire's earthquake "kit" was a flat of family-size pork and beans, a can opener, and a flat of bottle water.

While Dad fumbled with his keys, I studied the concrete courtyard, thinking I should do a marble test with the boys. We could prove that the building really was leaning. If it was condemned, they'd have to move somewhere safer.

"Maeve?" Mrs. Patel popped out of her place next door and held up a plate of samosas as a greeting. "You're here!"

"Mrs. Patel!" I gave her a hug.

"The plate. The plate!" She laughed, righting it before the samosas could slip off. She was wearing the same pink cardigan she always wore over her sari. There was a hole at one elbow now, and a dark stain beside the top button. "I hear we have you for six months?" Behind her and up the stairs, a commercial blared on her TV. *Gets out all grass stains! Guaranteed!*

"Six whole months." I took the plate.

"What's that?" Mrs. Patel cupped a hand to her ear.

"Six months!" I took a bite of one. "So good. I'm so hungry."

"Don't talk with your mouth full." She gave my wrist a playful slap. "Wait a minute. I have tamarind sauce." She disappeared and was back a moment later with a little dish.

"Come over tomorrow." She gave me a peck on the cheek. "I will deal the cards for rummy."

"I will. Thank you."

The last time I'd visited, I'd told Mrs. Patel that she needed a new sweater because she wore it in all the family photos on her wall, and so it seemed like she never aged past when she started wearing it. Mrs. Patel laughed and laughed. I like that very much, she said. Imagine, never getting old! This is my magic sweater, then. My fountain-of-youth sweater. I shall never stop wearing it. Not ever.

Used Furniture

When I'd visited in the spring, Claire announced a "family project" the moment I arrived.

"It'll be so much fun!" She handed out painting smocks. "We're all going to help turn the closet in the downstairs studio into 'Maeve's Space.'"

Usually they managed to clear just enough of the floor for the blow-up bed each time I came, but in the spring they—meaning Claire—had organized everything so that the room was tidy for the first time ever. Dad did commissioned portraits when he wasn't working on sets, so his easels and paints now lined one wall. Claire made dolls, so her bins of fabric and doll forms and her sewing machine lined the other.

The walk-in closet was empty, the beat-up walls patched and ready for paint. A double bed took up the space in the middle of the room. The twins were jumping on it, the gray cotton surface dappled with nondescript stains. I tasted bile.

"What's that face for?" Dad said. Corbin jumped into his arms. Then Owen. "What's wrong with it?"

"It's *filthy*."

"Claire steam-cleaned it. Both sides."

Nosebleeds, leaked periods, dried semen, vomit, the ghost of farts past, and everything that comes with all of that. Sex and violence and insomnia. Arguments in the middle of the night. Wet dreams. And the bugs.

Just think of the bedbugs.

Vancouver had an actual bedbug registry. You could look up any address and see if there was (or had ever been) a bedbug infestation there. Entire blocks lit up on the website, including several apartment buildings on streets far too close to Dad's place. I'd put in Dad's address once and an alert had popped up. I'd run screaming from the computer and all the way outside, where Claire had found me and explained that it had been isolated, at the other end of the building, and had been dealt with professionally.

Bedbugs are common in East Van, she'd said. As if that made me feel any better.

I knew why bedbugs were common in East Van. Because everyone was sharing their shitty old furniture. Dumped in the alley on moving day. Friendly trades. As seen on Craigslist. You take this couch; I'll buy that chair; need some new clothes; want this extra duvet? I have to get rid of this mattress, but it's still perfectly good. No bedbugs. I promise.

"I'll sleep on the air bed. It's comfortable. I didn't even want a new bed."

"Well, we got you one. And I'm still waiting for some sign of gratitude."

"I can't sleep on it, Dad."

"Maeve."

"Dad."

"Maeve! It's perfectly good."

And then Claire was beside him, a hand on his arm. "What's going on?"

"She won't sleep in the bed. She says it's dirty."

"I cleaned it," Claire said. "Both sides."

"This one looks like *blood*." I pointed.

"Just stains," Dad said. "That doesn't mean that it isn't clean."

"It's really comfortable," Claire said.

"What's wrong?" Corbin said.

"Maeve doesn't like the bed," Dad said.

They started jumping again. "We'll have it!"

"See?" Claire said. "Great springs. Good bones."

Claire made the bed and Dad told me the air bed wasn't available. When it was time to go to sleep and everyone had gone upstairs, I slept on the floor, well away from the dirty mattress. Which was where Dad found me the next morning. With a sigh, he hauled the mattress to the alley and pinned a sign to it: *Perfectly good. Her Highness wants something better. No bedbugs.* And he drew a picture of a scowling princess, which was supposed to be me, I guess. Crown and all.

"I'm sorry, Dad."

Next he brought home a bed from work. An iron bed frame and a brand-new mattress that had only been used for seven hours.

"By one of the three bears," he said. "The big one, I think. He was hardly in it at all."

By *three bears* he meant actors from the TV show he was

28

working on. The story line put a modern spin on fairy tales. A girl moves to a town and strange things happen and then she realizes that she's living in a bizarre parallel world where there are dragons in the supermarket and trolls using the ATM and evil witches who want her dead. It was scarier than it sounds.

"Seven hours?"

"Maybe less," Dad said. "Listen, Maeve. We don't have the money to buy you a new one, and props gave this one to me for a really, really good price."

"How much?"

"Beer."

"Beer?" I waited for him to say more. To explain. "You went into a liquor store?"

His expression shifted.

"Yes, I went into a liquor store." He turned to leave the room. "It's not like there's an alarm at the front door that keeps out certain people."

"Maybe there should be," I said under my breath.

"I'm the parent here. Not you. And I'm in charge of my sobriety. I'm in charge of staying clean. Not you. So mind your own business. And enjoy your new bed." He left, and then returned a moment later to add, "I'm going to build blocks to raise it up. We need to store a few things underneath."

"Sure." I sat on the edge of the new-not-new bed. "Thanks, Dad."

"I almost forgot." He came back into the room and took down a shopping bag from the closet. "Claire bought you this." New sheets, robin's-egg blue, with pillowcases to match. They were as soft as any of Dan's. Dan loved linens. People sleep better on delicious fabrics, he said. Truly.

"They're beautiful." Our sheets at home were so old that I could see the pattern of my mattress through them.

Dad set his hand on my head and kept it there—heavy and warm—for long enough that I started to wonder when the moment would end. But then he lifted his hand away and kissed my head where his hand had been and left the room, closing the door behind him.

"When you come in the summer, to stay, your little room will look amazing."

My little six-month space.

Before I made the bed, I crawled around it on all fours, examining the crevices along the piping—that's where you'll find the bugs—and then I made the bed and pushed it into the empty closet that was going to be my very own, micro-tiny room-not-room. My own space—albeit infinitesimally small—not a blow-up bed that squeaked and creaked and leaked in the middle of the room.

Keep Calm and Carry On

While I was back in Port Townsend, Claire and the boys painted the closet to match the sheets and hung white fairy lights along the ceiling. Claire put up a curtain rod for butter-yellow curtains with tiny white polka dots. She emailed me a picture when she and the boys were done. The subject said, *Look! PRIVACY.* Which was cute, considering the curtains—replacing the bifold doors—were nearly sheer.

Now there was a framed poster at one end: KEEP CALM AND CARRY ON.

As if it were that easy. As if that was all a person ever needed to do. The British government commissioned that poster as war propaganda in World War II. Sure, keep calm, everybody, while your street is bombed and bits of your children end up where your kitchen used to be. Keep calm while Hitler packs all those innocent people and families into train cars and sends them to their deaths. Keep calm as you fight over a tiny ration of sugar and the U-boats blow your husband's ship to smithereens.

I lifted the poster off the hook and leaned it against the wall. I had no intention of looking at that thing every time I was lying in bed. I hated that saying on posters; I hated it on pencil cases; I hated it on mugs and T-shirts and tea towels. I hated all the ways people had changed it. Keep calm and fill in the blank. Even Dan had one. KEEP CALM AND RIDE UNICORNS.

The poster was just as offensive where it was now. I turned it so I couldn't see it, but it was still there, nagging at me. I tried to slide it under the bed, but there was no room because of the boxes and boxes of fabric scraps and tubs and tubes of paint and stacks of blank or abandoned canvases, and rolls of wrapping paper and two different irons, and the ironing board, and a broken easel Dad said he was going to fix, and another easel that he didn't like but used as a spare when he was working on more than two paintings. All of that had been stuffed into the closet before Claire and Dad gave it to me, and now it was stuffed under the bed. They couldn't afford to give me that space, but they did anyway. Which was so generous of them. I could've been on that leaky air bed forever.

If I took down the stupid poster, Claire would notice right away. She'd be hurt, but she'd say that she wasn't.

And it was just a stupid poster.

She didn't mean any harm by it. She wasn't being sarcastic or ironic when she put it up there. She was being sweet and nice and thoughtful and supportive. I did need to keep calm and carry on. I knew that. However, to have a poster ordering me to do it every time I fell asleep or woke up was unbearable. But to hurt Claire's feelings was worse.

I hung it back up, but above my head, so I wouldn't see it unless I made a point of looking at it. I'd tell Claire that I wanted to draw something for the other wall. Maybe even paint a mural. She would be okay with that. She was always saying that I needed to take my art more seriously, because I was talented. You're so talented, Maeve. You have no idea. Just like your dad. You just do, and it comes easily. You have no idea how lucky you are.

Upstairs, I heard my dad walking from the living room to the kitchen and back. And then Joel Plaskett on the stereo. The creak of the couch. Two clunks, which would be him kicking off his boots. He didn't get to listen to his music very often. The twins preferred stuff that Dad referred to as "kiddie-pop barf," which was a little harsh. But he was more entitled to an opinion than most, I figured. Until I was five he'd been a professional musician.

The Railway Kings were almost famous. They filled small stadiums. Their songs got a lot of play on the radio. There were posters and T-shirts and autographed set lists. They had groupies—mostly underage pot-smoking waifs wafting patchouli and hummus, but groupies nonetheless. The Railway Kings had an image: part hobo, part hillbilly, part rock and roll. And it worked. They got people dancing. So much so that they had a "dust-kicker" clause in their contract for all the outdoor festivals they played. The organizers had to spray the ground in front of the stage with water before they started their set; otherwise, Dad said, his throat would be on fire for days after and he'd have to drink gallons of hot lemon juice with honey. As if that was what he was drinking. Sure.

That's how he met Claire—a waif, but not a flake. She waited by the tour bus one night, a warm and starry night, the way he told it, and when Dad saw her through the window, he brought out a bottle of wine and two glasses and they took a walk in the field behind the bus. She never went home, he said, because he was her new home. Claire told a much longer version, but the gist was the same.

One of Dad's ex-bandmates came over for supper once, and when I'd gone to bed, he ribbed them about the night they met.

Come on, did you even make it to the bus that first time, Claire? By my recollection it was backstage.

The details don't matter, Claire said quietly. Either way, it was love at first sight.

Yeah? You were both so shit-faced I bet you could hardly see at all. I bet your nose was full of it, right, Billy? We whooped it up back then, hey? He was laughing, but he was the only one. Good times, right?

And then Dad's voice, low and angry. Some scuffling, and then the door slammed. I never saw that guy again.

Keep calm and carry on.

That fucking poster. It was calling my name even though I wasn't looking at it. I scooted to the edge of the bed and stared at Dad's easel instead. He was painting a pair of dogs: a pug and a German shepherd. They were wearing crowns and had long velvet capes, none of which were in the photo he was working from. I crossed the room for a closer look. The customer's email was tacked to the wall beside the easel. She wanted Queenie and Prince to be painted in full royal attire. I was surprised that Dad would agree to paint something that looked so ridiculous. But there was the estimate, paper-clipped to the photo he was working from. He was charging double what he normally would. That made me smile. It was a shitty painting, and he knew it.

Shelves of paint pots, jars of paintbrushes and gesso, racks of finished paintings and half-finished paintings. Claire's workbench with the sewing machine at one end and a row of clear plastic drawers with bits of cloth all sorted by color. Since I'd been here last, Claire had reorganized the drawers to be a rainbow of colors. Gay pride. Sweet of her. She meant well. She always meant well.

This would be my home for the next six months.

One hundred and eighty-two sleeps. Four thousand three hundred and sixty-eight hours and some change.

And seventy-five days until the first day of school.

Claire had already registered me at Britannia High, the same school that had sent eleven kids to the hospital the year before, because of a suicide pact they were trying to carry out in the senior girls' bathroom with bottles of vodka and pills. The same school where Owen had found a dirty needle at the edge of the soccer field where the boys' junior soccer team practiced. The school in the background of the You-Tube video, the one of the kid getting his face kicked in by four other kids, and a whole bunch of kids crowding around, cheering them on.

Don't think about school.

Mom would be leaving for Haiti in four days.

Ninety-eight hours, to be exact.

I miss you. I can't do this. It hurts. I want to go home. Please don't go.

There was no text back. I held my phone in my hands and waited and waited and waited. I wanted to know I could reach her, even when she was so far away. I wanted to know that she was hearing me. But she wasn't, even though she'd said she would. She was with Raymond, and not thinking about me at all. I was sure.

There would be no keeping calm and carrying on. There would be panic, and reeling backward. Which would be fine if it took me home. All the way home. To my real home in the woods, with the garden all around, and the woodstove. I liked starting the fire on cold mornings. Usually.

Raymond's Penis

He'd come to Port Townsend to visit Dan, his younger brother, as in younger by almost twenty years. All it took was a couple of dinner parties and one bonfire with marshmallows and homemade wine before he invited Mom to join him in Haiti, where his charity had an immunization clinic. The flames reached up hot and orange into the black night, and I laughed. Actually laughed, until I heard my mom tell Raymond that she'd think about it. She poured more wine into his glass and then put her hand on his leg and slid it up just a bit and told him that she'd think about it.

For a moment, in the shadows beside the fire, I thought she was serious. But then Raymond left, and she never mentioned it, because it was a stupid idea. I was in Port Townsend, and so was Mom's job with the town, and her garden, and her friends, and her car, and her house, and all of her life, all in Port Townsend. Not Haiti.

But then Raymond came back a few weeks later, and

Mom went to pick him up at the airport, not Dan. And that was when I started to really worry. They'd been emailing, which I hadn't known about until I checked the computer while Mom was on her way to get him. It started out all nice-to-meet-you, but by the most recent ones he was calling her *sweetheart* and she was calling him *love*, and in the very last email—sent just before Mom got into the car and drove away—she told him that she knew of a little park on the way back. She told him no one ever went there, and that there was a corner of the parking lot that would be perfect for a "proper hello."

He spent eleven nights out of fourteen at our house, so I doubted that he'd come to see Dan at all, really. They weren't going to tell me that he was sleeping over, so the first morning was a surprise. I hadn't slept very well, because I could not get rid of the image of Mom and Raymond going at it in the back of the car, with the seats folded down and that old grimy blanket spread out. So I got up earlier than usual, rather than lie in bed thinking about it. It was cold, so I was kneeling by the woodstove, blowing on the kindling, when I heard a man's cough and looked up to see Raymond padding into the kitchen, entirely nude.

But he didn't see me. I tried to close the stove door as quietly as I could, hoping that he'd just get a glass of water or whatever and go back to Mom's room. But the door creaked, and he heard that and spun around, and I fell back and knocked over the side table by the couch, which sent the ceramic lamp to the floor, where it broke into a million little pieces.

"Maeve!" Raymond grabbed the dish towel and covered

himself. He scurried behind the cover of the kitchen island. "I certainly didn't see you there. Uh, good morning."

"Morning." I stood up, very reluctantly, and then bolted down the hall, hoping that we could just pretend that we hadn't seen each other at all. But then Mom came out of her bedroom, pulling her robe on as she did.

"What's going on?" She saw me, and she saw Raymond, and at first her face went pale. "Well, shit."

"I got up to make you coffee," Raymond said. "I was going to bring it to you before I went back to Dan's."

"You're naked."

"Sorry." Raymond shrugged. "Really sorry."

And then her face turned red and she got mad. "I have a teenage daughter, Raymond!" She steered me back into my room. "This is totally unacceptable, Maeve. I am so sorry. I should've told you that he was staying over. It was a bad idea not to, and I apologize. Give us a minute."

"Gladly." I shut the door and leaned against it, willing myself not to throw up. I'd seen three penises in my life up to that point: my dad's and the twins'. Raymond's made four. I'd been way too close to Raymond's old-man dick, all shriveled and wobbly and with great big sagging balls. It had practically been in my face. But worse than that—as if old-man penises weren't bad enough—I was upset about what his penis being there meant in the first place. My mom was going. And she wasn't just going in order to be helpful. To be charitable. For the greater good. No. She was going. As in, off in the direction of Raymond. Away from me.

. . .

Sometimes I still thought of the car parked in that empty lot.

I knew that park. Mom and I almost always stopped there on the way to Seattle.

Cedar trees swaying above. The little creek with soft loam and giant ferns on either side. The bear-proof garbage cans beside the trail. The outhouses. Sitting on the big rocks and eating salami sandwiches and oranges we'd brought with us and looking at the sky to see who would spot the first eagle. That's what I used to think about that place.

But not after reading that email. When I thought of it, I couldn't make myself think about the other things. The nicer things. I could only imagine Mom and Raymond having sex in the car, like a couple of desperate teenagers fumbling and humping and getting tangled in seat belts and each other. And then, when they were finished and had put their clothes back on, he'd get out and put the used condom in the trash. The bear-proof trash beside the trail. The one I'd put so many orange peels in.

I hated thinking about it. And I never wanted to. But if you imagine something once, it becomes a part of you. This was what made living hard. The fact that life happened all the time, in ways that I fully did not approve of, and then it just came pushing in and I couldn't stop it, and that was how I ended up tossing and turning on a bed in the closet at my dad's house while Mom and Raymond were fast asleep—or worse—in a big bed in his house in some random neighborhood in Chicago.

King Percival

I could go back to the bus station in the morning. It wasn't like anyone would stop me. I could go before anyone else was up. I could go now. I could tell Dad and Claire that I was going for a walk. The letter Mom wrote for the border officials—granting me permission for cross-border travel—was dated for the whole time she'd be in Haiti, just in case. I could call Claire and Dad when I got home. And what would Dad do? Come get me? Force me to come back to Vancouver with him? Or would he let me stay with Dan? If I could convince him? And besides, he quit high school and left home when he was my age, and he was playing with the Railway Kings by the time he was nineteen.

My phone buzzed. A text from Mom.

Deep breath. It's all good. I love you. Xoxo

As if she were reading my mind, all the way from Chicago, where it was the middle of the night and halfway to gone altogether.

That was what I was losing. The person who knew me best. The one person who truly got me. The one who knew how bad it could be for me. The one who helped me leave my room when it all got to be too much and all I wanted to do was lie in bed and stare at the wall. She was the one who'd collected me from the hospital that night when the ambulance came. Oh, Maeve. Sometimes it is just so hard, isn't it?

I wrapped her scarf across my palm. It was almost like she was holding my hand. But no, actually, it wasn't. It wasn't like she was holding my hand at all. It was just her scarf, and me, all alone.

You have no idea, I texted back. *I love you so much.*

And then I was crying. Big, ugly sobs, my shoulders shaking and my nose dripping with snot.

Upstairs, the front door banged open and Dad turned down the music. Claire and the twins were home. I grabbed a tissue and blew my nose. I wiped the tears away.

Steady, Maeve.

I could hear Owen crying, and Corbin hollering, and in the background Claire's singsong voice and Dad's low, reassuring tones, and then a jumble of footsteps coming down the stairs. The twins burst into the room and tackled me on the bed.

"You're here!" Corbin pulled at my arm. "Come on. Dad made baby foxes for Gnomenville. Ten of them. They have magic powers."

"Half of them are King Percival's." Owen handed me one of the gnomes Dad had been carving for years. It fit into the palm of my hand.

"A new one?" Sanded and painted, he had a bushy white beard and angry eyes. His arms were crossed.

"The new king." Owen beamed.

"He won't be for long," Corbin growled. "He made me one too. King Wren is plotting an attack. He'll win, and then he'll be the king again."

"He won't!"

"He will!"

"He won't!"

"He will!"

"Truce!" I pulled them off the bed. "Truce. Let's go eat cookies instead. Then you can commence the peace talks."

"War talks," Corbin said.

"Peace talks!"

"War talks."

"Peace talks!"

"Boys! Enough!"

And just like that, I could breathe again.

And just like that, things were a tiny bit less awful.

And just like that, my mind made room for things like little brothers, and warring gnome kingdoms, and cookies. I gave each of them a kiss on the forehead. Thank you. Thank you. Thank you for being little and loud and bursting with bright, shiny goodness.

Birth

We're having the babies at home, they told me. It will be a beautiful miracle, Maeve. You will be so glad you were there. I was ten—what did I know?

Me, two midwives, a friend taking pictures, Mrs. Patel in the kitchen stirring a pot of chai, Dad and Claire naked in the water up to their chests in the "birth pool" in the middle of the living room. I huddled on the couch not looking, covering my ears every time Claire screamed. When I did muster the courage to look, I saw Claire's vagina—blurry but obvious—under the water. Her vagina bulged between her legs, and then *a head came out.*

That was Corbin, dried off and given to Dad to hold. Claire wanted out of the tub, so the midwives helped her onto the floor, right in front of me. She groaned and rocked back and forth, and then, horror of all horrible things: she shit herself.

"Almost there," the midwife said.

I made a strangled sound.

"Maeve?" Mrs. Patel came out of the kitchen, wiping her hands on a tea towel. "Are you okay?"

"One big push, Claire. There's your baby's head." The midwife's tone suddenly sharpened. "Let's get this baby out fast. There's meconium."

Claire shit herself, and the baby shit himself.

Owen came out, covered in reeking slime. The midwife scrubbed him with a towel. He was blue and limp and tiny.

The room tipped. All I could smell was shit. Everything went blurry, and then black. When I came to, Dad gave me a baby to hold. I'm still not sure who it was. They were both pink and chubby and just fine.

Owen was still a lot smaller than Corbin now. After they updated me on the current political situation in Gnomenville over cookies and milk, Owen followed me back to my room, but he stopped at the door.

"What are you doing now?" he said in his raspy old-man voice.

"Not much." I pulled out my sketchbook and pencils. "Probably drawing. Are you coming in?"

"Mom told us not to barge in like we did when we got home. She says that this is your room, even if it's hers and Dad's too, but that it's yours for now and so we're not allowed to come in unless we're invited."

. . .

What if he'd stayed blue? And then gray? And then dead and cremated and nothing else at all except grief heaped on grief and one little baby where there were supposed to be two?

Now that Claire was pregnant again, there would be another baby who might die. Another baby who might be born with something wrong. Another baby who could die of SIDS, a fall off the bed, leukemia, a horrible chromosomal mix-up, a bookcase toppling over in an earthquake because Dad hadn't gotten around to securing them to the walls, even after living there for eight years.

Terrible things happened at home births. Not just blue babies covered in shit that could get in their lungs and cause pneumonia. Babies' heart rates could drop and the hospital might be too far away. Babies could get stuck. Arrested labor. Stillbirths, failed resuscitations, lawsuits. Grief.

When I looked up home-birth deaths, I found blog after blog by women who'd lost their babies. And they all had pictures of their dead babies. Posed, as if they weren't dead at all. Tiny fingers, perfect little feet. Soft, downy heads, eyes closed as if they were just sleeping. But the photos were almost always in black and white, so you couldn't see that the babies were dusky pale. Dead babies in the crook of their mother's arms. The father beside her, or arms around her, or touching the baby. No one smiled. That was the difference. Or sometimes—very rarely—they did smile. Which was worse.

There were dolls, too. Not like the soft, sweet ones Claire made, but realistic ones, with eyelashes and downy hair. Grieving parents could send in a picture of their dead baby, and a doll maker would make a life-size, weighted baby doll with the exact features of their dead baby. The parents could dress it, hold it, and lay it down in the crib at night.

"Maeve?" Owen was still at the doorway. "Can I sleep with you?"

"Sure," I said. "Come in and tell me a story about King Percival. I need a distraction."

"From what?"

From the fact that you almost died, I thought.

From the fact that not only did Dad and Claire want a home birth again, but they didn't even want a midwife there this time. When they told me in the spring, we were eating poached eggs on toast, which suddenly seemed too disgusting to even look at. Chicken embryos.

Claire beamed at me. How amazing would that be? Just you and the boys. Just family.

Such a trip, Dad said. I'll catch the baby in my own hands. The way it's meant to be.

Hospitals, clean beds, doctors: *that* was the way it was meant to be.

Owen fell asleep while he was telling me about King Percival's plans to storm the Wrens' kingdom.

Claire popped her head through the curtains. "Can I come in?"

"Sure."

"Do you want me to carry him upstairs?" She sat on the edge of the bed.

"No, he can stay."

"Okay," she said. "Tomorrow I want to hear about your trip, and the last weeks of school. I want you to tell me everything."

Not everything.

"Right now we should all get to sleep." She lifted Owen's hand and kissed it. "It's late."

"Claire?"

"Yes?"

"Are you still having a home birth?"

"Maeve—"

"I'm not going to argue with you," I said. "I just wondered if you were still doing it by yourselves."

"Well, your father . . ." She looked a little sad all of a sudden. "He's been working really hard lately. And I don't think he can—well, no. I have midwives."

"Oh."

"That should make you rest easier," she said.

"I'm sorry, I just—"

"You just wanted to know how much to worry."

I nodded.

"Good night, Maeve." She turned at the doorway, her big belly in profile. "Sleep tight."

Haitian earthquakes and decapitated people and Greyhound buses and dead babies and what it must be like to step in front of a speeding train. Why the train? Why didn't she kill herself in a different way? Hanging. Overdose. Carbon-monoxide poisoning. Slitting wrists in a bathtub. Jumping off a cliff, or into a river that was too fast and too cold. Why the train? How did she make that choice? Stop. Stop, Maeve. Focus on the distraction: Owen, one slender arm folded above his head, the other clutching Hibou, his eyes fluttering as he dreamt.

Hibou.

French for owl.

Sometimes things sound so much better in another language.

Worry.

Pain.

Fear.

Inquiéter.

Douleur.

Effrayé.

Maybe

At home in Port Townsend, I woke up to songbirds, the babbling creek, the smells of coffee and woodsmoke.

At Dad's it was crows shrieking, a garbage truck, the boys upstairs hollering, the low hum of the washing machine, a dog barking, Dad's heavy footsteps, the door slamming.

Maybe Mom wouldn't go. Maybe at the last minute she would realize what a dumb old asshole Raymond was, and she'd get on a plane and come home, and then she'd get in her car and come get me, and we could go home and take care of the garden, which was all alone and wondering where we were.

What time is it there? It's not too late. I love you. I love you. Don't go!

Maybe she would get the text and that would be the thing she needed to hear. Maybe she would read those words and come back to me.

My phone rang. "Blackbird," by the Beatles. And there

was her picture filling the screen. I'd taken that the past summer, just before Raymond happened. She stood at the garden gate with a huge basket of tomatoes under one arm.

Only it wasn't her. I could tell right away by the nasally exhale on the other end of the phone.

"Raymond?"

"Your mom is in the shower."

"Why are you calling me on her phone?"

"To let you know that she'll call you back. I know you don't like to worry."

I tasted bile in my throat. "You didn't need to call. I've waited a lot longer than thirty-five seconds to get a text back from her. Especially lately."

"All right, then," he said, his voice chipper. "Just thought I'd let you know."

"Gee. Thanks."

He sighed. "Look, Maeve, your mom—"

"Will call me back," I said as I hung up.

When she called back, she said hello and then dropped the phone.

"Sorry," she said. "Just loading up the car."

To go.

To the airport.

"How is it? How is everybody?" A car door opening, then closing.

"Is he with you?"

"He's locking up the house."

To go.

To the airport.

51

"Come *home*, Mom."

"Six months, Maeve. This is good for you. This is good for everyone."

"At least let me go home." I started to cry. "Let me go home. Don't go."

"I am going to Haiti, Maeve. Just a sec." She covered the phone and said something to Raymond. Then she was back and she was saying, "I love you. I love you. I love you. And you cannot stay at home by yourself. You know that."

"Maybe this time would be different?"

"Six months of different? I love you, Maeve, and I'm going to Haiti, and I need to get off the phone. Raymond says talk to you soon. I love you."

"I love you too."

She was gone, and then going even farther away, and I was bawling. I hurt everywhere. It literally hurt to miss her.

I missed her. I missed home. I missed my bedroom. I missed the garden. I missed picking beans and canning tomatoes. I missed sitting on the steps drinking iced tea with dirt under our fingernails. I missed the little fox with the limp, the one I left food out for sometimes. I missed sitting on the old couch on the covered porch, especially when it rained and the rain filled the gutters and spilled over, and I missed the staccato the rain made on the tin roof. Loud and peaceful at the same time. Sometimes I fell asleep out there, wrapped in my quilt, listening to the rain, and Mom would come home from work, or out from making dinner, and she'd wake me up. She'd shake my shoulder and whisper in my ear, Up, up, little one. Even when I wasn't little anymore.

Maybe terrible things would happen.

In six months, roughly twenty-eight million people would die in the world.

Cancer, murder, speeding trains. Hurricanes, poison, depression, starvation. War, shark attacks, random acts of chaos.

Cholera. The word was as ugly as it sounded. Some people could have it and never know it, but others could lose a liter of bodily fluids in one hour. I'll be drinking bottled water at the clinic, Mom assured me. Not even ice cubes from the tap. We have treated water at home. Don't worry, honey.

Maybe she would die in Haiti.

At her Haitian *home*.

She wasn't letting me stay home based on one night. The night after what happened with Ruthie. I hadn't told Mom, and I didn't intend to either. It was going to be our "test" night, and it had been planned for weeks. If I could do one night, I could try two, and then a week, and then she'd consider letting me stay home while she was in Haiti. I did okay all afternoon, and even through supper. But when it was time to go to bed, the house seemed darker and it was too quiet and my mind kept replaying what had happened in Ruthie's basement bedroom the day before. When I told 911 that I couldn't breathe, they sent two ambulances and a fire truck.

I hated thinking about the day at Ruthie's.

I hated thinking about the day that I spectacularly failed the test.

And this day too. I hated this day.

I hated Raymond for taking her away.

It was all his fault.

Maybe I wished he would die. Maybe it was that bad. A heart attack.

I wished he'd just keel over and die: a stroke, a clot in his lungs, a heart attack. That would be fitting. Dying of a heart attack just as he was falling in love with someone who was neither available nor suitable. Or even appropriate. Served him right.

Maybe not dead, though, because my mom would be so sad.

Maybe just a little heart attack. Just big enough to knock him over and keep him and my mom from going to Haiti.

Not while he was driving to the airport, though, because he might drive off the road and cause an accident with my mother in the car. But maybe as they were checking in. A sudden tightening in the chest, shortness of breath. The airline agent would notice first. Sir? Is something wrong? You look pale. And then my mom. Oh, Raymond, are you okay? Raymond! Somebody call 911!

A trip to the hospital instead of a trip to Haiti.

I could imagine my mother at his bedside, staring at him as he snored in his sleep, thin and sickly in his blue hospital gown, the fluorescent lights buzzing over his bed. She'd sit there and hold his hand and wonder. What had she been thinking? She did not love this man enough to be his nurse. And then she'd get on a plane, and I'd get on a bus, and we'd meet in Seattle, and Dan would drive us all home. Ta-da! The end.

A heart attack? What a terrible thing to wish on a person. I took back the heart attack. I hadn't meant it. Not really. I just wanted Mom to come home. And I wanted her to leave Raymond behind. I didn't want him—or anyone else—to have a heart attack. I was a bad person, to wish something like that on someone. Even if that someone was Raymond. I was a bad person, to think such bitter, dark thoughts.

Distraction

Sometimes distraction could take my mind off the worry, but sometimes it made it worse. Especially if it was Claire's idea. Distraction was Claire's favorite way of dealing with my varying degrees of weird. You just need to keep moving, Maeve. *Move.* Move your body and your brain and use up that nervous energy that clatters around in there, messing you up. Try new things! Meet new people! Get out there, honey. You think too much because you have too much time to think. When I was younger, she'd sign me up for things like circus camp, or kayak trips, or marimba lessons. That's why she tried to teach me how to knit. It's meditative, she said. You zone out and it's just the yarn and the needles and you, making something beautiful.

But I did not work that way. I lasted half the week at circus camp. I was so worried about getting hurt that I actually could not move the required muscles it would take to participate. And furthermore, I was sure that one of the other kids was going to fall to their death, so I could only sit on the bench with my hands covering my face, muttering, "I can't watch. I can't watch. I can't watch." They asked me to leave, and not very nicely, considering I was only eleven. One of the instructors actually said that I was jinxing the whole class. Circus = watching someone fall to their death. Kayaking = drowning. Marimba = failure. Knitting = way too much time to think. Claire didn't sign me up for that kind of thing anymore, but she was always pushing me: get out, go do something, find a friend.

As if.

Drawing worked, sometimes. Sometimes it could lift me out of myself. Sometimes figuring out the lines and curves and shapes of things around me was enough to stop the noise in my head for a while. But usually when the worrying about something stopped, it was because I'd moved on to worrying about something else.

Claire's latest idea of distraction was to send the twins and me to our grandmother's in Gibsons, on the Sunshine Coast, for a few days. We'd be going by ourselves. On a big ferryboat.

What if one of the boys fell overboard?

What if I couldn't find them when it was time to walk off the ferry?

What if there was an engine fire?

What if the ferry couldn't stop and it crashed into the wharf?

What if we got on the wrong ferry?

What if Grandma never came to pick us up?

What if the boys went into the men's bathroom and there was some creep in there?

"Do you let them go into the men's bathroom by themselves?" I asked Claire as she dropped us off at the terminal.

"Sure."

"You don't worry about them in there?"

"She means pedophiles," Corbin said.

"We know about pedophiles," Owen said.

"I'm not worried about pedophiles," Claire stage-whispered with a wink. "The boys know what to do if someone flashes a penis at them in the washroom."

And then there'd be the trip home. Alone.

So, so many things that could go wrong.

A few years before, a man was driving his minivan onto the ferry when the ramp suddenly went up and he drove right over the edge and into the water. He got out because he wasn't wearing his seat belt, but his two children, his wife, and his mother all drowned, buckled securely into their seats. That's why I never wore a seat belt when we drove onto the ferry. And I made everyone else take their seat belts off too. Because it would be way worse to be the only survivor than to die like that. They never protested. Maybe because they secretly agreed with me. Or maybe because it wasn't a big deal to them and they'd rather just do it than have me nag them about it. Which I would. Because I wouldn't want to be the sole survivor of an accident that left them trapped in the van underwater, slowly drowning, looking around through the churned-up murk and thinking they should've done what I said.

This time we were walk-ons, but that just meant different things to worry about. Up in the waiting room I was going through all the things that could go wrong. Malfunctioning ramps. Or computer error, like when that ferry rammed into the dock last year. Or operator error, which happened more than anyone would admit. Up north, for example, when a ferry actually sank and everyone ended up in the water until they were rescued, except for the two people they never found. All because the captain was having sex with one of the stewards on the control deck while the ferry sailed straight into a big rock.

Walk-on passengers could slip on the outside deck in winter, if someone forgot to ice it. They could press the wrong button and retract the walkway and people would just topple overboard, smashing into the water or catching the edge of the ferry, bones cracking and heads nearly getting knocked off. Being crushed between the ferry and the dock.

An earthquake.

The whole terminal would crumble, concrete and metal and cars and people and the wharf and the boats all thrown together into the deep harbor, shoved down by a gigantic overturned ferry.

No. Don't think about that. Rewind. Reverse. Refuse. Nancy's advice: If you get too far, stop in your tracks and rewind. Reverse the road to disaster. Refuse to go there.

Focus on the boys.

Stop thinking about catastrophic outcomes.

Think about something else.

I took out my book and sketched an old woman with a straw hat and bright blue eyeliner. Then a little girl playing with a yo-yo. A purple suitcase with the Eiffel Tower on it. The vending machine and Corbin standing in front of it, staring at all the things he would buy if he had any money.

Owen's red-and-white sneakers with the sparkly laces. He was sitting beside me, reading out loud to Hibou from *Owls in the Family*.

Right that very moment, there was nothing to worry about other than how to make Owen's laces look real. But I didn't want to draw anymore. I pulled Mom's scarf from my backpack and started worrying it, like it was some kind of silken rosary.

Don't think about Haiti.

Don't think about Raymond.

Don't think about dead babies.

Don't think about earthquakes.

Earthquakes. The Cascadia subduction zone was right underneath us, waiting to wreak havoc. Fifteen thousand people would die. We'd have fifteen minutes to get up to higher ground before the tsunami hit the shore.

Climb down, Maeve. Maybe it would be a small one, or medium.

Say it knocked the power out and the roads were jammed and the buses weren't running. How would I get the boys home? We could walk, but it'd take so long. Did we have enough food and water? Or maybe we could beg someone to take us to Grandma's in a boat. That might be easier than trying to walk back to the city from the ferry terminal. But what if there was a tsunami? Then we should run to high ground. Up to the highway. And start walking.

We should have a plan. A meeting place. Enough food and water for seventy-two hours.

I could smash the vending machine and take the contents for food. The drinks machine looked unbreakable, though. We'd have to find water somewhere else. Maybe we'd have to steal. But that would be okay, because life over death. Life wins.

Unless death gets you first. Unless we all died. Me, the boys. The old lady with the blue eye shadow. The little girl and her yo-yo.

> *The worst earthquake in recorded history claimed the lives of nearly twenty thousand people today, among them a teenage girl and her little brothers, innocently waiting for a ferry, which the resulting tsunami hurled up on the cracked and broken highway far above the terminal.*

Heart pounding. Hands getting sweaty. I clutched Mom's scarf until my fingers went numb.

Count, Maeve.

Slowly.

1, 2, 3, 4, 5—

What if there was another earthquake in Haiti? I pulled out my phone.

Likelihood of earthquakes in Haiti? Do you have a safety plan? Extra food and water?

No reply.

Tell me that I'm fine and to take a deep breath.

Tell me to take a sip of water.

Tell me to think about something pleasant.

Still no reply.

Staying in touch by text will not work if you NEVER TEXT ME BACK.

But if I was about to die in an earthquake, that would be the last text my mom ever got from me.

I love you, Mom. I'm just being stupid. You're probably on the plane.

And then I looked up information about earthquakes, because I just could not help myself.

"Oh, God."

Owen stopped reading. "What?"

I shoved the phone into my pocket. "Nothing."

"Here." He sat Hibou in my lap. "You can hold her. Sometimes that helps."

"Thank you." I clutched the stuffed owl tight. Like, white-knuckle tight. "Hey, Owen . . . do you have any of those little chew candies?"

"Yup." He fished in his backpack and found the tin. "Blackberry."

Stupid little herbal candies that were supposed to make you relax. Which was ever so slightly an improvement over the stupid herbal tincture that was supposed to do the same thing. Ruthie laughed at them. *Bach Flower Remedies? They're not even pretending to be something real, Maeve. Flowers? Where is the empirical evidence? How can they make these claims? Drug trials. Those are for real.*

But my mom bought the stuff in bulk anyway. And even though I had at least one little bottle of it in my backpack, I was so sick of the bitter, boozy taste and the whole idea of it that I could only just maybe stand one of the candies. Owen called them his "worry buttons," and he genuinely believed that they worked. He handed me the tin, and I took one.

Really, I wanted drugs. I wanted one of those little pill-boxes that had a section for each day of the week, with little happy pills in each one. Not some herbal hocus-pocus. But my parents actually agreed on a lot of things, and one of them was that they wouldn't let me take prescription drugs for my anxiety until I was an adult. Your brain is still developing, Maeve. You might grow out of it. It's too soon, they said. I disagreed. My brain was hardwired differently. What was the point of trying to put out a wildfire by pissing on it? Because that was what it felt like. If they actually realized how bad it was—if they truly understood—they'd let me have pills. If a leg is broken, put a cast on it. If you have cancer, do the chemo. If your head is messed up, take the pills.

"What's the matter?" Owen said.

"I'm just thinking too hard."

"I know what that feels like."

"I wish you didn't." I hated that he was a worrier too. It was my fault for always being a mess in front of him. I was a bad person for demonstrating what crazy looks like. I wouldn't wish it on anyone, and never on my sweet little brother. Never. "It sucks, right?"

"Yup."

Corbin was back now, emptying his bag onto the floor.

"What are you looking for?" I asked.

"I think there's a quarter in here somewhere." He pawed through the mess. "I went around and got four more, but I need a dollar seventy-five to get the chips."

"What do you mean, you 'went around'?" I straightened. "You got money from strangers?"

"Yeah." Two gnomes, his pocketknife, a rubber alien mask. "I do it all the time."

"What do you mean, 'all the time'?"

"He's good at it," Owen said. "He usually gets enough for us both to get something."

"I'm not sure if I'm more surprised that you share it with Owen or that you're panhandling in the first place."

"Mom says it's a job," Corbin said. "Like any other job."

"For bums, sure." I scooped the quarters out of his hand. "You're going to give these back. Who gave them to you?"

"I'm not telling."

"Yes you are."

"No I'm not!"

"Listen, Corbin, I'll give you money for the damn chips. But you can't go around begging off people."

"It's not begging!" he yelled. "Even Mom and Dad let me."

"They let you? Or you've heard them say that panhandling is an acceptable profession."

"I don't know."

"Do they even know about it?"

"Not really, I guess."

"Well, you can't say that they let you if they don't even know what you're doing! This is a perfect example of why six-year-olds should not be traveling by themselves." I grabbed his shoulders and spun him around. "Now, who gave it to you?"

"She did." Corbin pointed to a girl on the other side of the room.

"Go give it back."

"No!"

"Fine, then I will." I closed the quarters into my fist and walked over there with Corbin bouncing beside me, trying to pry my fingers apart. Halfway there I recognized her. The girl from the bus station. The one with the violin. The one who'd smiled at me. I stopped in my tracks.

"Maeve?" Corbin said. "What are we doing?"

She was reading a book and hadn't looked up yet. My panic attack shifted; it was about her now. About talking to her. Would she recognize me? Was it weird that I remembered her so clearly? Standing at the edge of that park, playing the violin with her eyes closed. Was that weird?

The PA system announced that the ferry would be loading soon, and with that news my resolve came back. Corbin would do the right thing, never mind how nervous I was feeling. "We're giving them back, and now you're not getting the chips at all. You're being a total brat, Corbin."

"And you're being a bitch!"

I tightened my grip on his arm. "What did you just say to me?"

"Hey, kid!" The girl stood up, and in two strides she was leaning over Corbin, glaring down at him. She was tall, and cute, and mad. "You do not talk to your mom that way. That is not cool."

"She's not my *mom*," Corbin sneered. "Just my stupid half sister."

"Whatever," the girl said. "You never call a woman a bitch."

"She's not a woman."

"Sure she is."

"She's just a girl."

"Corbin, give the quarters back." I could not stand them arguing about whether I was a woman or a girl. "Now."

"No!" Corbin hollered. "She gave them to me fair and square!"

"Begging off people is not 'fair and square.'"

"He didn't beg."

Up close to her now, I could see that the stamped letters

on her belt said SHIFT HAPPENS, and her eyes were apple green. On one hand I wanted to stare at her until I could draw her with my eyes closed, but on the other I would rather have become one with the dirty floor than be having this conversation. Or, no. I would rather be having an entirely different conversation. With the girl.

"Really?"

"He sold me jokes," the girl said. "A quarter each."

"Seriously?" I gripped Corbin's arm even harder. "You neglected to mention that part, Corbin."

"He did work for it. Fair and square." She stared at me. "I've seen you before."

"Bus station."

"Right." She blushed a little. Did she? Or was I imagining it? I was blushing, definitely. That much was for sure. "The truck on the sidewalk."

"My dad. Rock-star parking."

"Did he pay the ticket?"

"You didn't see him crumple it up and throw it away?"

"What do you call a dinosaur who crashes his car?" Corbin said.

"A Tyrannosaurus wreck," she said.

"Oh," I said.

"Yeah, oh." The girl grinned. "All good?"

"All good."

She looked at me. I looked at her. Corbin yanked his arm away.

"Meanie," he said.

"Ferry's boarding," the girl said.

"Yeah." The wonderful thing was that at that precise

moment I was not thinking of earthquakes. Not one bit. "We've got to go."

"Bye."

"Bye," I said. "Sorry about the misunderstanding."

"It's already boarding!" Owen said when I got back and began gathering our things. "You took so long, and I was going to come get you, but I couldn't carry all the backpacks and I thought you weren't going to be that long."

"Sorry." We lined up to board. The girl was ahead of us. She carried a beat-up violin case and had an equally beat-up backpack slung over one shoulder. There was a famous dead composer's profile silk-screened on a pinned-on patch. I didn't know which one, but it didn't matter. Because just below the dead composer was a rainbow patch.

Bingo. She was a friend of Dorothy.

After the thing with Jessica started, and before I came out to my parents, and when Ruthie still wasn't talking to me, I went to Dan's almost every day after school. He was supposed to be teaching me how to cook so that I could help with suppers at home. But mostly I overcooked chicken breasts and burned scones and put way too much salt into stews. I was so nervous that Dan might guess, just by looking at me. As if I'd changed when I came out to myself, and he could tell. As if gaydar was a real thing, which it might be and it might not be.

And then one day I was so nervous that I dropped a dozen

eggs and they all smashed on the tiles. I followed Dan out to his chicken coop to look for two new ones to use for the cake I was making for Mom's birthday, and when I found one nestled in the straw, I handed it to him.

"I'm gay," I said, when I'd meant to say, "Here's an egg."

"Well, my recruitment quota is now full." Dan gave me a big hug and made the cake for me while I fidgeted and stuttered and told him all about Jessica.

Jessica Elena Elliston-Haywood, who was as beautiful and stuck-up as her name, and such a good kisser.

I didn't tell him about Ruthie, because I wasn't sure what to say about her. And then later, after what happened, I didn't want to tell him at all. But that first afternoon, when I told him about Jessica, I felt buoyant and light. I kept holding on to the stool because it felt like if I let go, I'd drift up to the clouds, beaming and feeling ridiculously wonderful. It was so good to tell someone. And easier than I'd thought.

When the cake was cooled and decorated, Dan packed it into a box for me to carry home.

"Just a minute, sweetie." He disappeared into his bedroom and came back with a ratty old T-shirt. It had a rainbow on it, with FRIEND OF DOROTHY printed underneath in faded bubble letters.

"I get the rainbow," I said. "But who's Dorothy?"

"People used to say that as a way to tell each other that they were gay without actually having to say the word," Dan said. "Because it was so dangerous back then. So they had a code. Friend of Dorothy. Say I wanted to hook up with a handsome married businessman at a vacuum-salesman conference in Oklahoma in 1952. I'd sidle up to him and ask him if he was a friend of Dorothy."

"I don't get it," I said.

"As in Dorothy from *The Wizard of Oz*," he explained. "Which is the gayest movie ever. Somewhere over the rainbow? There's no place like home? Those fabulous red shoes?"

So the girl with the violin case and the rainbow patch was a friend of Dorothy. And I had a forty-minute ferry ride to let her know that I was too, if my nerves would let me.

Not Finding the Girl
You Are Looking For

I couldn't find her. I looked everywhere. Corbin sold more jokes for more quarters and spent the whole crossing in the arcade. Owen followed me around, so close that he tripped on my heels twice.

"Why don't you go join Corbin?"

Owen shook his head. "It's too loud in there. And he won't share his quarters."

"I'll give you some quarters."

"I don't like it in there. There's always big kids who push me around."

"Fine, then. But give me some space, okay? Hold my hand instead." He took my hand and skipped to keep up with me. "Where are we going?"

"We're looking for someone."

"Who?"

"That girl."

"What girl?"

"The one in the waiting room."

"The one we talked to?"

"Yes, Owen," I said with a sigh. "Could you just let me focus? I need to focus."

"Sure." Owen hummed a little tune. "I can do that." He lifted Hibou up into the air and turned her one way, then another. "Hibou says zero sightings."

The girl with the rainbow patch was nowhere. But I'd think I'd seen her turning a corner, or up ahead in one of the seats we were looking at from behind. She wasn't in the cafeteria, or the gift shop. She wasn't upstairs. When I pushed open the heavy door that led to the outside decks, Owen pulled me back.

"It's too windy," he protested. "It hurts my ears."

"Put your hands over them. Or wait here." He came with me, his hands pressed against his ears, Hibou tucked safely in his shirt. The wind was bracing, but it was warm. I checked that level, past the lifeboats and tourists with their cameras, a couple making out at the bow. I checked the upstairs deck too, while Owen whined about wanting to go back inside.

I even checked the bathrooms, waiting for every stall to empty, just to be sure. She was truly nowhere. As if she'd vanished off the boat altogether. I was more disappointed than I should have been. I should've talked to her more, as we'd boarded the boat. I should've made the boys go to the left, like the girl had done, instead of to the right, toward the arcade. We'd shared a look. It wasn't just a regular look. It was a *look*. Right? It meant something. Or, no it didn't. It didn't and I was just being a freak, making it into something it wasn't. Change the story, Maeve. There was no look. There wasn't anything. She was just being nice. She was just a girl.

Just one girl out of billions and billions of girls in the world. I told myself that, and believed it.

Only I didn't.

Or did I?

And then there she was, too far away to do anything about it.

We were walking off the boat, and she was nearly at the parking lot. She was the head above a group of little kids wearing red shirts with black violins on the back. She was ushering them onto a big yellow school bus, taking violin cases and piling them to one side and shaking parents' hands and talking to another girl who was holding a clipboard. Even if I sprinted up there, even if I could get to her before she got onto the bus too, what would I say? And whatever it was, I'd have to say it in front of those parents and those kids and that pile of violins and that other girl. That other girl was the worst. Did she know her? Were they friends? Clipboard girl smiled at violin girl. She reached out and touched her arm. Her ponytail bounced as she laughed at something violin girl was saying. Who was I kidding? I had no reason to talk to violin girl. And she had no reason to talk to me. The bus pulled away, and what did it matter anyway?

Grandma

Dad's chronic lateness came naturally to him, passed down by his chronically late mother. The passengers from our ferry all went their separate ways; then the next ferry loaded, another bus came and went, and still Grandma wasn't there. We went to the beach and skipped rocks and looked for baby crabs. By the time we wandered back up to the parking lot, I was considering getting the next ferry home. My phone buzzed. I hoped it wasn't Grandma, because if it was, it meant that she hadn't even left yet. It was my mom.

I do text you back. Perhaps not right away, but as soon as I can.

Earthquake risk? Remote. But I know you. You've already moved on to thinking about something else. Am I right?

Before I had a chance to text back, the boys shouted.

"There she is!" Corbin pointed. There was her old orange station wagon zooming down the hill. She careened to a stop across two parking spots and leapt out of the car, arms outstretched.

"My beautiful creatures!" she shouted. "Hugs! Immediately!"

With Grandma. I'm okay. I love you. More later.

"I'm so glad that you're here." Grandma flung open the trunk. Her gigantic dog slobbered in the backseat, leaning his big, blocky head over. "Sherman wanted to come too. Say hello, Sherman."

I didn't particularly like Sherman. He left slobber trails on my pants—or my bare legs. And he smelled like the fish oil Grandma put on his food, and like dirty old dog in general.

Grandma dangled the keys and grinned at me. "Want to drive?"

"No thanks."

"Good place to practice. Not much traffic."

"I don't want to drive."

"Your mother said we should be encouraging you."

"I never wanted my learner's permit in the first place. Did she tell you that?"

"Perhaps she's tired of being your personal chauffeur. Has that ever occurred to you? The moment each one of my boys turned sixteen, I handed them a set of keys to the car and told them I didn't want to drive them to any more parties or lessons or clubs or movies or jobs. I told them that unless we were going somewhere together, they were on their own or they could try to convince one of their brothers to take them or pick them up. With the exception of if they were drunk or stoned. I'd pick them up no questions in that case."

"I don't go to parties. I don't belong to any clubs."

74

"How about a job? About time you got one of those."

"I don't want to drive, Grandma. Please." I climbed into the passenger seat. Sherman hung his head next to mine and panted, leaving a pool of slobber on my shoulder.

"Come on, Maeve." Grandma leaned in, jingling the keys in my face. Everything was getting louder. The keys, the panting, the boys arguing about which side to sit on. The seagulls screaming outside. A logging truck gearing down. "Get behind the wheel."

"Grandma, I don't want to." I pushed Sherman's head out of the way. "And I wouldn't drive anyway because you don't have booster seats."

"No one is going to pull you over here."

"I'm not driving." I closed my eyes, trying to will away the panic. "I am not driving. Could we stop talking about it?"

"It's a Volvo, which happens to be the safest car in the world," Grandma said.

"Not true. Subaru has the safest car. And it depends on how—"

"We're hardly going far. And I bet you drive as slow as a little old lady. Or a typical little old lady. Those ones with the blue rinse in their hair."

"I am absolutely not driving, Grandma. I don't want to, and you can't make me." My voice was rising into a shout. "I just don't want to!" I saw Grandma's smile flatten, and I tried to calm myself down. "And it's the law that kids have to be secured in age-appropriate safety restraints until they are nine years old." Practically a whisper. "You want me to break the law?"

For a moment Grandma was silent. The boys were silent. Sherman was silent. Only the seagulls kept shrieking.

"All right." Grandma closed the keys in her fist. "Suit yourself. I'll drive."

I'd take the bus. A taxi. A train. I'd get a friend to drive. I'd ride my bike. I'd catch a ride with someone. I'd walk. But I didn't say any of that. She was like Dad in that she was all happy and full of jokes and smiles and hugs right up until the point that she was so pissed off she didn't even want to talk to you.

The boys did up their seat belts, which would choke them if we got into an accident. I turned around. "Maybe you should sit on your backpacks. They'd be kind of like booster seats."

"I don't want to sit on my backpack," Corbin said.

Owen shook his head in agreement.

"Maeve." Grandma drew out my name in one long, low growl. "Billy and Claire are fine with it. Just leave it alone now."

How hard was it to find two booster seats?

We could've carried them onto the ferry.

She could buy two and keep them in her car. The boys came over often enough. I would've bought two right then, if there'd been somewhere in that tiny town that sold them, and if I'd had enough money.

As we pulled onto the road, the boys argued about Gnomenville battle lines, and Sherman sat between them, watching the road more carefully than anyone in the car. Grandma drove, eyes straight ahead, not looking at me.

I tried to distract myself from my own catastrophic thinking by counting the driveways as they slid by. I got to sixty-three, and I was still thinking about car accidents.

Two thousand five hundred people died in car accidents

in Canada each year. Another twelve thousand were seriously injured. And Canada was not a big country. Well, it was big. But California had more people.

Over thirty-seven thousand people died in crashes in the US. Each year.

Over sixteen hundred of those people were kids under the age of fifteen.

Nearly 1.3 million people died in crashes in the world each year.

You shouldn't know these numbers, Nancy said. We need to work on that.

You should remember your calculus numbers instead, Ruthie said.

Why don't you learn the Latin names of the plants in the garden? Mom said.

Holy shit, Dad said. Those are some crazy numbers.

And Grandma wouldn't want to hear them at all.

> *Four people died in an accident on Marine Drive this afternoon, local artist Gillian Glover and three of her grandchildren: her sixteen-year-old granddaughter, Maeve Glover; and her six-year-old grandsons, Corbin and Owen Glover. If Ms. Glover had listened to the advice of her teenage granddaughter, perhaps the boys would have survived. Sadly, they were ejected from the vehicle due to being improperly restrained.*

It was not far-fetched. The year before, a Port Townsend woman had driven a minivan full of second graders to

Seattle for a field trip to the art museum, but when they were on the way back, she drove off the road and straight into a huge cedar tree. Five of the children were found scattered around the road and in the ditch. Two dead, three in critical condition. One seven-year-old sailed through the front window and wasn't found for four days. The reason no one could find him was that no one thought to look up. He was lodged in a tree, so high up that no one would've seen him even if they had. A helicopter pilot finally spotted his red jacket from above.

And then I read that he hadn't died right away. He'd died on the second day. Which meant he was up in that tree all alone overnight, bewildered and confused and scared and in so much pain.

None of those kids were wearing seat belts. None of them had been in booster seats. The woman said that she'd figured that because she was driving them on a school field trip, they didn't have to wear seat belts, as if her minivan had suddenly and magically been transformed into a great big yellow school bus.

I did not read the obituaries for those children.

Not even for the little boy who was stuck up a tree.

After supper we walked down to the beach so that Grandma could go for her daily swim, which she did every single day of the year, even in the dead of winter. I figured she'd probably die like that someday. Drowned. Her body would just drift on the waves until it finally washed ashore. She said she wouldn't mind drowning. She said if she had to choose between all the horrible sudden deaths, she'd choose drowning.

Maybe even out of all the ways to die, she said. Drowning wouldn't be so bad.

She waded in and then dove over the seaweed and did the breaststroke, fast and sure, until she was so far out we could hardly see her. Corbin followed her, yelping and groaning as he passed the kelp beds.

I did not swim in the ocean. Ever. I loved swimming in lakes—clear water, neatly enclosed, polite little fish—but even just the idea of swimming in the ocean was horrifying. The tide might suck me out and never bring me back. One of any number of big, wet mammals might suck me under and eat me or I'd drown. The ocean was rocky and weedy and full of floaty bits and weird creatures lurking in the dark and pebbly starfish and urchins and garbage and all kinds of writhing, wobbly, disgusting things. The salt felt caked on whenever I got out, and my hair was crunchy with it. It was not refreshing. It was not fun.

Owen felt the same way about oceans. He and I sat on a log, watching the waves and kicking the coarse sand at our feet.

"They're really far," Owen said.

"I know." I'd stopped watching because I could feel the anxiety pushing in. She did it every day, I told myself. She was a strong swimmer. And so was Corbin. She could bring him in if he got tired. But what if she suddenly had a cramp? Or what if something bit her? What if she had a stroke? And then Corbin would be out there all alone. I glanced up and tried to find them way out on the surf.

"There." Owen pointed.

I saw two tiny specks that looked like seals bobbing along. Too far! That's too far! But if I shouted, they wouldn't hear.

If I shouted, Owen would hear my fear and he would get scared too. Instead I circled my wrist with my other hand and found my pounding pulse and pressed down hard on the little blue vein, willing it to slow down. I pressed so hard that I winced with pain, and I knew there would be a bruise there later.

Broken Bones

After breakfast the next morning, the boys and Sherman headed into the forest behind Grandma's cottage to build a Gnomenville outpost while Grandma whooped my ass at Scrabble. I'd lost three games in a row when Owen came yelling at the top of his lungs down the path.

"He fell out of the tree and hurt his arm and he won't stop screaming!"

"Oh my God!" I grabbed Owen's shoulders. "What happened?"

"I don't know! I don't know! I don't know!" Owen hollered. "I think he might be dead!"

"Hold on. Just *hold on* a minute," Grandma said. "Owen, you *do* know what happened. You just told us. And you, Maeve, take it down a notch, for everybody's sake. Screaming people are not dead people. Now, Owen, go get the first-aid kit from under the bed and meet us on the trail."

Not even a minute into the forest, I could hear Corbin screaming.

"We're coming!" Owen hollered as he caught up with us. "I got Grandma and Maeve and the first-aid kit!"

"I'll take that, thank you." Grandma lifted the kit out of his arms.

"Help!" Corbin screeched. "I need an ambulance! I need a fire truck! It's broken!"

Everything I had learned in my first-aid courses fell out of my head and trailed behind me like Hansel and Gretel's crumbs. By the time we got to Corbin, I had no idea what to do, even though I'd rehearsed this kind of thing in my head over and over.

Sure enough, Corbin's arm was broken between the elbow and the wrist, twisted into a very wrong S shape. When I looked at it, I wanted to vomit. I actually had to look away.

I knew it. I knew it. I *knew* it. I knew something bad was going to happen. I should've gone with them into the forest. I should've been watching them. Let them go, Grandma had said. They're little kids, playing. That's what kids do, Maeve. You have to let them be kids.

Including this? Sprawled on the forest floor with a broken arm and so pale that he looked dead, even if he wasn't?

"Accidents happen," Grandma said as she opened the first-aid kit and handed me a splint.

Accidents could be prevented. Accidents wouldn't happen if people weren't so careless. Accidents happened when people weren't paying attention, or when they ignored the obvious. Like how stupid it was to let two little kids play alone in a forest teeming with bears and coyotes and a swift-water creek and trees and trees and trees to fall out of.

"Unroll the splint, Maeve."

So I did. I unrolled the splint and threw it at her. She gave me a quick, cool look and then went to work splinting Corbin's arm while Owen hopped nervously, chewing his fingers, and Corbin screamed his head off.

"I need a fire truck," Corbin said once his arm was splinted.

"You don't," Grandma said.

"I need an ambulance!"

"No you don't," she said. "You didn't break your leg. You can walk to the car. Now let's go."

Back at the cottage, Grandma arranged Corbin in the backseat with a bunch of pillows to prop up his arm and gave Owen strict instructions to help keep the pillows from toppling over. The nearer we got to the hospital, the less Corbin wanted to go. But within the hour he was wheeled into surgery, protesting at the top of his lungs that he was about to be de-limbed by an embedded agent from King Percival's army.

"That's a good sign," I said as we found a bank of seats in the lobby and settled in to wait for Dad and Claire, who were already on the next ferry.

Parental Marital Tension

When Claire and Dad rushed in about an hour later, Claire went straight to the nurses' station to ask about Corbin, and Dad went straight for Owen, picking him up and clutching him as if he was comforting Corbin by proxy.

"I can't believe it," Dad said. "Surgery!"

"It's just a broken arm," Claire said as she lowered herself into the chair beside me.

"Just a broken arm?" Dad set Owen down and sank into one of the chairs. "A broken arm is serious, Claire. Especially one that needs surgery."

"It might be serious if he was stranded in the wilderness for days on end."

"It can be serious," Dad said. "Infection. Nerve damage."

"Well, Billy, of course you're right," Claire said brightly. "So let's all sit here sick with worry. I'm sure that will be very helpful."

Whatever was happening, it was not about Corbin's broken arm.

"What do I know?" Claire added, and then she pushed herself up and headed for the vending machine. She fed it some coins and punched some buttons and came back with a handful of granola bars. "Anyone want one?"

"No." Dad folded his arms. "I don't."

"Have one." Claire held one out to me and Owen and Grandma. "You probably haven't eaten since breakfast, right?"

I took the granola bar and nodded. Claire sat down again. She pulled a side table in front of her and kicked off her sandals and rested her swollen feet on the table. Dad grimaced.

"It's a hospital, Claire. Put your shoes on."

"Plenty of people here do not have shoes on."

"They're patients."

"What's the difference?" She fished in her bag. "I've got apples and some cheese in here, but I didn't have time to put together anything else. Or we would've missed the ferry." She aimed a pointed glance at Dad.

"We caught the ferry with plenty enough time for you to get a chocolate bar before we boarded, right?"

"Barely." Another icy glance at Dad.

What was this about? Why were they acting like this? Other parents acted like this. Other people spoke to each other like this. Not Claire and Dad.

"You had a chocolate bar?" Owen sat up.

"And she bought one for Corbin," Dad said.

"Pregnant women can have chocolate whenever they want," Claire snapped. "So can children with broken arms."

"That's not fair, Mom."

"No, it's not fair. Go break an arm." This was such an un-Claire-like thing to say that the three of us stared at her, amazed.

"Oh, Owen." She reached for him. "That was unkind. And I have no excuse. I didn't mean it. I'm sorry."

Owen, confused and bewildered, began to cry. Claire awkwardly pulled him into her lap. "I'm sorry, baby. So sorry."

"Can I have a chocolate bar?" Owen asked through his tears.

"Of course, baby. Of course." Claire set him on his feet and looked up at my dad. "Will you please take him outside for some fresh air? Go across the street and buy him a chocolate bar." She said it so formally, but instead of sounding polite, it sounded like Claire was really telling him to take Owen across the fucking street and get him a fucking chocolate bar, and, by the way, fuck you.

Once Dad and Owen were gone, Claire put her face in her hands. "I didn't know where Billy was," she said. "When you called."

"But you found him," Grandma said.

"Where was he?" I asked.

"He said he was going to work, to get a few things done before shooting starts on set next week." Claire shook her head. "I called his cell. Ten times. Then I called the production office, and whoever picked up that line went to look for him and couldn't find him. Finally he called me back after I left a bunch of messages and texts. I asked him where he was. He said work."

"So he was at work," I said. But I thought of the night I arrived, how he'd been so late. All the long days on set. Too long.

"So he says," Claire said. "He says that whoever answered the phone was just a PA who didn't know where to look. He says it's a big lot. But I don't think he was there. I don't think he was there at all."

"You're overthinking it, Claire." Grandma put a hand on Claire's arm. "He's been sober for five years this time. And he's not having an affair. If that's what you're worried about. He is head over heels in love with you, and only you. You know that."

"I know it's not drugs. I'd know. I'd know it in my gut."

"You would."

"And I know he loves me. And the kids. And the baby." She put her hand on her belly.

"Did you ask him outright?" Grandma said. "'Are you having an affair, Billy? Are you using drugs again, Billy? Are you drinking again, Billy?'"

"No."

"Why not?"

I didn't want to be hearing any of this. When I stood up, my knees trembled.

"He insists that it's work," Claire said. "He says it's crazy busy."

"Then he was at work."

I was halfway to the bathroom, but I could still hear them.

"I can't help but think about when he was with Deena," Claire said. "And what happened."

Deena. My mom.

Claire was talking about the affair that ended my parents' marriage. What was her name? Shelley? Kelly? She was a single mother who worked at the café up the street from the recording studio in Seattle. She had no idea who the Railway Kings were. She didn't know that he was nearly famous. She only listened to popular country music. He told her that he worked in a warehouse, packing paper cups into boxes. When the band went in together, he said they worked together. Paper cups. Paper plates. Plastic knives and forks and spoons. He said he liked that she didn't know about the band.

She also didn't know that he was a husband, and a father to a toddler, and a drunk. She didn't know that he put a lot of money up his nose. She didn't know how angry my mother was. The woman in the café was the one who changed everything. She was the one who wrote her number on his coffee cup. She was the one who opened her door to him, night after night, while my mom was at home with me asleep in the bed beside her and didn't know what to do. That woman was the one who changed everything. It didn't matter that I couldn't remember her name. She could've been anyone.

I locked myself in the bathroom and sat on the toilet. The fluorescent light buzzed overhead. I sat on the toilet for a long time, staring at the red emergency button on the wall. I wanted to press it. But it was for the wrong kind of emergency. Dad was messing up. Claire was angry. The baby was coming. Corbin's arm was broken. My mom was in Haiti. I even lost the girl from the bus station on the ferry. It all felt like an emergency.

Bumping into People

Claire stayed with Corbin at the hospital, even though Dad had offered. In the morning, we all went up to get them. About five minutes after we arrived, Dad said that he had to catch the next ferry.

"I've got to get to work."

"On a Sunday?" Claire was wearing one of his old Railway Kings T-shirts, threadbare over her belly, and a pair of sweatpants. Her hair was a mess, and her eyes were ringed with red. It looked like she hadn't slept at all. "Really?"

"Yes, really." He kissed the boys and me. He didn't kiss Claire at all. "To finish what I was supposed to be doing at work *yesterday*."

Once he was gone, Grandma rallied the four of us. "Let's go have brunch," she said after Corbin was discharged.

"I'm not hungry," Claire said.

"Your baby is." Grandma shook her car keys. "Let's go."

Corbin was the first one out of the car when we pulled into the Gumboot Garden parking lot.

"Waffles and whipped cream!" He started to run, but then he stopped with a yelp and held his casted arm closer. "Is it still supposed to hurt?" Grandma and Claire followed him inside, while I hung back with Owen. He surveyed the rock bed at the edge of the road.

"Looking for skippers," he muttered. "Got to be flat. Smooth. Like this." He indicated the ideal size with his finger and thumb. I found a good one and offered it to him.

Someone was playing the violin nearby. And they were playing one of Dad's songs: "O'Ryan's Train." When I was little, Dad brought me a big black dog that he said was for me—even though I wanted a puppy. Mom said he was just dumping him with us because he was going on tour and no one else would take him. His name was Mars, but I called him O'Ryan, after that song. It was my favorite song, until years later when Dad told me that it was the last one he wrote before Hank—the drummer—overdosed on heroin and they all cracked apart. That song was a hit. It even made it onto the charts. A crossover favorite, the critics said. Their best work, just as it was all coming apart.

I followed a hedge to the end and looked across the road to see who was butchering the song. It was supposed to be fast and twangy, but this was mellow and slow. I was ready to resent whoever it was. But it was the girl from the bus station.

It was the girl from the ferry.

She stood with her face turned to the sun, her violin case open in front of her, playing my dad's song.

Owen appeared at my side, his shirt folded up and weighed down with rocks.

"That's Dad's song!" Owen said. "She's playing Dad's song. Let's go listen!"

He took off at a run, stones falling out of his shirt as he did.

"Check for cars!"

He lurched to a stop and had a quick look, and then he was running across the street and hollering. "Hey, you're playing my dad's song!"

She stopped. "Your dad's song?"

My stomach flipped. I wanted to cross the road, and I didn't want to cross the road. I wanted to go talk to her, but I wasn't sure that I could. But it didn't matter, or it couldn't matter, or I wasn't going to let it matter for once, because I was going to do both.

As I crossed the street, I could tell that she was trying to figure out where she'd seen Owen before, but then she saw me, and I could tell by the look on her face that it was all coming together.

"I remember you," she said. "The evil joy-killing half sister. Where's the other one?"

"The Gumboot." I gestured behind me. "My stepmom loves their wasabi scrambled eggs."

"Really?"

"She's pregnant."

"Ah, okay." She laughed. "That explains it."

I stood there. She stood there. Owen waited for something interesting to happen, and when it didn't, and the moment stretched on and on, he gave up and headed back to the café with his skipping stones.

"Traffic!" I shouted as he neared the edge of the road. I kept my eyes on him until he disappeared into the café.

"So." She cradled her violin. "The Railway Kings. Your dad?"

"He played guitar, mostly," I said. "But he wrote, too. He wrote 'O'Ryan's Train,' actually."

"That's very cool."

"If you're into the Railway Kings. Not many people are. Were, I guess. It's a certain type."

"Definitely. My parents were big fans. Are, I guess."

"Mine too."

The girl squinted.

"That was supposed to be a joke."

"Ah. Right. Got it." She picked a quarter out of her violin case and held it out.

I took it. "What's this for?"

"That's the going rate, right?" She grinned. "As set by your entrepreneurial little brother. His jokes are pretty funny."

"Yeah?"

"Knock, knock."

"Who's there?"

"Iguana."

I knew this one. "Iguana who?"

"Iguana be your friend."

"Funny." I blushed and gave the quarter back. "My jokes are free."

"Cool." The girl nodded.

"Cool." I nodded too. I should go join the others at the Gumboot. They would've ordered by now. But I didn't want to leave. Not yet. "Do you busk here a lot?"

"Not really." The girl looked around suddenly, as if she

wasn't exactly sure where she was. "I came up to teach a couple of classes at the fiddle camp."

That was the bus. Those were the kids. The girl with the ponytail. "You teach? That's cool." I took a deep breath. I was going to keep this conversation going as long as possible. "Have you been playing the violin for long?"

"Since I was five."

"That's a long time," I said, wondering how old she was. As young as fifteen? As old as twenty? "My dad tried to teach me guitar, but I don't have a musical bone in my body. I draw, though."

"What do you draw?"

"Everything." I had my sketchbook with me, but I wasn't about to show it to her. I never showed anyone. "Objects. Little things. Teacups. Keys. Bicycles." It sounded silly, in a list like that. "People who catch my eye." Which I regretted saying almost immediately. I felt my cheeks get hotter.

"Does your dad still play music?"

"Sometimes. He's a set painter in the movie industry now."

"Still cool," she said. "In Vancouver?"

"Yep."

"So you live in Vancouver too?"

"For now." I told her that my mom was in Haiti. But I didn't tell her about Raymond. Or what I thought about it all. "You?"

"East Van, born and bred."

"Really?" I felt a catch in my throat. "M-m-my dad lives in East Van too."

I took a deep breath, willing away the stutter.

"We should get together, then." The girl grinned. "Do you like mochas?"

"I love them! They're so good. I love the whipped cream." I sounded like one of the twins. Not smooth at all. Eager, and utterly graceless.

"Great," the girl said with a laugh. "Then we have to go to Continental?"

"Chocolate whipped cream, yes! Absolutely." I said it too quickly, and I could feel another spew of excitement brewing. Calm down, Maeve. Take your time. "Breathe."

"Pardon?"

"Nothing." I was flustered; the stutter was back. She was probably already regretting suggesting coffee together. "I m-m-mean, yes. That'd be g-g-great. Coffee. Sure. I could do that." Then I had to actually press my fingers to my lips in order to stop talking altogether.

"We should probably know each other's names, then."

"Good idea."

"I'm Salix." She tucked her violin under one arm and reached out a hand.

"I'm Maeve."

We shook hands and both held on for one second too long, then two seconds, and then Salix let go first.

"That's an interesting name," I said, recovering. "How do you spell it?"

"S-a-l-i-x."

She slipped her phone out of her pocket. "What's your number?"

A girl was asking for my number. That had never happened before. Jessica had already had my number from being

95

my lab partner, and Ruthie had always had it. If I was going to count Ruthie at all. Which I shouldn't. Not really.

I was so shocked that a girl was asking for my number that I actually couldn't remember it. I had to take out my phone and check before reciting it, and then I tucked it back in my pocket, fully expecting to never hear from Salix again. She was being polite, that was all. She probably was a very busy person and would forget. But then my phone buzzed while she was still standing right in front of me.

Continental. 2pm Friday?

"Just to make sure that I got your number right," Salix said. "While I've still got you here."

I stared at my phone. Even though I'd been participating in the entire conversation, I still couldn't believe the words on the screen.

"I don't get back to the city until then," Salix said when I still hadn't said anything. "Is Friday okay?"

I texted back, my fingers shaking so much that I had to correct the autocorrect several times.

Ill beat

I'll be three

I'll be there.

Salix's ringtone was a piece of violin music. She glanced at her phone. "Great! I guess I'll see you on Friday."

"Friday." And then, as if the wind had shifted, doubt flooded me. I felt suddenly bloated with it, swollen. Maybe this wasn't a date at all. Maybe Salix was just being nice. Maybe she was just shopping for a new friend. But I didn't want a new friend. "I—I—I—" I stuttered. "I like your r-r-rainbow patch."

"Thanks." And then her eyes found the ground and she said shyly, "I didn't see a rainbow on your backpack."

"No. Wait, you looked? When did you look?"

"At the terminal, when you were wrangling your brothers. No rainbow."

"Speaking of the ferry, I didn't see you. Where were you?"

Salix lifted her eyes. Bright green and sparkling. "You looked for me?"

I nodded. The wind shifted again, and the doubt began to ease. "And I didn't find you."

"I was down on the vehicle deck in the corner where walk-on passengers leave their dogs. I like to play for them. Keep them company. Know where that is?"

"I know it." The one place I hadn't looked. I wished that I had. I wished that I could've found her like that, serenading the dogs. "That's really sweet."

"Or really silly."

It was time to make an exit. Dan said it was always better to be the person who hung up first. Or, in this case, walked away first.

"I should g-g-go," I stammered. "They're probably wondering what's taking me so long."

"See you Friday," Salix said. "You know the place?"

"I do," I said. "My dad buys his coffee beans there."

"Mine too."

"Rock on, Railroad Kings."

"Long live 'O'Ryan's Train.'"

"A certain type, right?"

"Definitely a certain type," I said. "Bye."

"Bye."

I backed away, so distracted that I only remembered at the last second to check for cars. A truck sped by, and a car, and then I crossed the street and ducked behind the hedge to call my dad. I wanted to thank him for being one of the Railway Kings. I'd never thought twice about it before, but now it mattered. It was currency all of a sudden, and it had bought me a date.

Gut Instinct

I stood behind the hedge and phoned Dad. It rang and rang while Salix started playing the song again. It sounded absolutely perfect this time, even though she was still playing it her way, which didn't sound much like the Railway Kings' version at all. Dad's phone went to voice mail, but I didn't want to leave a message. I wanted to tell him all about it. Remember that girl from the bus station? Remember her? You won't believe it, Dad. I called again. And then a third time, and it rang and rang. And then I saw her again, back at the ferry terminal, and now she's right here. Rang and rang, and then he finally picked up.

"Maeve!" He barked my name so loudly that I had to pull the phone away from my ear. "What the hell? Why do you keep calling? Is everything okay? Is it the baby?"

"No, no, Dad. Everyone is fine. I'm great!"

"Jesus," Dad said. "Then why are you calling and calling? Why didn't you leave a message?"

"Do you even know how to listen to your messages?"

"Beside the point. I'm busy here, Maeve." His tone was short, his words staccato. "What do you need?"

"There was this girl, on the ferry. . . . Well, before that, at the bus station. Did you see her? She was playing violin outside? At the edge of the park?"

"No, I did not see a girl playing the violin."

"Well, I saw her again, in the waiting room at the ferry terminal, and Corbin was telling jokes, but I thought that he was begging for money."

"Can this wait?" He wasn't getting it. He didn't understand how it all came together and lifted up into something bigger. He didn't understand how serendipity was at play here. Or luck. Or chance. Or God. He wasn't even listening. Not really. He didn't care. That was the message I was getting. He didn't even care.

"I guess." I wasn't mad. I should've been. But I was just sad. Because it would be different to tell him later. I wanted to tell him now, with all the excitement like a sparkling halo. That wouldn't last. "I—I—I just really wanted to talk to you."

"Everybody's okay?"

"Yeah," I murmured. In the background I heard the noon chimes from the steam clock in Gastown, which made no sense at all. The movie lot he was working on was far away, down by the Fraser River. Nowhere near Gastown. A half-hour drive away at least. My stomach tightened. He was lying. "I thought you were at work?"

"I had to come downtown for an errand."

"Oh." Suddenly there was an edge in his voice. Something

dark. Something that could cast shadows. Or doubt. The conversation in the hospital came flooding back, pushing away my sparkly excitement. "You didn't mention that yesterday."

"Why would I?" Darker and darker. Sharper and sharper. "Look, I have to go." Then he was saying something to someone with him. "Just a sec, man. I told you."

"Who's with you?" I wanted to know. And I didn't want to know.

"One of my crew."

I wished I hadn't called him in the first place. I wished I'd kept it all to myself.

"Okay. Well. Bye, Dad."

"Aw, come on, Maeve." His voice buoyed up suddenly. "Don't say goodbye like that."

Maybe he cared. Or maybe he didn't want me reporting back to Claire that he'd been an asshole on the phone. An asshole who was in Gastown doing who knew what when he was supposed to be on the movie lot. An asshole who was the boss of a big crew. An asshole who could have sent any one of them downtown on "an errand."

"I can give you two minutes," he said.

"And then what?"

"I have to get back to the set."

"What was so important downtown?"

"Really?" The edge was back. "You're wasting your two minutes? Tell me. A girl. Bus station. Ferry terminal. You're going to meet her at the airport next?"

Was it a woman he was with? Was that it? He didn't sound drunk. It had to be a woman. Another affair.

"Dad?" Is it a woman? Are you with a woman, Dad? But the words wouldn't come, and I gave up.

"One minute, Maeve."

"It doesn't matter."

"Did you ask her out?"

"It doesn't matter."

"Sure it does!"

"You have to go."

"Don't make me fish here, Maeve."

"Fine. Yes. She asked me on a date. Or at least I think she did."

"That's really great, Maeve." Behind his voice, a siren wailed. So close that we couldn't speak for a moment. When it faded, he said goodbye. "Give my love to everyone. Kiss Claire's belly for me. Love you guys. That's so great about the girl. I'll give you money. You can treat. Where are you going?"

"Continental."

"You drink coffee?"

"Only if it has whipped cream." Now I was the one who wanted to get off the phone. "Anyway, you need to go, right?"

"Right. Love you. Kisses for everybody, got it? The belly baby too."

"Love you too."

"Bye."

Salix was still playing, but it was a different song now. Nothing that I recognized. I wanted to go back across the street and take her hand and walk to the beach and sit on a log and count the seagulls, or the dogs running up and down along the shore, or the children building sand castles. I didn't want to go into the restaurant and sit there with the others and tell them everything, or parts of everything, or nothing at all.

I wanted to tell them that Salix wasn't just some girl. I wanted to tell them that she was the one from the bus station and the ferry terminal and how that meant something, it really did. And the phone call with Dad. Would I tell them that he said hello and he loves us all? Or would I tell them that he was in the wrong place, and he was a jerk, and I didn't believe for one minute that he was at work at all? I could see the twins and Grandma and Claire at a table by the window, laughing as Corbin stuck raspberries on the tips of his fingers of his broken arm.

I texted Mom.

I met a girl. Her name is Salix. She asked me out. I think. Also, Corbin broke his arm.

And *Dad is acting weird.*

For the first time since I'd left, she texted back almost right away.

A date! Email me the details. I want to know everything. Sign Corbin's cast for me, will you? Hot here. Very hot.

And then a second text.

Raymond says hi.

I doubted that, but okay.

Salix was playing something classical now. Something that sounded like it could be happy or it could be sad. Like the composer wasn't quite sure. I peeked around the shrubs. Salix had moved into a slice of shade at the edge of the forest beside the store. The music, the trees, the blue sky, the girl who looked like she could be a boy apprentice to a composer a hundred years ago, or a hundred years from now. It felt good watching her, but when I turned toward the restaurant, my stomach flipped with worry. Dad was messing up again.

Dead Bodies

When we got back to the city and unpacked, the boys went straight out to Gnomenville to return the troops and see how the rest of the Wrens and the Percivals had managed while they were gone. I put in a load of laundry, and when I came back upstairs, I noticed a box beside the couch that hadn't been there before. It was open, a stack of disposable bed pads resting on the top, and a small brown bag with a label on it: LABOR TEA. And an illustration of a goddess pushing out a baby, her legs spread, stars raining down, smiling blissfully.

"Birth supplies." Claire sat on the couch with a book. *Birthing from Within.* "They came while we were gone."

The pads would be for the mess. When her water broke. The blood and mucus and shit.

I will not be at this birth.

I will not be at this birth.

I will not be at this birth.

"I'm going over to Mrs. Patel's," I said. "I owe her a game of rummy."

"Sure." Claire pointed to the counter. "Can you take that plate back to her?"

I knocked on Mrs. Patel's door, but there was no answer. I could hear the television from inside, so loud that I could tell it was a soap opera. Someone was breaking up with someone else. Crying, dramatic music, then a commercial. I knocked again. No answer.

The door was unlocked, so I stepped inside. Just like I had a thousand times before.

"Mrs. Patel?" I slipped off my flip-flops and parked them beside Mrs. Patel's sensible old-lady shoes. She liked footwear to be neatly lined up. "It's Maeve."

When there was still no answer, I put my hand on the banister and leaned up the stairs.

"Hello?"

It made sense that she didn't answer, because the TV was so loud. Mrs. Patel was pretty deaf. If she didn't have her hearing aids in, she might not hear me at all. Even with them in, I had to holler sometimes. I climbed the stairs into the living room.

"Mrs. Patel?"

She was slumped on the floor in front of her butter-yellow recliner, a deck of playing cards scattered around her. Half sitting, half lying, her head resting on one shoulder, vomit streaking her hair and her pink cardigan—the one with the hole at the elbow and the missing button. The smell of piss and shit, and for a moment it all got confused in my head and I thought that maybe I was still next door looking at the disposable pads and thinking about Claire shitting herself and bellowing like a cow. But that wasn't right. This wasn't right.

"Mrs. Patel?" I dropped the plate. I glanced at it. I should pick it up. I thought, What a relief that it didn't break. I thought, None of this makes sense at all.

And then all those first-aid classes came to mind, and I rushed to her side and dropped to my knees. I grabbed her arm and shook it hard.

"Mrs. Patel!"

Her head rolled forward, her chin resting on her chest, her lanky gray hair a curtain across her face. I groped for her wrist and pressed my fingers to where her pulse should be. I must be in the wrong spot. I walked my fingers in tiny steps around Mrs. Patel's bony wrist. No heartbeat. No pulse. Just cold skin, and Mrs. Patel's hand flopping, lifeless.

Lifeless.

Dead.

I scrambled backward, knocking over the TV table Mrs. Patel kept beside her chair, spilling her phone and her crossword magazine and an abandoned dinner of fries and samosas to the floor. The soap opera hollered at me. "He's leaving you! And he's never coming back! He never loved you. Never! Not ever!"

Time fell onto the floor too, and slithered away. I have no idea why I didn't just run. I have no idea how long I sat there beside Mrs. Patel's body. I have no idea how long it took me to call 911. But I must have picked up the phone and dialed. Just as I must have reached for the crocheted throw from the couch and covered Mrs. Patel with it.

Mrs. Patel died suddenly in her living room, where she was found by her sometime neighbor Maeve Glover, who was shocked and horrified. She is survived by—

I wondered about all of this after. Of course I did. After the paramedics came, and the cops, and it was only then that Claire showed up, summoned by the commotion.

"Maeve?" she called from the door. "What's happening?"

But I couldn't answer. The two cops stood on either side of Mrs. Patel's body like sentinels. She was still propped up by the chair. The paramedics hadn't even slid her onto her back. She was that dead, as if there were degrees of deadness, which I had never considered before. The paramedics threw questions at me instead of helping Mrs. Patel. What's her name? How old is she? Did she have any medical conditions? When was the last time you saw her?

"Hardeep Patel. Seventy-two. Or three. Or one. She takes a lot of pills. Last Thursday," I said. "She was wearing that pink cardigan. And I thought, Oh, she needs a new sweater."

"But she was okay then?" the paramedic said. "Had anyone seen her since?"

"I thought, Oh, she needs a new sweater."

And then Claire was pulling me away, down the stairs and outside, where the smell of lilacs hung in the thick, hot, windless city air and it wasn't any easier to breathe.

Back home, Claire steered me to the couch. But I didn't want to sit. I just stood there, staring at the far wall. Mrs. Patel was on the other side. Still dead. "Maeve?" Claire stood too close.

I could smell garlic on her breath. I almost gagged. "What do you need? A glass of water? Something to eat? Are you cold? Do you want a blanket? Sometimes people in shock get the shivers."

"I want to talk to my dad."

"Of course," Claire said. "I'll call him for you. Right now." She dialed and then held the phone to her ear.

"He's not answering." She dialed again. "It's just going to his voice mail."

I put my hand out. Claire gave me the phone. I had the idea that if I was the one to dial him, if I was the one to call, then of course he would pick up. Of course he would. Because he was my father and I was his daughter and there should be a telepathic connection that would give him the knowledge that this was an emergency. A true, genuine emergency. I needed him.

It rang and rang and rang. Claire stood even closer. The smell of garlic made me want to retch. Her face was so full of sadness and sympathy and concern that I had to look away.

You've reached Billy Glover, scenic artist and portrait artist. Please leave me a message and I'll get back to you as soon as I can.

The phone felt suddenly hot in my hand. I tightened my grip.

"Dad?" The word caught in my throat. "Daddy? I need you. I really, really need you. Please come home right away."

I gave the phone back to Claire and kept standing there.

Of course he'd call back. It was an emergency. He was my father. I needed him.

But he didn't call. And he still didn't call. And he didn't come home. And I was so, so mad at him. Furious. I had just had the most devastating day of my entire life, and he just was not there. He was somewhere in the city, near enough to come to me. Mom would probably have come all the way from Haiti, if I'd asked her to. He was close enough to get here fast and pull me into the hug that I needed from him, not from Claire. From *him*. I wanted to be held by my dad, his big arms tight around me, holding me so that I wouldn't have to hold myself. But he just wasn't there.

Killing Someone

The boys went to bed without protest, climbing the stairs with heavy steps, glancing back with red-rimmed eyes. For an hour the house was still and quiet. I sat on the couch, still staring at the wall we shared with Mrs. Patel. Claire busied herself with one of her dolls, stitching the yarn hair to its head. We both looked up when we heard soft, slow footsteps coming down the stairs. It was Owen, his face blotchy, the tears still coursing down.

"Can I sleep with you, Maeve?"

"Oh, honey." Claire put down the doll and went to him, hugging him to her. "I don't think Maeve wants company tonight."

"He can sleep with me," I said. "I don't mind." I hadn't spoken since leaving the message on Dad's phone, and my throat was dry and my words were scratchy. "Come on." I took his hand. "Let's go to bed."

"Thanks, Maeve."

111

"Thank you, Owen." I squeezed his hand.

"I didn't want to be all by myself."

"Me either."

I couldn't get Mrs. Patel out of my mind. I tried thinking about my mom in Haiti. I tried thinking about Salix. I tried thinking about all the things I could come up with, and nothing stuck. I tried counting sheep, counting up to one hundred, counting down from one hundred. All I could think about was Mrs. Patel. Dead Mrs. Patel.

Mrs. Patel was dead.

Mrs. Patel was dead.

Whenever I closed my eyes, I saw her. The TV tray toppled over. The folds of Mrs. Patel's sweater. The image of the man and woman on the TV, arguing, gripping each other, their faces contorted in anger. I don't love you! Go away!

Sleep just never came.

Every once in a while I would slide one hand across until I found Owen's. I'd hold his wrist lightly, my fingers resting on his pulse. I was glad he was there, to remind me that life was the common denominator, not death. Although I supposed one equaled the other when it came right down to it.

Sleep just never came.

It didn't come and it didn't come, until I finally got up and turned on the light beside the bed. Owen didn't stir. I found Dad's illustrated anatomy book and looked up *heart*.

One page showed a human heart, sketched in black, suspended in white space. Another image was in color: reds of all shades, and purple, and black, white plaque, blue blood pumping out one side, red blood flooding in the other. On the next page the heart was sectioned. Halved, and then quartered. It looked like meat. Like each quarter should be wrapped in butcher paper, a label on the front, priced accordingly. This week, on sale. A quarter heart. A dollar ninety-nine a pound. Or a million dollars a pound? What was it worth when it didn't work anymore? When it was just meat?

Did Mrs. Patel still have her heart?

Did the morgue man cut it out? Did it rest in his gloved hands, wet and cold? Did he put it in a bowl? Did he look at it and examine it and poke it and slice it open? And then did he put it back, placing it in her chest cavity, held open by angry metal spacers?

I found an empty page in my sketchbook and drew the outline of a whole heart, intact. Not butchered quarters. Not sections revealing the clockwork. Just a heart. A vital muscle so strong it could power the whole body. So vital that if it didn't work, a person died.

According to the book, Mrs. Patel's heart would've been about the size of her fist. She had tiny hands, with short slender fingers, like a child's. I read on. The heart was located not so much to the left, but almost midline. I made a fist and placed it where my heart would be. Where her heart had been.

Myocardial infarction. Ischemia. Death of heart muscle. The heart couldn't function without oxygen. It started to die as soon as the vessels were blocked by plaque or a coronary spasm or a thrombus—a blood clot—which could be sudden.

That was when I realized that I had killed Mrs. Patel.

She'd died from the heart attack I had wished for. The one that had been meant for Raymond. The one I'd tried to take back.

Mrs. Patel died suddenly in her living room, where
she was found by her killer and sometime neighbor
Maeve Glover, who was shocked and horrified when
she realized what she had done—

What had I done? The heart attack had been for Raymond. And then I'd taken it back. I had! But somehow it had still been floating around, and it had found Mrs. Patel.

This was my fault.

Her *death* was my fault.

Unintentional homicide. But murder nonetheless.

This was a terrible, terrible realization, and I wanted to rewind so badly.

I hadn't wanted Raymond to have a heart attack. I hadn't meant it. I hadn't wanted that awful thing to float out of my grasp before I could pull it back in and throw it away. But it got away from me and made it as far as Mrs. Patel's house, where it slammed into her while she was just sitting there, watching TV and doing absolutely nothing wrong. It gripped her and set off all those tiny explosions as she clutched her chest and gasped and then slid to the floor and died right there with her slippers on, her scrawny, hairy legs splayed out in front of her.

I felt too dizzy to sit.

It was ridiculous. There was no way to *conjure* a heart attack. Superstition. Voodoo dolls. Magical incantations. Spells with a strand of hair and a torn picture. It couldn't be.

It couldn't be.

No.

Impossible.

But I couldn't shake the idea.

What if it was true? If so many people could believe in a power they couldn't see and call it God or Allah or whatever, and if all those people believed that God could make things happen or *not* happen, maybe this was no different.

I wouldn't have believed it before.

But now I did.

I set my pencil down and lowered myself to the floor, where I lay on my back and squeezed my eyes shut. My heart—healthy, galloping, robust—thudded faster and faster. It had no right to. No right at all. The drawing of the heart glowed in the small circle of light from the lamp. I stared at it so long that it started to pulse, right there on the page. Terrified, I lunged for the lamp and switched it off, plunging the room into that extra-black darkness that happens at first. After a few moments I could see, but the shadows in the room were even worse. Large and looming and strange.

"Maeve?" Owen's small voice, exquisitely alive, and tremulous.

"Yeah?" I flicked the light back on.

"I wet the bed."

I almost laughed. It was such a living-person thing to do that I didn't mind how gross it was. I didn't even mind the smell. It was just so basic and real, and had everything to do with being alive. Not like Mrs. Patel, whose bladder had relaxed when she died, releasing one last, passive flood of urine, soaking her nightie and the carpet underneath.

Owen had wet the bed. Normally, I would've been so disgusted. Normally, I wouldn't have wanted anything to do with cleaning it up, but right then I was just so glad I could actually do something to help.

"It's okay." I turned the overhead light on too. No more

shadows. "It's okay." He blinked against the brightness, and I helped him out of bed. I gathered up the soaked sheets and the blanket. I handed him his owl, which was still dry. Owen followed me silently to the washing machine. I stripped off his pajamas while he stood there. He yawned and shivered while I loaded the washer. I found one of Dad's T-shirts in the dryer and helped Owen into it. It made him look even smaller, the sleeves draping down to his elbows, his knobby knees, pale, peeking out. "Better?"

He nodded, yawning again.

I couldn't find any linens, but there were sleeping bags in the closet at the end of the hall, so I collected two of those and steered Owen back to bed. I unrolled the bags, a blue one with glow-in-the-dark stars on the inside for Owen, and a musty old green one for me. I settled Owen into his and zipped him up, and then I crawled into mine beside him and turned off the light.

"I'm sorry," Owen whispered, his voice thick with sleep.

"It's okay," I said, when I really meant *thank you*. But he wouldn't understand how much he'd helped me. He'd pushed away Mrs. Patel and the bloody hearts and the pulsing heart on the page. Not far, but enough that I could finally fall asleep, to the throbbing of my own pulse, angry and exhausted.

Parents Arguing

I slept for an hour. An hour filled with wretched dreams featuring too much blood and too many samosas and a very loud soap-opera soundtrack. While I was lying awake, trying to go back to sleep, I heard the unmistakable sound of a key in the front door.

It was Dad, coming home at last. At almost four a.m.

I still wanted to see him. I still wanted him to hold me and tell me that everything would be all right. What I really wanted was for him to tell me that it wasn't my fault, but even just a hug would do. I hurried upstairs to catch him before he went to bed, but I stopped short at the top when I heard him and Claire talking.

"You just threw five years of sobriety down the toilet?"

"*Whoosh.*"

"This isn't a joke. Fuck, Billy. Five years!"

"You know the sayings. 'Keep coming back,'" Dad said. "'One day at a time.'"

"Maeve needed you, Billy. We needed you!"

"My phone was in my truck."

"And where was your truck?"

I sat on the second step, the wall hiding me. There was a pause. A long pause.

"Where was your truck?" Claire said again. "Where were you? Where were you getting drunk while your daughter found Mrs. Patel's dead body? Where were you, Billy? Answer me! Where the hell were you?"

"Stop it, Claire." His voice was thick, drunk. "You want to know where I was?"

"Yes."

"Well, here's a fucking news flash. I don't have to explain myself," he slurred. "I'm a grown man. I can do whatever I do without checking with you first, or after. Or ever, for that matter."

"You're a grown man with a family."

"You want me to stand here and grovel?" He dropped his keys. When he bent to pick them up, he almost toppled over. "You'd have a comeback for everything, so why bother? I say one thing; you say another. Back and forth and back and forth. Yadda yadda. Blah, blah, blah. I'm wrong. You're right. Done. Why not just go to bed instead and save ourselves the grief?"

"Grief?" Claire let out one barking laugh. "Talk to your daughter if you want to know about grief."

And then her footsteps, stomping up to the third floor.

And his stomping across to the couch.

And me, crouched in the dark, still wanting to talk to him. Still wanting him to take me in his arms and listen to me tell him how awful it was. But I waited too long, and then he was snoring.

I peeked around the corner. He was sprawled on the couch, his boots still on, one arm covering his eyes. He didn't care about Mrs. Patel dying. He didn't care about me finding her. In that drunken, slumbering moment, he didn't care about anything. He just slept, deep and easy, as if he'd earned it. But he hadn't. He was just some drunk, insensitive asshole passed out on a couch.

What Happens
After You Die

Ruthie was with her dad when he had an aneurysm and dropped dead in the produce aisle at the Seaside Market, a head of lettuce in one hand and a bag of carrots in the other. We were eleven, and when I saw her at the funeral, she said her mother bought the vegetables he'd been holding, in case some of his spirit was in them now.

"Which is dumb. That's not how death works," Ruthie said. "You're alive, and then you're dead. Nothing happens after. Nothing at all. It's science."

But there was a window between when the organs stopped functioning and cells actually began to perish. Only minutes, maybe. But there was a time when the body was dead but the soul remained. When my dog, O'Ryan, died I could tell. Even after half an hour, O'Ryan looked alive, but just very, very still, and yet I didn't believe that he was actually dead, except that his jaw was slack and his bowels had let go.

Just like Mrs. Patel.

With O'Ryan—old and arthritic and riddled with cancer—I didn't truly believe he was dead until Dan came over with his stethoscope and showed me that there were no heart sounds. No lung sounds. He fit the stethoscope to my ears and placed the bell over O'Ryan's heart, and it was true.

There was no guessing with Mrs. Patel. It was obvious that she was dead. And even though it was far-fetched, and even though I tried to tell myself that I was being ridiculous, I just kept thinking that it was my fault. I had wished a heart attack on Raymond, and it had landed on the wrong person. *My fault. My fault.* The heart attack was *my fault.* That looped in my head, so loud that I couldn't make any other sense of it.

Dad looked rough the next morning. He sat at the table with a piece of dry toast and a mug of strong coffee in front of him and opened his arms to me. I sat awkwardly in his lap and he wrapped his arms around me and leaned his head on me. His hair reeked of alcohol and cigarettes. His face was greasy and bloated.

"I'm sorry that I wasn't here for you, kiddo."

I didn't say anything. I glanced at Claire, but she looked away.

He was talking. He was saying the words, but they were flat and drifting. I wanted to be here. Cell phone in the truck. Out a bit too late. Had no idea. You two were close, I know that. So sorry. I wish I'd been here. No excuse. How awful for you. What do you need, kiddo? Have you called your mom? Can we do anything? Have you called your counselor?

Before I left, Nancy had said I could call or email anytime.

But I didn't want to talk to Nancy. I knew what she'd say. *I am so, so sorry for the loss of your dear friend, Maeve. This is not your fault. This is just life. It was her time. Now, Maeve, I have names of counselors up there. There's no need to try to do this alone. What about a grief group?* Or she'd recommend Al-Anon *again*. Nancy, who refused to accept that I would never, ever join a group like that. A bunch of people whining and moaning about their drunk father or mother or sister or boss or kid. All of them in some basement somewhere, shoulders hunched miserably, commiserating, huddling around stale doughnuts after, crying into napkins. *A place for you to build relationships. A place to make friends.*

I wanted Ruthie. I wanted one of her pragmatic summaries. *Heart-attack curse? Don't be stupid. The heart dies because of a medical emergency that cannot be fixed in time.* That's what she'd say. Science. It comes down to biology.

"Have you called your mom yet?" Dad asked again as he got ready to leave for work.

I shook my head.

"Why not?"

I shrugged.

"Call her," he said. "She'll want to know."

So I texted her. *Mrs. Patel died.*

That was it. So much had happened. Too much. When she left, she'd said that she wanted to know about everything. She wanted to know the details. She wanted to know how I was *feeling*. *If we keep in touch, nothing will change between us*, she'd said. But so much had already changed. There was too much to tell her. There was nowhere to start, because there was nowhere to end.

When she called, I told her that I didn't know when Mrs.

Patel had died. Or how she'd died. Claire told me, I said. Bandhu had called her. Oh, and Dad came home drunk.

She said all the right things. And she didn't ask any of the right questions.

"Mrs. Patel is in a better place."

"I guess so."

"Your father has slipped before, and recovered from that. Don't worry."

"I suppose."

"What about your date?"

"My date?"

"With Salix." I could tell that she was pleased that she remembered her name.

"Oh. That."

"Yes, that!" She was being excited for me. She was missing the point. "When is it?"

"Friday."

"Well, I want to hear all about it. Let me know how it goes."

When we hung up, Haiti seemed even farther away. It was at the edge of the planet. Or I was at the edge of the planet. Either way, someone was going to fall off.

Of course I was going to cancel the date. I didn't deserve to go on a date. I didn't deserve to feel the excited butterflies. I didn't deserve to think about what to wear, or what to say, or to imagine a first kiss with her.

I'd *killed* Mrs. Patel.

I turned the phone over and over in my hand until I finally sent a text.

I'm really sorry, but I can't make it on Friday. Something came up.

My skin prickled with disappointment, and I almost started to cry. But then I reminded myself that I was the one to blame. I thought of Mrs. Patel on a cold metal gurney in the morgue. Her life had ended because of me. I had no right to be happy.

Little Kids and the Subject of Death

"Hindus do death really fast," Corbin said as he and Owen and I walked up the street to get ice cream a couple of days later. Mrs. Patel's service was the next day, as soon after the death as possible, according to tradition.

"When Bobs died, we had a funeral the same day," Owen said. "Remember? And Dad pretended to be the priest."

"It's stupid to have a funeral for a cat," Corbin said. "Nana Jenkins says animals don't have souls."

Claire's mom. Also dead. Fundamentalist Christian who was certain beyond a doubt that she was going to heaven. Died of lung cancer. Smoked for fifty-two years out of sixty-four.

"To each their own," I said. The boys looked up, puzzled. "Thoughts. Everyone is entitled to their own ideas about death and what happens after."

"Louie in gymnastics died," Owen said.

"He wasn't a kid," Corbin said. "He was the janitor. He was really old."

"Mia Wong died."

"Car accident." Corbin picked up a long, thin stick and stuck it down his cast.

"Corbin!" I grabbed the stick and tossed it into the street. "You could get an infection."

"And die," Owen said. "We were at Mia Wong's birthday party just before she died. She had a lion cake. And party hats with polka dots."

"I ate too much cake and barfed," Corbin said.

"That robin died."

"So did the rat."

"We buried them," Owen said. "Is Mrs. Patel going to be buried?"

"Cremated." I didn't want to talk about any of this. And I didn't want ice cream, either. Mostly, I wanted to throw up.

We were outside the ice cream shop, and all of a sudden I did not want to go in. Mrs. Patel's favorite kind of ice cream was mango. She sometimes sent me to buy a small tub of it from here. Not when she was slumped by her chair with her hair sticky with vomit and the soap opera blaring. No! I will never leave you! No matter what you do! I don't care! Come back! Come back! I love you!

"You two go ahead." I gave them my wallet. "Get whatever you want."

"When you die, do you want to be buried?" Corbin said. "I want to be burned up."

"I want to be buried," Owen said.

They looked up at me, waiting for my answer.

Over two million people died in the US each year.

That meant about six thousand five hundred people *every day*.

Two hundred thousand people died in Canada each year.

Thirty thousand people died in British Columbia each year.

That was only eighty-two people a day.

Should I count myself at risk for the American statistics? Or could I adopt the Canadian risks while I was there?

"Maeve?" Owen took my hand as Corbin pushed ahead into the store with his good arm. "What kind do you want?"

"Nothing, thanks."

People swerved around us on the sidewalk. A pair of Chihuahuas tied to a parking meter yapped and yapped, straining at their leashes. A car honked. Someone was screaming at a cyclist to get off the goddamn road and use the bike path.

"If I was dead," Owen said, "I'd look down on you and hope you had some good ice cream."

"Thanks," I said. "If I was dead, I'd look down on you and hope you'd have some good ice cream too."

Dead People's
Empty Houses

When we got back to the building, there was a moving truck parked out front and a guy smoking a cigarette while he arranged furniture and boxes in the back. Another two men ferried a couch through the courtyard.

"That's Mrs. Patel's!" Owen waved his arms. "Hey! Stop!"

The movers carried Mrs. Patel's tired old couch up the ramp and into the truck.

"Watch out, kid." One of the men patted him on the head as they strode by, heading back to Mrs. Patel's.

"You can't take her stuff!" Corbin raised his casted arm like he might clobber them with it.

"Yes, they can." I pulled the boys away from the ramp. "Her family probably arranged it."

The movers came back again, this time with Mrs. Patel's china hutch wrapped in blankets.

"Let's go inside." I took the boys' hands.

"No!" Corbin pulled away. "I'm not going inside. I'm going to make sure they don't break anything." He faced the truck, hands on his hips. "You better not!"

"Me too," Owen said quietly. He sat on the curb and chewed on a finger.

So I went home by myself, but I didn't quite get there. One of Mrs. Patel's sons was sitting on a kitchen chair outside her door, talking on the phone in Hindi. He motioned for me to stop as I walked by.

"Maeve, hi. Hold on." He ended the call. "How are you?"

My hands started to shake so much that I had to shove them in my pockets. "I'm okay." My voice trembled. The thick weight of guilt I'd felt for days pressed down even harder. I wanted to tell him. *I killed her, Bandhu. I loved your mom, and it's my fault that she's dead. I deserve to be haunted by the stench of shit, spilled samosas, and blaring soap operas. I love you! Damn it, I love you! And Mrs. Patel slumped on the floor and the vomit and the playing cards scattered all around.*

He was talking. Saying all the things he should. *I'm so sorry that you found her like that. Thank you for giving the police my number. It must have been so hard for you.* And then he was saying something about her pink cardigan.

"Excuse me?"

"It's funny that she died in that sweater." He smiled a little. "But it's no surprise."

How could he smile like that? How could he just stand around and talk on the phone and talk to me and watch the movers take his mother's things away? And where would those things go? To Goodwill? To the dump? To his house?

"I gave her a new sweater every year on her birthday," he said. "And every year she folded it so nicely and put it in her drawer with a piece of tissue between it and the sweater I bought her the year before. She only liked the pink one. That was the first one I bought her. I wasn't much older than you."

I was thinking of gin rummy, and how she never let me win. I was thinking of her slippers, worn right through. I was thinking of her cupboard full of jars of loose tea. I was thinking that it was all my fault.

"I'm so s-s-sorry for your loss."

"Thank you," he said. "How are you coping, Maeve? I know it must've been very upsetting. I can only imagine."

I was not coping. I was terrible. I kept seeing her dead body over and over again. I kept hearing that soap opera, and in my head it was always even louder than it actually was. It was deafening. I love you! No, no! Don't leave!

"I am so, so s-s-sorry," I whispered.

We stood out of the way for the movers to go back in.

"You know, we told her to get one of those buttons she could wear around her neck, to call for help if she fell or if she was sick," he said. "There were a few times that she was almost unconscious from the diabetes. But she always said that when her time came, she didn't want to miss it."

Diabetes?

She died from *sugar*? Not from my wishing anything on anyone?

Diabetes killed more people each year than breast cancer and AIDS combined. I knew that much. Insulin. Glucose. Something about carbs and proteins.

"Diabetes?"

"Yes. There is a history in our family."

I could feel a shift.

"It had gotten much worse lately," he said. "She might have had many more years if she had agreed to get one of those buttons."

"That's what happened?" I felt lighter all of a sudden. "That's how she died?"

I gripped the railing with both hands. I was so weightless that I could float away. I could soar overhead and look down and everything would look tidy and perfect from above. And it would be. I hadn't killed Mrs. Patel. Of course I hadn't killed her. Ruthie would've been the one to stop all of this from happening in the first place. If I'd been able to talk to her, she would've made me realize what a stupid idea it was. Science. It's always about science. Empirical evidence, Maeve.

Science or superstition, it didn't matter.

I hadn't killed her. That was all that mattered.

A mover came out with Mrs. Patel's recliner on his back. He probably had no idea that that chair had held her while her sugars plummeted, and her heart beat valiantly along, until it couldn't anymore.

"Could I ask a favor?" Bandhu said.

I wanted to laugh. There went the chair, bobbing through the courtyard, bright and absurd, a greasy patch at the top where her head had rested. But not at the very end, I wanted to say, as if it were a punch line. Mrs. Patel's head had rested on her chin instead, vomit trailing down. *Bam! Pow!* Cue the applause. I hadn't killed her, and now everything seemed a bit too hilarious. Of course I hadn't conjured a heart attack. I wanted to laugh and laugh, because it was such a stupid idea. Ridiculous!

Bandhu was still talking. "I have to pick up my uncle from the airport. Would you mind keeping an eye on the movers? I've already paid, including tip. And I'll give you twenty dollars for your time."

"You don't need to pay me." I had to bite my lip to stop from laughing. "I'm happy to help."

And so absolutely, deliriously happy that I hadn't killed Mrs. Patel.

"I'll see you tomorrow?"

"We'll be there."

"My mother would like that." He pressed the twenty-dollar bill into my hand anyway, and then he said goodbye and left, just in time so that he wouldn't see the smile I couldn't hold back any longer.

When the movers were done, the one who'd carried the yellow chair on his back returned to walk me through the empty rooms so that I could sign the form saying they hadn't damaged any walls or doorways.

"You need to come inside," he said when I balked at the door.

"I can't, sorry. I'll sign now."

"Eyes inside. Contract says so."

"But I can't. She died in there. She was my friend."

"Sorry for your loss. She's not in there now, and I need a signature."

So I followed him in. He pointed out a gouge in the wall, a piece of missing baseboard, a crack in the bedroom door.

"Those were all here already. I can show you the pictures we took." His voice echoed, and the walls looked dirty, and the linoleum was sticky underfoot, which seemed so odd. Mrs. Patel had been a meticulous housekeeper, but her furniture and her pictures and her shelves of books and china teacups had hidden years of grime underneath.

"Where do I sign?" I said. "I have to go."

He held the clipboard while I signed at the bottom, and then he left and I was alone. All the curtains and drapes were gone; the sun streamed in through the windows, the rectangles of light meeting in the middle of the room. I put my hand on the banister. I took the stairs one at a time, hesitating on each one, but ending up at the top nonetheless. There were divots in the carpet where Mrs. Patel's furniture had been, and a grimy trail where she'd walked from the kitchen to her chair and back a million times or more. Someone had cleaned the spot where the piss and shit and vomit had been, but only just there. So the patch of carpet stuck out, cleaner than the rest, but still dirty. A broom leaned against the kitchen counter, beside a black garbage bag, half full. I swept the kitchen, and then I took the broom and the dustpan and the garbage bag downstairs and swept the linoleum by the door.

The place still smelled of her. But it smelled of dusty furniture and musty books, too, and the cleanser that was used on the carpet where she died. Even though I was the only one there, it was a different kind of quiet. A garbage truck rumbled down the alley, and it was louder, like the noise came right in and bounced off the bare walls. I could hear the children in the park across the street. Mrs. Patel's home was a sad, grimy, lonely place now. I shut the door and took a breath of fresh air in the courtyard. That was that.

Funerals and Fathers

I composed about a million texts to Salix in my head and sent exactly none. Too much had happened. I'd messed it up. She would think I was a flake. Which, clearly, I was. Because who would believe for *one minute* that a person could conjure a heart attack that could actually kill someone?

Someone who was crazy. That was who.

I didn't tell anyone about the heart attack. Not even as a joke. And I never would. Instead I carried on, looking after the boys, sketching, and feeling like I blew it with Salix. Three days after Mrs. Patel died, Claire and the boys and I went to the Hindu temple for Mrs. Patel's service.

"She's been our neighbor for almost seven years!" Claire was on the phone with Dad as she fished in the dryer for a clean pair of underwear. I was in my room, brushing my hair and listening, brushing my hair and listening. "You should be there, Billy. Take a longer lunch. Explain it to Nigel; he'll understand." There was a pause, and then Claire slammed the dryer door. "I hope so, Billy. Because there's no excuse not to be. She wasn't just a neighbor. She was our friend. She was *your* friend." Another pause. "It starts at two o'clock. You can meet us there."

Dad didn't show up.

Claire left me outside the temple to wait for him while everyone else filed in and she settled the boys inside.

"Are you coming in?" It was Bandhu.

"I will," I said. "I'm just waiting for my dad."

I kept my eyes on the parking lot, but he never showed up. Finally I went inside too, and instead of concentrating on Mrs. Patel's service, I sat and stewed in anger. Where the hell was he? What if he'd left work but hadn't made it to the temple? What if he'd stopped to get drunk in the middle of the day? He wasn't injured. He wasn't dead. He was just an asshole.

"This is inexcusable," Claire whispered, about ten minutes into the service. She was as restless as the boys, as we all focused on a service in a language none of us understood.

She put a hand on Corbin's leg to stop him from bouncing.

"Mom, Mom," Owen whispered. "I don't understand what they're saying."

"I have to get out of here." Claire gripped my wrist. "I can't breathe."

I took her arm and helped her up. The boys followed behind. People stared at us as we left, but Claire just doubled over a bit, holding her belly, as if that was the reason we were leaving. When we'd pushed through the doors and into the hot summer day, she straightened for a minute and took a deep breath.

"What the hell is going on? Where the fuck is your father?"

The three of us didn't say a word as we followed her across the parking lot. She unlocked the van, got into the driver's seat, and kicked off her sandals.

"I'm going to find him." She gripped the steering wheel. "I'm going to find him, and he is going to get the full wrath."

"What's *wrath*?" Owen asked from the backseat.

"Because if he thinks this is in any way acceptable, he is sorely mistaken."

She drove back to our neighborhood and—starting at the south end—stopped at every single bar and restaurant and pub and sent me in to check if he was there.

He wasn't.

"I'm hungry!" Corbin hollered when we stopped at a place that sold beer and fish and chips. "I have to eat good to re-build my bone. The doctor said!"

"Eat *well*." Claire put on her sandals.

"And get plenty of rest, and drink lots of water."

Claire hefted herself out and stalked into the shop and ordered four fish and chips combos, and when they were ready, we sat in the van and ate, and then we headed farther north to where the microbreweries had tasting rooms and tiny bars.

We drove around for hours and hours—so long that we had to stop for gas. Claire offered to drop us off at home, but we all wanted to stay together. Claire finally drove home as it got dark. When she took the boys upstairs, she found Dad sprawled across their king-size bed, snoring softly.

"For real?" She slammed the door. Then she opened it again. "Billy! Wake up!" But he didn't or he pretended not to, so she slammed the door again. She stomped downstairs, leaving the twins standing in the hallway, each of them holding a picture book, a dazed look on their faces.

"It'll be okay." I ushered them into their room. We sat on the lower bunk, quiet until Corbin offered up his book, and then Owen put his on top, and then they had something to argue about.

I read the stories and tucked them in before I went downstairs.

"I don't know what to do." Claire was on the phone. "Remember before the boys were born? Remember how bad it was?"

I didn't want to listen. I didn't want to know.

Missing Ruthie

I wanted to talk to Ruthie.

Not my mom, because I didn't want her to know that it was getting worse.

Not Claire, because she was so deeply into it that she was nearly drowning.

Not Nancy, because I never really did want to talk to her.

Not Dan, either, because he always turned everything into a joke. He made light of all the hard things and expected me to do the same. Sometimes that was okay. But not now.

I wanted Ruthie, no matter what had happened between us. I used to be able to tell her anything. She knew all my other secrets, and even now that we weren't speaking, I knew she'd never tell. I'd always trusted her before. I wanted Ruthie, who was so scientific about things. She could always apply a formula, and if one didn't exist, she'd invent one. She'd listen to me cry, but she'd never cry along with me. She'd listen, but she wouldn't sympathize.

I didn't know what else to do, so I wrote to her anyway, even though I wasn't sure that I did trust her anymore. I told her about Mrs. Patel, and about my dad. I even told her about Salix, because if I didn't, it would make things worse.

I don't even think it's legal for me to go into a bar, I finished. *Let alone twenty-six of them. Can you believe it?*

My finger hovered over the delete button. I'd written it, and now I did not have to send it. That was what Nancy said. Write the letter. Win the catharsis. Erase the letter; burn the letter; delete the letter; rip it up; shred it. But don't send it.

I hadn't received an email or text from Ruthie since she'd invited me over that afternoon, after Jessica had already moved back to California. It was a couple of weeks later, and I had a good reason to email her, so I did. She emailed back almost right away, as if she'd been waiting.

I still had the email. And the identical text. I opened both.

Come over and help me make a bunch of hexaflexagons?

And I have something I want to show you.

I'm home. Come in.

r.

But that was a lie. Or if she did have something to show me, everything happened before she had a chance. Or, thinking back on it, maybe she did show me.

I'd tried writing her a couple of times since then, but what was I supposed to say? She should be the one getting in touch with me. Right? Or was I supposed to ask her all the questions and hope that she'd give me some answers?

I was mad.

I was embarrassed.

I was ashamed, and confused.

I was hurt.

And she should be all those things too. Plus she should be sorry.

Why should I be the one to reach out now, after all this time?

I should let her come to *me*.

She was the one who needed to apologize.

But I sent it anyway. And once I had, there was no way to take it back. For better or for worse.

For better: I missed Ruthie, and I wanted her to be my best friend again.

For worse: she'd delete it before even reading it and never talk to me again. Everything would stay weird. I started another email.

I miss you.

Send.

And then one more.

I don't even know if you'll get any of these. Or if you'll read them.

And then it was almost funny.

I'll stop now.

Send.

And lastly, a joke. Because she told terrible jokes.

Q. Why did the mushroom get invited to all the parties?

A. Because he was such a fungi!

Send.

Maybe she would delete them all.

But maybe she would read them. And maybe she'd remember what it was like before Jessica.

Surprises

On Friday morning, my phone buzzed. I groped for it, knocking my sketchbook and pencils onto the floor.

Just on the ferry now, coming back to Van. See you this afternoon!

Salix?

Salix!

But I had sent that text. I'd canceled our date. And then Salix hadn't texted back.

But there was my text, still open. Not sent. I *hadn't* sent it. My stomach flipped. I hadn't messed it up after all! Salix hadn't ignored me. I had just beaten myself at my own impulsiveness, for once.

I deleted the one from before and then, with shaking hands, texted her back. *2pm, right?*

Salix texted back immediately. *The trick will be getting an outside table.*

Inside would be okay too, I texted.

No. Salix's reply came quickly. *It's a beautiful day. Leave it to me. I'll get an outside table. Don't worry. See you then.*

I sat there, stunned. There was still a date, and it was that afternoon. My first date. Only, no. Not really. But sort of. Did Jessica count? We held hands at school. She sat on my lap during lunch. We kissed a lot. But we never went *out* out. I went to her house on the weekends and we watched movies and baked cookies. She was so bold at first, up to and including that amazing—and also awful—first kiss. Just before she moved back to California, she passed me a note in class. *Want to sleep over and do stuff?* With *xoxoxox* and a happy face. I was sick with nerves while her parents served supper. I was sick with nerves when we watched a movie, holding hands and pulling away whenever her mom came downstairs. I was sick with nerves when we went to bed, locking her bedroom door and stripping until we were naked. Absolutely naked. When I slid into bed beside her, my nerves went away. But hers didn't. She lay rigid beside me, and so we hardly touched. All her talk, and I don't think she knew what to do with a girl. And I never claimed that I did either.

Jessica

When I told my dad and Claire that I was gay, Dad laughed. I can see why, he said. And then he winked. I like girls too. I cringed. And then Claire: I knew it! She hugged me. You know, I had a girlfriend for about three months back in college.

But one girl crush back in college didn't make her gay. Not really. I never said I was, she said when my dad teased her about being a lesbian. I suppose that I'm technically bisexual, she said. If you want to label me.

He gave her a look that I had no trouble deciphering.

Being queer was also about *not* being into boys. Just as it was about attraction, it was also about an absence of attraction, like white space. There wouldn't be white space if I liked both. But I didn't. Girls shimmered, as if all the light shone on them and not on the boys at all. Boys were hardly there, just shadows and background noise. I liked how girls talked, and moved, the way they smiled, or tucked their hair behind an ear. I watched the other girls as they changed for gym class, pulling off T-shirts and shorts, shrugging out of dresses. How they fixed their hair and teased each other. The lines of their arms and the curves of their bodies. I was always itching to draw them, even in the locker room. Which sounds weirder than it was. All those girls ignored me. They would never even have noticed me, sitting there with my sketchbook and pencils. They thought I was a loser. A geek. One of the invisible ones. And that was okay too, because the less they noticed me, the more I could admire them, even if they were bitches.

Until Jessica saw me. Actually *saw* me, as if I were suddenly in the light too. She was putting her clothes back on after gym. She slid tight jeans up over boy-cut underwear, a tiny, blurry tattoo of a star on her hip.

"My girlfriend did it," she said. "With a needle and ash. That's how they do it in the Russian prisons."

I looked away, blushing.

"Not that I've ever been in a Russian prison."

She'd come from California the week before. Some mess having to do with her dad losing his marbles and coming to her school and screaming in the office about alien abduction. Now she was living with her mom, but she hadn't quite mapped the school population yet. Who was land. Who was water. Or maybe she didn't care.

"I saw you looking," Jessica said.

I was going to deny it, but I stammered an apology instead. "S-s-s-s-sorry."

Jessica laughed. "No problem." She grabbed her bag and closed the locker with one finger, which she then dragged lightly across my locker, the one next to hers. "I like to look too." She patted my head, as if I were a little pet. Which was kind of how it played out, in the end.

Dates

A ponytail. A headband. Hair down. Hair up. Skirt. Shorts. A dress. Tank top and jeans. No. What the hell. Earrings? No earrings. Small earrings? Or a cute T-shirt? No. Tank for sure. Too hot for a T-shirt. Shorts to be casual. It was casual, right? Mom's scarf as a belt. Nice touch. Too bohemian? What did it matter. Did it matter? What did *bohemian* even mean? What the *hell*.

Tank top.

Shorts with the scarf belt.

Done.

By then I had to leave, so there was no more changing my mind unless I wanted to be late. On my way out, I found Claire leaning against the kitchen counter, wincing.

"Are you okay?"

"I'm fine." She let out a breath. "Braxton Hicks."

"Who?"

"Braxton Hicks contractions." Claire straightened and

smiled. "That's better. Practice contractions. That's all. Baby's fine."

"It's way too early."

"Absolutely." She reached for my hand and placed it against her ribs. "That's a kick. Feel it?"

Nothing. Nothing. But then I did feel it! It was like a kick, and then a push, like the baby was stretching.

And then I *was* going to be late, so I hurried out of the house and up the street without thinking about what I was wearing at all.

I slowed to a stop about a block away from Continental.

Was I wearing totally the wrong thing?

I should've worn a dress. I looked down at myself. Too casual. I looked like a slob. And had I even put on deodorant? I closed my eyes and tried to think. That morning? No. The text from Salix had thrown me off. Squeezing my eyes shut tighter, I cringed. I was pretty sure that I hadn't.

"Hey." A hand on my shoulder. When I recovered from the surprise, Salix was laughing. "What're you doing?"

"I was j-j-just thinking."

"What about?" Salix was as cute as I remembered. Maybe even more so. She was wearing skinny pin-striped pants folded up to her calves, and red suspenders and red Converse sneakers and a tight black tank top with the word *almost* printed on it in big white letters.

"Nothing, really. *Almost* what?"

"Just 'almost.'" She started walking. "Come on. That's our table."

Our table? Outside tables were highly coveted at Continental. People came in the morning and set up to stay for hours, with newspapers and knitting and friends and books and computers. And when they did finally decide it was time to leave, there were always people hovering nearby.

But there it was. An empty table with a coffee cup holding down a piece of paper with Salix's name on it and *Reserved* scrawled above a skull and crossbones and signed, "Evil Pirate Overlords of Management."

I reached for a chair, but she beat me to it and pulled it out for me.

"Thanks."

The sidewalks were crowded with couples and old men and children and dogs and all the bustle that came with a Friday afternoon on the Drive. A bus pulled up and emptied, and a little old lady struggled to get her shopping cart off. Salix ran to help, and when the woman turned, her smile was wide and her eyes were pinched at the corners and she was wearing a pink cardigan. Instead of asking about the table, I heard Mrs. Patel, loud and clear.

Come over tomorrow.

She gave me a peck on the cheek.

I will deal the cards for rummy.

But I hadn't gone. I hadn't even thought about it. We went to visit Grandma. So the cards ended up on the floor instead.

I didn't want to think about her.

I'd spent so much time thinking about her. Surely that was enough?

I could think of her later.

But images kept pushing in. An ace of hearts by her limp hand. The old pink cardigan. And the TV with the soap opera blaring. The broom and the dustpan. The walls with the shadows where frames had hung.

Salix took the seat across from me. "Are you okay?"

"Yes." The paramedics and the firefighters and the police, all just standing around her dead body. I knew there was nothing they could do, but still, they should've done *something*. I sat up and smiled. "I'm fine."

"I used to work here," Salix said. "For about three weeks. I broke seven glasses and three mugs and got a third-degree burn on my wrist. I was fired, thank God. But they still love me. So they saved me a table, in case you were wondering about the miracle."

"I *was* wondering, I just . . . got lost in my thoughts for a moment. So awesome about the table." Nothing in my voice conveyed *awesome* or *miracle* or even *interesting person*.

"What can I get you?"

"Oh. I don't know—"

How would this go? Should I get up and go inside with her? Or should I let Salix order and then give her money? Was this her treat?

"My treat," Salix said.

Had I said that out loud?

"What do you—what's something that—" I stammered. "I d-d-don't . . ." I took a breath and tried again. "What's good?"

"The mochas. Iced or hot."

"Sure. That sounds good. I've got money." I dug in my bag for my wallet, but it wasn't there. I pulled out my sketchbook and pencil case before finally finding a handful of coins at the bottom. I stared into my bag, horrified. My cheeks were suddenly hot. Should I go back home to get it?

"It's on me, Maeve." Salix put a hand on my wrist. "Don't worry about it. Iced or hot?"

"Iced, I guess. Thank you."

149

"Done."

She held the door open for a mom with a baby on her hip—that made three people she'd helped so far, if the baby counted too—and then followed her inside and up to the counter, where she leaned on her elbows and chatted with the boy working the espresso machine. She looked out the window and saw me watching her. I quickly looked away and flipped through my sketchbook.

Salix returned with four glasses: two big ones—the iced mochas with chocolate whipped cream—and two little ones filled with water. She set them down. "It's amazing that I did that without dropping one." She pulled a wax paper bag out of her pocket and lifted out a big cookie. "Gingersnap." She broke it in two and then set the pieces on top of the bag in the middle of the table. "You pick. The person who breaks it gets second dibs. That's how it goes."

"You're obviously not an only child."

"I have an older sister." She pushed the cookie my way. "Take your pick."

"Thank you." I took half. I broke off a corner. My mouth was dry. I chewed and chewed. When I swallowed, I reached for the water. My hand was shaking, and the water sloshed in the glass as I brought it to my lips.

"So, hi."

"What?"

"We never said hi."

"Hi." I laughed, and the knot in my stomach began to loosen. "How was fiddle camp?"

"Great. I had the little kids. They're so funny. It's like a bunch of feral cats trying to sing in tune, only it's fifteen violins. There was a lot of screeching and yowling."

Salix's violin case sat at her feet, along with the same beat-up backpack. "Who's the guy on your backpack?"

"Beethoven," Salix said.

"The blind guy?"

"That's Bach."

"Ah." Stupid. Stupid. Stupid.

"What kind of music are you into?"

"I like to listen to it. Does that count?"

"Depends on what kinds."

"Pretty much anything except country and soapy jazz."

"Soapy jazz?" Salix laughed. "What's soapy jazz?"

"Sleepy and slippery and oozy. My dad calls it soapy jazz." My throat was dry again. I took a sip of my mocha, but there was so much whipped cream that I had to tip the glass way up before the coffee made its way to my lips. And then it was in a rush, and it sloshed down my chin. I pulled the cup away, ending up with a sizeable whipped-cream mustache.

"I asked for extra whipped cream." Salix offered me a napkin, and I wiped it away. "Sorry."

"That's okay," I said. "Elevator music."

"What?"

"Soapy jazz."

"Okay, sure. I know what you mean. But what about real jazz?"

"I like real jazz." Was that the right answer? "My dad has a huge collection of great jazz."

"Good, because I don't know if we could continue sharing this table if you didn't like real jazz."

"Define 'real jazz.'"

"I like the old stuff. Louis Armstrong and Bix Beiderbecke. Django Reinhardt. That kind of thing."

"Never heard of Bix Blahblahbeck, but everyone knows Louis Armstrong. Who doesn't love 'What a Wonderful World'?"

"It's not my favorite."

"Blasphemy." This was feeling easier now. "And I know Django Reinhardt. My dad loves him. Can you play his stuff?"

"I can. Want me to play a bit for you?"

"Sure." A cute girl playing the violin for me at a sidewalk café? I wouldn't have been surprised if a *Tyrannosaurus rex* had lurched down the street and swallowed me whole. It was about as likely.

When Salix stood up and began to play, everyone turned to listen. All the people at the other tables, people walking by with their groceries and dogs and toddlers and cell phones in hand. The guy who ran the used-book store next door came out, and so did his customers. Salix played for about five minutes, and when she stopped, everyone cheered.

"Where do I put the money?" one woman said.

"That was a freebie. By request."

"That was amazing," I said. The people hung around for a long moment, but when she put her violin back in its case, they slowly drifted away.

"Thanks." Salix took a drink of her coffee. "You said you don't play an instrument?"

"No."

"Not even the school band?"

"No." Speaking of school: "Do you go to Brit?"

"Windsor House."

"Where is that?"

"Strathcona. It's a democratic school, which basically means we can do whatever we want whenever we want and go whenever we want."

"I'm registered at Brit."

"Change that. Windsor. Definitely Windsor. We even have a carnival band, which I think you should join."

"But I don't know how to play anything."

"That's the beauty of a carnival band. No one will notice." She shook her head, marveling. "I can't believe that Billy Glover is your dad and you don't play an instrument. You have to in my family. It's a rule."

"Not many rules in my house."

"You're lucky."

"I don't know about that," I said. "You're an awesome violin player. Would you have learned it if your parents didn't push you to?"

"Probably not."

"I kind of wish my dad had kept trying to teach me to play the guitar."

"There's still time."

Neither of us said anything for a beat too long, and then I wasn't sure what to say, so I didn't say anything, hoping that Salix would say something first. And then she did.

"How was your week?"

Not a hard question.

I could've come up with something. But actually, I couldn't. I should've known she'd ask that. What have you been up to? Do anything interesting since I saw you? How was your week?

"M-m-my week?" Mrs. Patel's legs sticking out. Samosas and French fries spilled on the carpet. A queen of spades. A bloody splotch of ketchup. "It was f-f-fine."

"Really?"

I blinked.

"Your face says it wasn't fine." Salix looked genuinely worried. Which made it even worse. "What happened?"

"It was j-j-just that . . ." But there was nothing *just* about it, and all of a sudden I was telling her about finding Mrs. Patel in her pink cardigan, and the paramedics and the police and the soap opera blaring on the TV, and the movers. Salix listened, her face shifting from worried to curious to horrified to sympathetic.

"Oh, I . . . that's horrible," Salix said. "Absolutely horrible. I don't even know what else to say."

And just like that, I wrecked the date. Why would Salix want to hang out with someone who could recite the entire soap-opera conversation that was happening in the background while she knelt beside her dead neighbor?

"I should go." I stared at my drink. I couldn't look at her eyes, kind and inquiring. If I did, I might cry.

"Are you going to go to her funeral?"

"It was yesterday." I was nearly breathless. I didn't want to tell her that we walked out of Mrs. Patel's service. I didn't want to tell her about driving around and looking for Dad. I didn't want to tell her that we didn't find him. "Look, I'm really sorry. I have to get going."

"Already?"

I nodded quickly. "I have to look after my little brothers."

"Oh." Salix stood up. "Uh. Okay. Maybe we could—"

But I had already stuffed my sketchbook into my bag and

was gone, stuttering a goodbye over my shoulder as I resisted the urge to run down the sidewalk. I paused after a few steps. I should say something. I should make it less weird. I should let her know that it had nothing to do with her. It was all me. All the weird was all me. I turned, and there was Salix staring at me, and she looked so confused, and I couldn't think of anything to say, so I turned again and bumped into a spinner of books. It tipped over, scattering cheap paperbacks onto the sidewalk. I tripped on one and then broke my fall by reaching for the produce display in front of the Persian market. A cascade of oranges fell, rolling into the street. The next car ran over them, bright little explosions against the hot black asphalt.

"Maeve!" It was Salix, coming to help. Of course she would come to help. But I didn't want her to. I leapt up and took off at a run. I kept running. "Maeve! Stop!" But I didn't stop, and I didn't look back. I ran all the way to the park and turned the corner and caught my toe on a split in the sidewalk. There was nothing to break my fall this time, and so I ended up on my hands and knees.

Whatever Hope died suddenly today, surprising no one in particular. Survived by Salix Unknown-Last-Name-Because-It-Didn't-Even-Get-That-Far, who narrowly escaped the mess that is Maeve "Stupidity" Glover. Donations can be made to Whatever Hope's future that wasn't: "Two Girls in Love." There will be no service, because there wasn't anything in the first place to have a service about.

Humiliation

Salix texted seven times from when I got back onto my feet to when I stumbled through the courtyard.

Hey.

Are you okay?

What happened?

You didn't finish your half of the cookie. It's very sad about that.

Then a picture of the cookie sitting on the paper bag, with a sad face drawn on with marker.

I'll save it for you.

Hello?

As if we'd see each other again. Because I'd genuinely blown it this time, no mistaking. She was just being nice. I did not text back. I sat on the curb and cried, so thankful that no one was in the courtyard. Why are you crying, Maeve? Oh, I don't know. No reason. I just found my lovely neighbor's dead body. That's all. And I messed up a date with a girl I really liked. Or I was crying about all the other things. It's not always obvious, Nancy said about crying. Sometimes you're sure it's one thing, but it's something else. I didn't want to think of all the things it could be. I wanted it to be about the date. This was about screwing up with a really cute girl. A girl who helped little old ladies off the bus. A girl who could make an entire city block of people stop what they were doing to listen to her play her violin. The girl I wanted to hold hands with. The girl I wanted to kiss.

Which would not be happening now.

I rooted in my bag for my keys but couldn't find them. I tipped my bag out and sifted through the pencils and sketch-book and erasers and coins and there was my wallet, jammed under a water bottle. It had been there all along. And my keys, too.

I let myself in with an enormous sigh. I flopped onto my back and lay splayed on the dingy carpet, staring at the dust motes in the sunshine, the silence echoing with all the wrong and the stupid and the regret. I tried to see each particle, forcing my eyes to focus on the impossible, if only to distract me from thinking about anything else that had happened. Or hadn't happened. Or was happening, even now. A hierar-chy of happenings.

A game of rummy that never happened

A date that only halfway happened.

Mom and Raymond happening and happening and happening.

Whatever was happening with Dad.

The baby who was happening, at a home birth that shouldn't be happening.

Mrs. Patel's place so empty next door, and the images of her dead body that just kept happening.

Ruthie and Jessica and everything that happened. And didn't happen.

Ruthie, and the friendship, not happening.

Ruthie

Ruthie translated the world through *Doctor Who* episodes
and intricate plotlines from obscure Japanese video games.
She saw numbers and formulas in the same way that I
could see lines and shapes of objects and draw them to life.
Ruthie, who lumbered up and down the locker-lined hallways at school, awkward in her broad-shouldered body, her
big feet shoved into gigantic sneakers with Daleks on the
sides, her Tardis-shaped backpack snugged to her back with
both straps. Nobody used both straps. No one at all. All the
other students hung their backpacks on one shoulder, with
one strap. Not two. I tried to explain this to Ruthie once,
but she only shrugged and said what did it matter how she
carried her backpack. But it did matter. These little things
mattered a lot.

I met Ruthie at social-skills class when we were in fifth
grade. I was pulled out of Mrs. Henshaw's class, and Ruthie

was pulled out of Mr. Randhawa's class at the other end of the hall. We were brought together with three other kids once a week and made to do things like practice looking each other in the eye and then not looking each other in the eye. Or ordering a meal and remembering to say thank you. Or excusing ourselves politely when our tics or our anxiety or our wild rage or pre-psychotic disposition dictated that we should.

Ruthie was just weird, maybe too smart to be normal. And I was just worried. The two of us seemed pretty harmless compared to the other three, all boys who'd been suspended for various acts of violence, and in one case for having set the school on fire. A small fire, but still.

We had nothing in common, really, but we liked each other's company and filled that best-friend-shaped space that everyone seems to have. And then I got used to her, and I loved her. Ruthie was an only child, and I was an only child most of the time, so maybe that had a lot to do with it. Whatever kept us together, it was strong. We did everything together. We tried to get classes together, we had lockers beside each other, and we ate lunch together in the loser corner every day. On weekends I would go to her house and sketch while she built tiny models of robots and airplanes, delicate and perfect despite her beefy hands. Or she would come over and read me weird science articles while I drew, or she'd follow me around the garden and tell me that 93 percent of gardeners grew tomatoes, or that the biggest tomato ever grown weighed seven pounds, or that Japanese scientists were studying mosquitoes to help them design a painless needle.

Mostly these articles came from *Scientific American*, which her dad subscribed to, and which for some reason never stopped coming after he died. One day at lunch she was reading to me about how developing brains fold like crumpled paper to get their convolutions. Which is where Jessica found us after I saw her tattoo in the locker room. She sat beside us, as if that were an acceptable thing to do—join us at our table in the corner. On purpose.

"What are you doing?" Ruthie held the magazine to her chest, as if it were secret.

"I'm Jessica. I met Maeve in the locker room. She was looking at my ass. And you are . . . ?"

"I wasn't looking at your—" I felt my cheeks heat up. "I wasn't l-l-looking at you."

"You were so." Jessica grinned. "It's okay. I don't mind."

"I wasn't."

Jessica stared at me, eyebrows raised. Ruthie stared at Jessica, mouth agape.

I looked from one to the other, not sure what to say, so I introduced Ruthie.

"Nice to meet you." Jessica flicked a piece of popcorn into Ruthie's mouth, which was still hanging open. Ruthie gagged and spat it out. It landed on Jessica's tray. She flicked it off with a finger and thumb and offered Ruthie the bag of popcorn instead. "Your mouth was open, so I went with it."

But before that. The spring before, when we were waiting for my mom to pick us up in Seattle after watching a roller-derby match between the Rat City Roller Girls and the Bellingham Betties, Ruthie stood there beside a bus stop full of graffiti and garbage and mumbled something about the match and the Betties' jammer and then she kept mumbling and it sounded like she said she liked girls.

"What?" My mom's car was at the intersection. She honked her horn and waved.

"I like girls," Ruthie repeated.

Three little words. And I knew exactly what she meant. Because I did too. But I didn't want to talk about it. I didn't want to say it out loud. And I'd never thought that Ruthie was gay. Not in a million years. I'd thought of her as one of the weird science nerds who would one day find another weird science nerd and have a few weird-science-nerd babies.

But then I thought, Who says that the weird science nerd has to be a man?

Whatever. I was already dealing with my own confusing thoughts about girls; I was not ready to deal with Ruthie's, too. I pretended that I didn't hear her, and I waved frantically at my mom as she pulled in. And then it occurred to me. What if Ruthie thought of *me* that way? As a *girl* girl.

No.

I was not a weird science nerd. I was her type just as much as she was mine, which was not at all.

She was not cute. And she was not interesting. Well, not in that way. Not to me. She was interesting, sure. But she'd be more interesting to the weird science nerd who would fall in love with her and want to read tedious articles from *Scientific American* together. And *cute* was not a word that I would use to describe Ruthie. Someone would. She would find her weird-science-nerd match, I was sure.

Mom pulled up, and Ruthie got in the front, because there was more room for her. It wasn't that she was fat—not at all—but she couldn't pull herself together to fit into anything. Clothes, groups, backseats. Ruthie always seemed to spill over.

Ruthie avoided me for a while after that. She hid in the science lab at lunch and after school and during every second of her free periods. When I ran into her in the bathroom one day, she blushed and finished washing her hands and walked straight out, not bothering to dry them. I followed her into the hall.

"Ruthie! Where have you been?" I wanted to tell her that I'd heard what she said by the bus stop. I wanted to tell her that it was okay with me. I wanted to tell her that I was too. Me too, Ruthie! But none of that came out.

"I've been working on the molds," she said. "The ones for the state science fair. That's all."

And then I didn't see her for another two weeks. Not until after the science fair, which I was supposed to go to with her, but when she didn't call and she didn't text and she didn't email, I figured that was her way of uninviting me.

"I won," she announced the Monday after the fair. She sat across from me at lunch and lined up her yogurt and her sandwich just so, and arranged her carrots into a hexagon shape on a piece of paper towel. As if nothing had ever happened. Which it kind of hadn't. But it kind of had, too. Had she been ignoring me? Or had it really been about the molds? The half conversation in the parking lot seemed so fuzzy now. Had I heard her? Had she said that? She slid her medal across the table. "First prize."

"That's great," I said. "Congratulations, geek."

"Thanks, freak."

And things went back to normal. Sort of.

Jessica laughed at Ruthie's carrot-stick hexagon when she sat with us for the first time the next spring. She helped herself to one while Ruthie looked on, horrified.

"That was mine."

"You can spare one." Jessica's hair was shorter than Ruthie's, but it looked much better. Ruthie's hair was choppy, a fuzzy helmet that stuck out about an inch all the way around and didn't look any better when it was long. Cursed and damned in that department, she sometimes said. Not Jessica, though. Her sleek black hair was choppy in all the right places, a pixie cut that looked expensive, with long, dyed-pink bangs that were definitely expensive.

I wondered if Jessica was gay, but I didn't outright ask her. And then I didn't have to, because she came to school one day about a week later wearing a T-shirt with two woman-figure symbols like the ones on bathroom doors, side by side, holding hands—or handless arms—with the words SORRY, GUYS underneath. We were standing outside before the first bell, and it was cold, but optimistically spring cold, so no one was wearing jackets or coats, except Ruthie. Ruthie and I stared at Jessica's shirt (which essentially meant that we were also staring at her breasts), both of us blushing. Ruthie stammered and swallowed and garbled something about petri dishes and extra credit and fled to the science lab.

"I can tell so much about you when you stare at me." Jessica pushed her bangs out of her face. And then: "Don't tell me that you didn't know that I'm a dyke. I've been dropping hints from the moment I met you."

And then she grabbed my hand and held on to it, pulling me into the school as if it were no big deal at all.

Ruthie scowled when Jessica asked to be the third in our group for the end-of-term biology project later that day.

"It's worth thirty percent of our grade," Jessica said. "Of course I want to be in Dr. Ruth's group."

"Don't call me that."

"Come on, it's a compliment."

"She can join us," I said. "Right, Ruthie?"

"You want her to?"

"Sure."

"Fine." Ruthie stacked her textbooks and binder to make room.

"Thanks." Jessica beamed as she sat down, inching her chair closer to mine.

I hadn't told Ruthie about us holding hands, and no one else would've told her. No one else really talked to her, except for the other geeks in the science club and Mathletes, who would be clueless about it too, no doubt. I was going to tell her, but then I was thinking that maybe I didn't want to. Maybe it was something that I wanted to keep all for myself. Just for a while. Just until I'd have to tell her. I knew by the fierce red splotches on Ruthie's cheeks that she had a crush on Jessica too. Was that what it was? Did I have a crush on Jessica? But she took *my* hand, I reminded myself. *She* took my hand. She held tight. *She* pulled me in.

A third for a science project was one thing. But a third in

a friendship sent everything off-kilter. And a third for anything more than that? A disaster.

The next day Jessica and I were sitting on the floor in Ruthie's basement ripping newspaper into shreds so we could start on the papier-mâché cell model, while Ruthie was upstairs mixing flour and water for paste, and getting snacks.

"We need snacks," Jessica had said. "It's the hospitable thing to do, Ruthie." And so Ruthie had hefted herself off the floor and tromped upstairs. I could hear her crossing the kitchen. A cupboard door slammed. The fridge opened and closed.

"I better do this now," Jessica said. She leaned over and kissed me on the lips. I froze, and Jessica kissed me again, and then I was kissing her back, and that's how Ruthie found us, with our mouths glued together and Jessica's hand up my shirt, the strips of newspaper scattered around us. Ruthie dropped the tray, and the bowl of paste; a plate of cheese and crackers and three glasses of apple juice crashed to the floor.

"Ruthie." I sprang to my feet. "Let me help."

Ruthie just stood there, her jaw slack.

"I'll get paper towels," I said, too loud and too fast. I ran up the stairs and grabbed the paper-towel roll from beside the sink. When I got back downstairs, Ruthie was still standing amid the broken bowl and the broken plate and the broken glasses, the paste oozing onto the dingy carpet, and Jessica was standing on the other side of the mess, chewing on her lip, hiding a smile.

Ruthie said it was no big deal, and she might have been talking about the mess, or maybe she was talking about me

166

and Jessica, but it didn't matter, because she disappeared. She switched to another biology class, arguing that she wanted to learn from a teacher who was working on his PhD, not the one who'd just graduated from college, and so the principal signed off on her request. She was the top science student, after all.

That could've been the worst of it. But it wasn't. It got much worse, and so much messier than a heap of broken dishes on the floor.

I wasn't off to a good start when it came to girls. Jessica—and then what happened with Ruthie after—and now Salix. Each time I thought about texting Salix back, I didn't. A couple of times I'd start a text, but I never sent them.

Tell the cookie that I'm sorry for leaving it behind.

Or *Can I buy you a sorry-I-bolted coffee?*

Or *Django called from beyond the grave and he wants me to tell you that he was listening that day and to tell you that you're really good.*

Stupid.

Or *Do you know Grandview Park? It could use a really good violinist. It's all hippie drummers and one guy on a trumpet who sounds like a dying goose.*

Stupid and pathetic.

So I just didn't text her back.

New Neighbors and
Drunk Dads

The new neighbor moved in exactly a week after Mrs. Patel's service. He was an old man—older than Mrs. Patel—short and pudgy, with shaggy white hair and thick glasses barely perching on the tip of a bulbous red nose. A wino nose, my mom called them. The boys and I watched the movers bring his things in from the street. Dollies stacked with boxes, a leather armchair, and so many bookshelves that I lost count. When the movers left, he disappeared inside and came out a few moments later with four ice cream sandwiches.

"I always keep a box in my freezer," he said. "It's the only thing in there right now. Let's introduce ourselves when our fingers are filthy with chocolate, shall we?" But he took out a handkerchief and dabbed at the corners of his mouth as he said it. "I'll go first. I'm Oscar Heidelman." He had an accent. German, I guessed, although I didn't really know.

"I'm Corbin," Corbin said with his mouth full. "And this

is my brother, Owen. We're twins. Only, we don't look alike. And I have a broken arm."

"I see."

Owen looked at Mr. Heidelman, unsmiling. I knew what he was thinking. No one should be living in Mrs. Patel's place except for Mrs. Patel. Ever. Especially not so soon after she died *in the apartment*. The building owners could've waited until the end of the month at least.

"I'm Maeve."

"Lovely to meet you all, neighbors." A horn honked from the street. "Excuse me." He pushed his glasses up. "My babies have arrived."

"Babies?" Owen said.

"Come see."

So we followed him through the courtyard. A bright yellow truck was parked at the curb. ELLIS PIANO MOVERS. Mr. Heidelman popped the last of his ice cream sandwich into his mouth and greeted the men. He stood at the foot of the ramp while they wheeled a small grand piano down. I tried to count the instruments. Another smaller piano. A bass. A cello. Five violins, and maybe a viola, all with cases as beat-up as Salix's.

"Do you play all of those?" I asked.

"I do." Mr. Heidelman nodded as one of the movers carried in another black case.

"What's that one?" Owen asked.

"A French horn."

"I was looking for you guys." Claire joined us at the street, her feet bare and swollen. "Lunch is ready." She turned to Mr. Heidelman. "Care to join us?"

"No, thank you," he said. "I'm far too eager to get settled. Perhaps the boys would like to come help me unpack a million boxes of books after lunch? I pay in lemonade."

Corbin came home after only twenty minutes and one glass of lemonade.

"It was too sour," he said. "And the books are really dusty."

Owen was there until it was nearly suppertime.

Just as Claire was pulling things out of the fridge, Dad texted to say that he was on his way home with pizza—early, for once. He had hardly shown his face since the day of Mrs. Patel's funeral.

So pizza was a big deal.

Usually when Dad came home, he went straight upstairs and had a shower, almost before even saying hello. But he didn't that day. And there wasn't any pizza.

"Where's the pizza?" Corbin asked, the disappointment clear on his face.

"I said I was going to order it."

"No, you said you were bringing it home," Claire said. She pulled up his text and showed him.

"Thanks, Text Officer Claire." He saluted her.

Something was off. It wasn't just the pizza. It wasn't just that he was home early. He wasn't himself. Had he gotten fired? Had he gotten stopped for drunk driving? The worst thing was that neither of those things would have surprised me.

Claire started to tell him about her friend in Toronto who'd just won a major environmental award for a rooftop garden she'd designed, but he wasn't really listening to her either.

All of a sudden, and with a great war cry, Dad grabbed Corbin and flipped him, pinning him to the floor.

"Gotcha!"

Corbin's expression went from shock to glee, until he was squealing with laughter and pummeling Dad with his cast.

They were still wrestling when Owen appeared at the door, with Mr. Heidelman behind him.

"Billy, we have a guest," Claire said. "Meet our new neighbor. Mr. Heidelman."

Dad shoved Corbin off him and leapt up.

"Hi!" He thrust out a hand. "Billy Glover."

"He was in the Railway Kings," Claire said. "Remember them? 'O'Ryan's Train.'"

"Not my genre, I'm afraid."

"I don't blame you, Mr. Heidelman," Dad said, tossing Claire a withering look.

"Oscar, please." His eyes drifted to the art on the walls. "Patrons of the arts, I see. As am I."

"We try." Dad ushered Mr. Heidelman in to show him the enormous painting of the horse and ogre that hung in the stairwell. It was hideous and awful, and at first glance it looked hundreds of years old, done in dark oils and grim colors, with highlights placed exactly where they should be. It looked like the horse was just about to rear up and gallop right out of the canvas, except that it had one rotten leg, red and oozing and chewed to the bone. The ogre was large and scowling, dressed in a business suit, its eyes glistening. I hated that painting.

"This one is by a good friend of mine," Dad said. "It was a wedding gift. We do lots of trades. Barters. That sort of thing."

"Billy is an artist too." Claire pointed out the painting hung over the dinner table. "That's one of his." It was my favorite: an alpine meadow, with me and Dad asleep on a patchwork quilt in the corner. Dad was curled around me, his arm curved protectively above my head. I was about two years old, with chubby legs and rosy cheeks. My parents were already living apart by then.

He was doing it again.

Drinking.

Not coming home.

And now he was acting high.

It was only a matter of time, even though Claire had said he would never go back. She'd said he would not be a statistic. She'd said she believed in him. As if that was all it took, when the fact was that over 50—and up to 90!—percent of addicts relapsed. The numbers didn't lie.

He was pushing Claire away, just like he had done before. Just like he'd done with my mom, using the woman at the coffee shop to ruin it permanently.

Maybe he was hardwired to fuck up his family. His *families*. Every time a new baby—or two—came along, he fell apart. Maybe he wasn't meant to be a part of a family at all. My heart constricted at the idea. He couldn't do this to us. He wouldn't.

"It's a very good painting." Mr. Heidelman peered at it, hands locked behind his back. "Beautiful detail. Skillful brushstrokes." He glanced at the date in the corner. "Fourteen years ago. Your new work must be very, very good."

"Yeah, it's not bad."

"He's being modest," Claire said. "If he was willing to sign with a gallery, he'd be very successful."

"No galleries." My dad shook his head. "I like doing my own thing." He sniffed. "So, can I help get you settled at all? Need anything? Pictures hung? Furniture arranged?"

"No, but thank you." Mr. Heidelman laughed. "I am very tired. I am going to make a cup of tea and then take myself straight to bed. Everything else can wait."

Once Mr. Heidelman was gone, Claire ordered the pizza. While we waited, Corbin and Owen staged a battle between the kings, but Corbin wasn't really into it. He kept glancing up at Dad. Corbin let King Percival win too soon, and then he got up and took a running leap at Dad, tackling him. Dad rolled onto the floor and they started wrestling again. At first Corbin was laughing, but then he was yelping in pain.

"Ouch, Daddy!" He scuttled away.

"Aw, it wasn't that hard." Dad yanked him back by his good arm, and his cast clunked against the table leg. He was being too harsh. Too rough. Even for Corbin.

"It was so." He pulled away again, back up to Claire, who folded her arms around him.

"Are you okay, baby?"

Breathless and sweaty, Corbin nodded.

Owen and I sat on the couch. All of us stared at Dad.

"Billy?"

"What?"

"Are you okay?"

"I'm fine."

"I hope so."

"Lighten up, people." Dad rolled his eyes. "Come on, Corbin. I'll go easy on you."

"Mom?" Corbin said quietly.

"He's had enough." Claire pressed her head to Owen's, her eyes on Dad.

"Corbin can speak for himself," Dad said.

But Corbin didn't say anything.

"We were just playing." Dad sat back on his knees. He was panting too. His cheeks were red. He pushed his hair off his forehead. "What?" He met Claire's gaze and held it.

"That was too rough," Claire said.

"We're talking about Corbin, here, right? I had the right twin. It's not that hard to tell them apart."

Owen made a little noise. I put my arm across his shoulder.

"That was uncalled for, Billy."

Owen trembled for a moment, trying not to cry, but then he couldn't help it and he started to sob. I hugged him while Claire glared at Dad.

"So I'm the bad guy. Okay. Sure." Instead of apologizing, Dad jumped up and headed for the door. "I can be the bad guy." He spun his keys on a finger, and they flew right off, hitting the wall. "Someone has to. And it's never going to be you, Claire. Right? You're the good one. The perfect parent." He picked up his keys, smashed a baseball cap onto his head, and opened the door, where the pizza delivery guy was just about to knock. "Great. Pizza's here!" He took the two boxes and threw some money at the man, and then he tossed the boxes behind him like Frisbees. One of the boxes opened, and a pizza slid onto the living-room carpet. He slammed out the door, leaving the four of us staring at the mess.

The marriage between Claire and Billy Glover died today under suspicious circumstances. Not much is known at this time, but resuscitation is unlikely. The marriage leaves behind a confused wife, three bewildered children, and a fourth blessedly oblivious one on the way. In lieu of flowers, the family asks that Billy get himself some goddamn help.

Running Away

When I'd said goodbye at the bus station in Seattle, I'd told my mom I'd tell her everything. I'll email you every day, I said. You'll know everything.

But she didn't know everything, because it was so much harder to tell her than I'd thought it would be. She hardly knew anything. Sure, I told her about Mrs. Patel. I told her about Dad. But not really. I didn't tell her that I was the one who found Mrs. Patel, and how I thought I was the one who killed her. I didn't tell her that Dad's drinking was getting worse, and how he was messing everything up. I told her about my date, but not how I ruined it. And she had no idea that I was planning to get on a bus and go to Dan's. After what happened with the pizza, I emailed him. He said I could come. I told him it was just for a visit. I told him that I was so depressed and lonely that only a piece of his red velvet cake would make it all better. But I was planning to stay.

Who would stop me from leaving? Who would actually stop me? Dad and the boys wouldn't have a clue. Claire was too busy barely holding everything together. She'd probably be relieved to have one less person to worry about.

Mrs. Patel would've cared. Now, now, Maeve, she'd have said. Come. Sit. Think this through. I'll put on the kettle. You deal the cards.

But I couldn't leave. Not until I knew that Claire would be okay.

Two days after Dad's pizza fit and a week after falling flat on my face, figuratively and almost literally—the scrapes on my knees had finally healed—I was in the park checking the bus times while the boys played. There was a bus at five a.m. and a bus at seven p.m., the same as every other day since I'd started checking. It was comforting to see the times in their little boxes on the schedule grid. As soon as I could, I'd get on one of those buses and cross the border and get off in Seattle and call Dan to come get me.

I put my phone away and opened my sketchbook. I scanned the park to find someone to draw. A man sitting against a tree, reading a book, sunglasses perched on his head. Sneakers kicked off, socks stuffed inside, his jeans rolled up, bony white feet pointed at the sun. A long nose and bushy eyebrows. Ears that stuck out. And then someone was standing in front of me, blocking the light.

"Hey."

Salix.

Books scattered on the sidewalk. Oranges rolling into the road. Django Reinhardt. Everybody watching. So much embarrassment that it was coming off the pavement in hot waves.

Salix pointed up the grassy hill, to where a man was play-ing the trumpet. "Is that the dying goose?"

"Look, about the other day. I'm really sorry."

"It sounds like it."

"I'm sorry that I didn't text you back."

"That was rude."

"It was, and I—"

"Why, though?" She put up a hand and shook her head. "No, I can guess. You were upset. You were embarrassed. You didn't know what to say."

"All those things."

"All those things that I don't mind. All those things that don't matter. I mean, I'm sorry that I upset you—"

"It wasn't you. It wasn't anything you said."

"How was I supposed to know that? You never texted me back after. You just figured you'd let me be worried about you? You just figured that I wouldn't care? You just figured you had somewhere else to be? Somewhere better?" Salix paused. "Help me out here."

"I'm sorry."

Salix put her hands in her pockets. Then she took them out. She looked away for a moment, up at the trumpet player, and then back at me. "You're okay, though?"

"Now." I lifted a knee. "I did end up falling. Just over there."

Salix crouched beside me and touched the yellow bruise that circled the scrape. "Ouch."

Her fingers felt soft and warm. My breath quickened. "Wh-wh-what are you doing in the park?"

"You texted me."

"No, I didn't."

Salix pulled out her phone and showed me. A text, from about twenty minutes ago. The one I had composed a week before and had never sent. In all my fiddling to find the bus times and text Claire that yes, I'd pick up bread and milk, I'd somehow sent the text that I'd never deleted. Maeve Glover, technical genius.

"Right," I said. "The trumpet guy."

"The trumpet guy." Salix sat beside me.

"You don't have your violin with you."

"Nope."

Neither of us said anything for a minute or two, and then Salix reached into her pack and pulled out a little waxy bag. I knew what it was right away.

"The cookie."

"The cookie." Salix offered it to me. "It might be a bit stale."

I held the cookie in my lap.

"So." Salix bumped my shoulder with hers. "If I said that I'd be back in ten minutes, would you still be here?"

I nodded.

"You won't run away?"

"I'm watching my brothers. They're in the playground." I pointed.

"I'll be right back." And then she was walking away, across the grassy hill. I put my hand over the bruise on my knee. Salix's fingers there, and her shoulder pressing against mine. This wasn't the plan. I was going home. As soon as I knew that Claire and the boys would be okay. When would that be? When she kicked Dad out? When he got himself together? After the baby came? I wasn't sure, but I was sure that I wanted to leave. That was my focus. Get on one of those buses and cross the border and go home with Dan: a dark drive through the forest and then my house in the woods and the garden all in a tangle. My dad's mess, my mom and Raymond in Haiti, even the cookie in my lap—none of it added up. Salix was supposed to be out of the equation. But here she was, coming down the path with a tray of plastic cups. She headed to the playground first and offered drinks to the boys, who took them happily and chatted with her, even though they hardly knew her. I'd have to talk to them about that. It was far more likely that they'd be abducted by someone they knew than a stranger.

She headed my way, and at the last minute I realized that she was watching me watching her.

"Iced mocha, part two." She sat beside me and handed me a cup. "I got chocolate milk for the boys. In case you were wondering."

I'd been too nervous to wonder. The noise of the playground got louder all of a sudden; the children's colorful T-shirts and shorts were little pops of light bouncing and flashing. I wanted to look at Salix. I wanted to look at her up close. Study the line of her jaw, the curve of her lips. But I couldn't look at her like that. I found Corbin instead and watched him on the swing, holding on to one chain with his hand, his cast hooked around the other, pumping higher and higher.

"Hey." I did look at her then, but I tried not to stare. Salix took the cookie back. "Let's give this to the birds."

"Good idea."

Salix broke off a little bit at a time and sprinkled it at our feet. Starlings fluttered down nearby and hopped skittishly toward the crumbs.

"Tell me about the funeral."

"What?"

"That's what you were going to tell me about before I scared you off."

"You didn't scare me off." I didn't want to tell her about the funeral. I didn't want to think about Mrs. Patel.

"Okay, forget the funeral." Salix chewed on her straw. "Tell me what three things you'd take with you if your house was burning down, not including people or pets."

That was her changing the subject? To house fires? Really?

"Did you know that over three thousand people die in house fires every year? That's just in the States. And that's not including firefighters."

"I'd take my violin, and my computer—because it has all the pictures of my family," Salix said. "And my earphones."

"That works out to be about one every hundred and seventy minutes."

"One what?"

"One person, dead." I knew that I should be saying something else—I should be telling her those three things—but my brain took over and brought up the statistics instead. "Every hundred and seventy minutes. I think it's actually one hundred sixty-nine minutes."

"And if you narrowly escaped being one of the dead people, what would you take?"

I pressed my lips tight, biting them shut. A ticker tape of facts ran through my brain: Stay close to the floor. More Americans die in house fires each year than in all natural disasters combined. Change smoke-alarm batteries twice a year. I would not say anything at all until I could be sure that I would not recite even just one more statistic about house fires or charred bodies or arson or smoke inhalation or the best way to survive a house fire. Three things—think about those three things.

When I decided, I said them over and over in my head before I said them out loud. Just so that I wouldn't end up telling her instead that most house fires start in the kitchen.

"My sketchbook and pencils—that counts as one. My computer—same about the photos—and the painting of me and my dad."

"Show me."

"The painting?"

"Your sketchbook." Salix put a hand out, as if I would just give it to her.

"No," I said. "I don't do that. I mean, I don't show people. I never do."

"I played my violin for you."

"You play your violin for a lot of people."

"Show me."

I put my pencils into my case and zipped it shut. I placed my sketchbook in my lap, and my hands flat on top of it, pressing it down, as if it might drift over to Salix despite everything.

"Okay," Salix said. "You're a tough audience."

"I'll show you," I said. "But not today."

Salix grinned.

"What?" I said.

"That means I'll get to see you again."

I grinned. "Yeah?"

"Yeah." Salix beamed. "Let's see. Other introductory stuff. My dad is a bus driver. My mom works at the grocery store. But before that they lived in a bus and sold crappy jewelry at folk festivals, until my sister was born. In the bus. Her name is Linden. After the tree. Salix means 'willow.' You get the picture. Linden is two years older than me. She's at Juilliard now. She plays the cello. We used to busk in this park, actually. Up by the cenotaph. Pretty much right where the dying goose is."

"Juilliard," I said. "That's impressive."

"I'll be going too. If I get in, that is."

"You'll get in." I wasn't thinking about house fires anymore. I was thinking about Salix's parents, on a bus. Having a baby. Don't go there, Maeve. Leave the babies alone. Step away from the potentially dead babies.

"It's almost impossible to get in."

"Your sister did."

"So maybe that's it for family luck." Salix lifted her necklace, the same one she'd worn each time I'd seen her. Even that first time at the bus station. "Linden gave this to me for good luck. She wore it for her audition."

"But it's not luck," I said. "It's talent. Which you have lots of."

"Maybe," Salix said. "But it'd have to be a full scholarship, like Linden. I have a plan, though, for if I don't get in."

"Another school?"

"No. I'd just take off. Europe. Or Australia. Maybe Thailand."

"Thailand? But what about earthquakes? What about tsunamis?"

"In Thailand?"

"Over two hundred thousand people died in that one in 2004."

Salix emptied her drink and squinted at me. "You know, we have earthquakes here, too."

183

"Or hepatitis," I blundered on. "You can catch hepatitis from water. Or spa treatments. Tattoo parlors. Tourist sex." I heard myself say it, even as I wished I would just shut up. Or have a normal conversation. Like a normal person. I took a sip of my drink just to stop my verbal diarrhea.

"I'll stick to bottled water," Salix said with a laugh. "And I'll be sure to avoid spa treatments and dodgy tattoo parlors. And tourist sex."

"What if you meet some guy on the beach and he plays the guitar and he's really nice and then he says, 'Hey, let's meet up in Bangkok.'" The words just came spilling out and spilling out and spilling out. "Only he tucks a brick of cocaine in your backpack and you get caught at the airport and then you get thrown into a jail in Thailand. And then what? It happens."

Salix stared at me, dumbfounded.

"It happens," I repeated. "It does."

"It'd be a girl."

"What?"

"On the beach. It'd be a girl."

"Oh."

"Where are you from?" Salix said.

As in what planet? As in who says shit like that? What kind of person goes on and on and on about shit that won't happen and why it would happen and basically insinuating that Salix would be stupid enough to have whatever the hell "tourist sex" is or carry drugs across an international border, as if she wouldn't notice a brick of cocaine in her backpack? As if.

"That is such a good question," I said.

"Seriously," Salix said. "You said your dad lives here. Where's your mom again?"

"Haiti."

"Your mom is in *Haiti* and you're worried about me going to Thailand?"

"I worry about her, too," I said. "Trust me."

"Why is your mom in Haiti?"

So I told her how it all happened. I managed not to tell her about Raymond's shriveled-up penis, or Mom and him in a parked car beside the bear-proof garbage cans, or the man who was questioned at the border, or Tim McLean, who'd had his head cut off by a madman on a Greyhound bus.

I told her about Dan instead, and the unicorn pajamas, and the FRIEND OF DOROTHY shirt, and even about Jessica. But I didn't tell her about Ruthie, or how Dad was ruining everything, or how I was thinking about getting on a bus and going home, even though no one was there. That maybe I wanted to go home while my dad ruined his second marriage. I told her that the baby was kicking. I told her about Mr. Heidelman and the ice cream sandwiches and the moving truck full of instruments.

"I wish I could stay," she said when I finished. "But I have a student."

I collected the boys and we walked with her as far as the store. She came in and held the basket for me while the boys ran up and down the aisles. I took a loaf of bread off the shelf, and a carton of milk, and when we were outside again, we stood in the middle of the sidewalk, the boys running circles around us.

Salix shoved her hands into her pockets. "If I text you, will you text me back this time?"

"Yes. I will. Definitely."

"Okay, then it's probably safe to say goodbye. So, bye."

Corbin grabbed my arm. Owen grabbed the other one. "Let's go!"

"You should go too."

"Looks like it."

"Bye, Maeve."

"Bye, Salix."

She strode down the block and turned the corner without looking back.

Forgetting About Someone You Love

What I wanted to do was go home and replay every second of the time with Salix. What happened was that when we got home, there was an email from Raymond. Seeing his name pop up set me on edge immediately. The subject line said *DON'T WORRY, YOUR MOTHER IS FINE!*

> *Hi, Maeve,*
>
> *We got into a minor car accident on the way back from the beach today, and your mom is staying overnight in the hospital. No broken bones, but she knocked her head pretty good, so they're keeping her just to make sure it's only a concussion. She can't text or email from the hospital, so she asked me to let you know. Here's a picture, so that you know she's okay.*
>
> *She says not to worry.*
>
> *We'll be in touch soon,*
>
> > *Raymond*

I scrolled down to the picture. She was sitting up in bed wearing a hospital gown, holding a piece of paper. On it, in her writing: *I'm fine! xoxo*

I zoomed in and searched every inch of that picture, looking for something that would tell me that he was lying, that she wasn't okay. But there were no bandages, no scrapes, not even a bruise or a black eye. Or was that a shadow of a black eye? I tried to check if her pupils were equal, but the picture was grainy that close up. I emailed Raymond back, cc'ing Mom.

> *If you broke her, I'll kill you. Not kidding.*
> *Tell her to phone me the MINUTE she can.*
> *—M*

I looked at the photo again. That was a shadow of a black eye, I was sure of it. What if she looked and acted fine at first, and so nobody figured it out? What if she had a bleed so tiny that no one noticed, and then during the night it bled and bled, and she had a stroke? What if she *died*? What if it wasn't an earthquake and it wasn't cholera? What if it was a minor car crash instead?

> *Deena Glover died today from the result of a minor car accident, shocking her loved ones and the old man who was with her. She leaves behind a garden in desperate need of attention, and a daughter, also in desperate need of attention. Not that she'd know, considering the daughter has been ignoring her. Or avoiding her. As for the old man, he is entirely at fault for this whole mess.*

188

I calculated the time difference. Almost eleven p.m.

"Maeve?" Claire stood in the doorway. "I just got an email from Raymond. He said he sent you one too. And Billy."

"I have to talk to her." I could hardly breathe. "Right now. I have to know that she's okay."

Claire sat beside me with her computer and looked up all the possible numbers for hospitals in Port-au-Prince and read them out while I called and asked for my mother in terribly accented French. On the fourth call a woman said something in French, and after a click and a pause I heard my mom's voice.

"Maeve? Is that you? Are you okay?"

"Am *I* okay?" I started sobbing. "No. No. Are *you* okay?"

"I'm fine, honey. I was going to call you in the morning."

"In the morning?" I said through the tears. "In the *morning*?"

Claire patted my knee. "I'll leave you two alone," she said as she left the room, shutting the door softly on her way out.

"I really am okay," Mom said.

"How do you know? Did they do a CT scan?"

"They checked me out. Thoroughly." The line crackled.

"I miss you so much, Mom."

"I miss you too, honey. It's harder than I thought, being so far away from you. I love you."

"I love you too."

We talked about Haiti. The charity. Raymond. Home. They'd both had an email from Dan, saying that he found a bear on the porch when he went to check on the house. My mom laughed.

"It was probably napping on the couch."

The old couch on the porch, where I spent hours and hours

189

sketching blue jays and crows, the chickens in the coop, the cedar trees, the fox, and the garden.

"After it shopped in the garden," I said.

It was so sad that we weren't there to pick the greens, the baby carrots, and the peas. It was symbolic, and I wished it weren't. The garden going on without us. The house all alone in the woods.

And all the while, in between the words, all the things I wasn't saying. So I said some of them. I told a little bit more, like I was letting out string on a kite, just a bit at a time. I told her about Salix and how I ran away on that first date, and about sitting in the park with her. I told her that I found Mrs. Patel. After I told her that, there was a long silence on her end. So long that I thought the call had been dropped.

"Mom?"

"I'm so sorry that you found her," she said. "I'm so sorry that I wasn't there to comfort you."

And Dad. What could I tell her about Dad?

"He's doing okay, I guess."

There was a pause. "Really?"

"No. He's not okay."

"Maeve." Another pause. "You know you can't make him stop. This is his thing to fix."

"It might be too broken," I said with a catch in my throat. "I think he and Claire might break up."

"Oh, Maeve. I'm so sorry. Are you okay to stay there?" she said. "Should I call Dan?"

This was my chance to go home.

It hadn't occurred to me, until that moment, that Dad was the reason I was there, and that if he was a mess, he could be the reason Mom would let me go home. I could get the

190

five a.m. bus. I could be home the next afternoon. I could be standing barefoot in the garden with the light cutting through the trees and the dirt underfoot and the smell of all the green all around. But I didn't want to go. And it wasn't just because of Salix. It was because of Claire and Owen and Corbin and the baby. And it was because of Dad, too, because even if I couldn't fix it, it didn't seem right to walk away.

"No more car accidents," I said. "No more hospitals. Okay?"

"You didn't answer me," Mom said. "Do you want me to call Dan?"

"Not yet."

"You'll tell me when?"

"I'll tell you when."

After we said goodbye, I sat on the edge of my bed and stared at Dad's unfinished painting of the pug and the German shepherd, which was supposed to have shipped two weeks before. He'd started another painting on the other easel, but I couldn't tell what it would be. So far it looked like a mess. A complete and utter mess.

Braxton Hicks

When I woke up the next morning and went upstairs, I could tell right away that Dad hadn't come home. Claire was silently fuming as she made breakfast, slamming cupboard doors, kicking the fridge shut, wrestling toast out of the toaster and tossing it onto the plates. The boys sat on the couch, not playing, not arguing. Just watching Claire scrape peanut butter across a piece of burned toast.

"Have you heard from him?"

"I have not." She did not look up.

"Can I help? Have you called him?"

She dropped the knife into the sink with a clatter. She put both hands on the counter and sighed.

"Let's get out of the city," she said. "Let's go to the lake."

We got ready in record time, even the boys. Either we all really wanted to go swimming, or we all really wanted to be away from home for the day. When we were down in the garage with the van packed, Claire offered me the keys.

"You drive."

"I don't want to."

"What's the point in having your learner's permit if you never use it?"

"I might use it," I said. "But not here. Did you know that three thousand two hundred eighty-seven people die in car crashes every single day on this planet?"

"No one in this van is going to die."

"You're the one who told me that highway is called Sea to *Die*."

"It's a joke," Claire said. "It's Sea to *Sky*, Maeve. You're not supposed to take it seriously."

"We should all take it seriously," I said.

"Oh, *Maeve*." She dangled the keys. "Take a chance. Come on."

"'Oh, *Maeve*' will not be driving today."

"Fine. Make the enormous and very sweaty pregnant woman drive."

"Claire, I . . ." I should drive. I knew that. But the disconnect between the idea and the action was too vast. "I want to . . ."

"No, you don't. Not really." There was an edge in her voice, but then it vanished. "It's no big deal. Let's go swimming."

About an hour later we turned off the highway and onto the road that led to Alice Lake. My phone buzzed in my pocket.

What are you doing today? Let's get iced mochas and go to the park to listen to the dying goose. He's improving. Meet me at the park in half an hour?

We're just about at Alice Lake, I texted. *But I'd love to. Later? I'll text you when we leave.*

But it didn't send. I tried again as we turned into the parking lot. No service. No service. No service. I rolled down the window and stuck the phone out, but still no service.

"No service at the lake," Claire said.

"Apparently." I reached the phone out as far as I could, this time in another direction. "Can we just turn around for a second?"

"There's no reliable service until Squamish."

"But I got a text from her when we turned off the highway."

"Then that was a fluke. I'm not driving all the way back to Squamish." Claire parked the van. "It can wait."

Before she could even take the keys out of the ignition, the boys grabbed their backpacks, tumbled out the side door, and raced for the beach.

"There's no way I can herd those boys back into the van to drive you back to the highway, Maeve." Claire suddenly brightened. "But you could!"

"No way."

"You can do it. I know you can. You drive in Port Townsend. And this isn't the city. It's a quiet road in the middle of nowhere. It doesn't even have painted lines. Your mom said you need to keep practicing. It's less than five minutes to the highway."

"I can't drive unless there's a licensed adult with me."

"Less than five minutes." Claire pulled the cooler out of the back. "Help me with the wagon."

I lifted down the wagon and loaded it with all the beach things.

"What if I went and got the boys and brought them back and we just drove down super quick?"

"They're probably already in the lake." Claire offered the keys. "You'll be fine. Go for it. Break the rules. Do something that makes you uncomfortable. Be a rebel."

And if I hit someone? Or someone hit me? Or I drove into a ditch? Or the brakes failed? Or the engine died? Or the police pulled me over because they could see the guilt blazing through the window like a spotlight?

"It's illegal."

"When I was sixteen, you had your learner's for thirty days and then you took your driving test. Boom, thirty days later, full-fledged driver. So they've changed the rules. So what? You'll be fine. Go ahead. You have my blessing." She held up a finger to stop my next protest. "We're not going to force the boys back into the van so you can send a text to your girlfriend. It's not going to happen."

"She's not my girlfriend." At least I didn't think so.

But I did need to text her. I wouldn't be able to think of anything else. I'd be looking at the mountains and drinking lemonade and swimming in that beautiful water and getting a tan and building sand castles, and all of it would be flattened because I'd be thinking of Salix waiting for my reply. I'd already brushed her off that way. I did not want to keep her waiting again.

How long would it take to walk back to the highway? Half an hour? But then what if Claire was right and there was no signal? Then it would just be stupid. Stupid, stupid, stupid. And I'd miss out on the lake.

"Look, Maeve. Help me haul this to the beach, and we'll get settled, and then you can go for a swim to clear your head." She hitched a beach bag onto her shoulder. "I can't leave the boys alone for this long. People are going to think they're here by themselves, and the lifeguard already gave me a warning the last time we were here because they were out too far. I had to tell him that they were eight, just so he'd leave us alone, but I know he's got a hate-on for me, so let's just go already. Okay?"

Mostly defeated, I picked up the handle of the wagon and started for the trail ahead of Claire.

"Come on, Maeve," Claire called from not far behind me. "It's just a text."

"Okay."

"She'll understand."

"Sure."

"You could always go by yourself." That little edge was back.

The wagon bumped and crunched on the gravel.

"Wait up, Maeve." Claire caught up and put a hand on my arm. "Give a pregnant woman a chance, would you?"

Salix would understand. She wasn't like me. She didn't leap from assumption to assumption, adding everything up wrong. She'd go to Thailand on her own. She'd move to New York. She'd wear a rainbow patch for everyone to see.

"*Whoo*," Claire puffed. "Whoo, whoo. Okay."

"What is it?"

"Nothing." She winced. "Braxton Hicks. That's all."

I dropped the wagon handle and took her arms. "Are you sure?"

I'd been reading. Collecting evidence for my argument

against home birth. I'd read a lot. *Spiritual Midwifery. The Essential Homebirth Guide. Birth Your Way.*

"Positive."

"If you have more than four in an hour, we should call the midwife." I found a bottle of water in the cooler and gave it to Claire. "Dehydration can bring them on. It's been so hot. Have you been drinking enough water?"

"I'm fine, Maeve. Let's go make sure that the lifeguard hasn't seen the boys yet." Claire started down the path ahead of me. She got a few steps and then stopped and turned around. "How do you know so much about Braxton Hicks?"

It was the same lifeguard, but this time he was busy chatting up a flock of bikinied teenage girls, lined up on beach towels, slick with tanning oil. I doubted he'd even noticed that Corbin and Owen were out on the dock by themselves. By all the gesturing and flailing I could tell that Corbin was impressing the other kids with his waterproof cast. Owen stood beside him, shivering, his nose looking beaky even from that distance, his nose plugs squishing it shut.

I set up Claire's folding chair and a shade umbrella. She sat, digging her swollen feet into the cool sand, and guzzled the bottle of water. She let out an enormous belch after.

"God, the gas." She winced again, hands on her belly.

"Still having them?" I offered her another bottle of water.

"No thanks."

"We should go home."

And if we did, I could be texting Salix in about half an hour. But it wasn't about the text anymore. Not at all, really. It was about watching Claire wince and cringe and hold her belly.

"I'm fine," Claire said. "I'm *fine*, Maeve. The baby is *fine*. I'm not going into labor today. Or tomorrow. Or even this week, or the next, or the next after that. And Salix will wait. I promise. You want to be with someone who won't get upset if you take your time getting back to her. She's that person, right?"

I nodded. Be with someone. Girlfriend. Claire was a lot more optimistic than I was. And way ahead of things too.

"There's no need to worry. Now go swimming."

"You're sure?"

"Can you even imagine if I went into labor here? That lifeguard would be horrified."

"So would those girls."

"He'd come running over with his big red first-aid box and open it only to find there was nothing in there to help. But at least he has one," Claire said. "The boys took the one from the van to Gnomenville. King Percival fell from a tower. It was quite gruesome, apparently. We have one under the sink in the bathroom, but I think most of its contents were used in the last big battle between the Wrens and the Percivals."

"Then the first thing that I'm going to do when we get home is restock it." I stripped down to my swimsuit.

"That's Billy's job." Claire sighed. "He has a list of things to do before the baby comes. Updating the first-aid kits is on it."

"What else? Maybe I can help."

"But I don't want you to. I want him to do it."

"Maeve!" Corbin hollered from the dock. "Come out here!"

I glanced at Claire.

"I'm fine. Go ahead."

The water was cold at first, but it felt good. It washed the dusty drive off, and it washed everything else off too. I dove down into the deep, where the water was colder. It was black and silent and cold, and I felt blissfully alone for the first time since stepping off the bus. I swam deeper still, and then my chest tightened and I ran out of breath. Four minutes for the brain to die without oxygen, yet this was where I wanted to be. I headed back up with my eyes open, watching Corbin and Owen from below, their skinny pale legs churning awkwardly, their small hands bright against the watery dark.

I didn't drive the van down to the highway illegally. I didn't walk down either. I stayed in the water until my fingers were prunes, diving under again and again. It felt perfect under there, and it was how I held off from panicking about texting Salix back. When we left, I didn't get a good signal until Squamish.

"Told you so," Claire said as I started to type.

"You said we shouldn't say that," Corbin said.

I was at Alice Lake with no service. Sorry!

Bad trumpet music! Mochas! Yes, please!

A moment later, she texted me back.

Teaching tonight. Is tomorrow morning good?

Very good.

Very good.

"All good?" Claire said. "Your cheeks are red."

"All good," I said. "Very good."

I'd see her in the morning. I'd see her that soon. It wasn't soon enough. Or was it too soon? It had to be just right, because that was how it was, unless something happened between now and then. I needed my dad to keep a holding pattern: come home, don't come home, it didn't really matter; I just needed him to not rock the boat for once. I needed all the interested parties to keep the status quo. I didn't want anything to mess this up. My heart raced and my fingers tingled and I could feel my cheeks blazing. I was nervous already, but for all the good reasons.

A very small section of Maeve Glover's neuroses drowned in Alice Lake today. Though it is survived by the bulk of her anxiety, which is kept alive by an infinite list of things to worry about, we are delighted to bury this one tiny piece. There is great hope that this death is permanent.

All the Beautiful People

The dying goose wasn't at the park, but Salix was, playing in front of the cenotaph with her violin case open, a few dollar coins tossed in.

"Not bad for so early in the day."

"Those are my fakes." Salix stopped playing. She took a step toward me, as if she was going to hug me, or maybe kiss me on the cheek, but she didn't. I took a step forward, wondering if I should do either of those things. But I didn't. Instead we ended up standing very close to each other but not touching. "I put them in there so people will think that other people have already given me money. No one wants to be the first. Linden taught me that." She put her violin away and pocketed the coins. "Come on."

.   .   .

We stood near the back of the crowded bus and held on to the bar over our heads. While I hoped that my armpits didn't stink, Salix bumped into me playfully.

"How much time have you got today?"

"All day."

"Excellent. Let's go a little further." We got off that bus and onto another, where we got two seats on the long bench in the middle. "I would drive us there, but my mom has the car today."

"You drive?" I said. "Here? In the city?"

"Sure. You don't?"

"I have my learner's permit. I can drive with someone who has five years' experience."

"How old are you?"

"Sixteen and three-quarters, and not in a rush to drive by myself," I said. "Or at all. Especially not in the city. How old are you?"

"Seventeen and getting rid of my N as soon as possible."

"Your N?"

"You get your L here first, and then after a year you get your N—which stands for 'novice'—and after two years with your N, you get your real license."

"I don't want any license, to be honest. Then maybe everyone would stop pestering me about driving."

"But don't you live in the country? Doesn't every kid who lives in the country want their driver's license right away?"

"All the more deer to hit," I said. "All the more drunk drivers to avoid. All the more ditches and ravines and rock cliffs to crash into."

"But just think, as soon as you have your license, you can

go places by yourself. You don't have to ask for rides. That's worth it, isn't it? To go where you want to go? To be free?"

"Not if it means that I have to be responsible for the safe and correct handling of a one-ton death machine."

"You won't kill someone."

"I might," I said. "I almost killed a deer."

"But you missed it?"

"Barely."

"So you didn't kill it. Imagine being able to get up and go whenever you want. That is definitely worth the risk. The risk is small."

But it wasn't small. So many car crashes. So many mechanical failures. So many slippery roads and blizzards and moments where one wrong move could kill. I would not start reciting facts again. I would not. Focus on the girl, Maeve. You are on a date with a very cute girl, and she is taking you somewhere, so don't do the fact thing. Just don't do it. Think about something else. Anything.

In about a year, Salix could be in New York. Or Thailand. In five months and twenty-one days, I was going home. So why were we even pretending that this could be a thing? Or maybe it was just me. Maybe this was no big deal to her.

Not what I had in mind when I told myself to think of something else.

This thing that hadn't started? It was going to end, no matter what happened between now and the end of the five months. Goodbyes. Last moments. Hopeless.

The bus shuddered to a stop, and I bumped against Salix.

"Sorry."

"It's okay. Honestly."

A large woman with a rolling cart full of groceries squished into the seat on the other side of me, so I ended up pinned against Salix, our bodies pressed together from shoulder to knee. The two of us sat very still. I liked being that close, and maybe she did too, because when the woman got off, we didn't move apart. We stayed pressed together on purpose, slowly relaxing into it until it felt completely natural, as if we'd sat like that a million times before.

"This is our stop," Salix said. I could hear the reluctance in her voice. I wanted to stay sitting against each other like that too. But we both got up, our sides warm from where we'd touched. When we stepped off the bus, I realized that we'd traveled clear across the city. I'd never gone that far alone on the bus.

"Ta-da!" Salix pointed to the beach across the street. "Welcome to my office. I make good money on this beach. And I promise you there won't be anyone trying to slip a brick of cocaine into your backpack."

"What?"

"The girl on the beach in Thailand? My life, wasting away in a foreign jail? Tourist sex?"

I cringed. "You had to remind me?"

"Come on." Salix took my hand. "I'll play for a bit and then I'll buy you an ice cream cone."

"I have to tell you that I have pretty sophisticated taste in ice cream. I only like the ones that come in boxes. The expensive ones."

"No problem, princess." Salix did a little bow. "Your wish is my command."

. . .

The beach was full of Beautiful People, like the girls on the beach at Alice Lake, except this beach was packed with them and their boyfriends. Sinewy teenagers who played beach volleyball like they were in a commercial, leaping high without breaking a sweat or dislodging their expensive sunglasses or perfect ponytails. And adults who still had their adolescent bodies, chiseled and tight and smooth. I could hardly see the sand for all the lithe sunbathers posed just so on their blankets and towels, sunglasses on every single one of them.

"We're definitely not in East Van," I said.

I felt frumpy in my tank top and capris. My flip-flops were two years old and had been purchased at a gas station after I lost my sandals at the beach. The capris were a hand-me-down from Ruthie's cousin and had a paper clip instead of a proper zipper pull.

"Definitely not in East Van." Salix swept an arm in front of her. "Behold, the land of the lotus-eaters."

"Lotus-eaters?"

"It's from that poem by Tennyson. About a ship that ends up at an island where all they eat are enchanted lotuses, which make them dreamy and happy and they forget all their troubles. So much so that the captain has to drag his men back to the boat against their will because they want to stay there forever. People call Vancouver the land of the lotus-eaters. But I think they mean people like this, more specifically."

I blinked. "I love that you know that."

"Thanks." Salix lifted her sunglasses and grinned at me. "I love that you don't think that knowing that is completely dorky."

A trio of glisteningly tanned girls with rolled-up yoga

mats under their arms hurried past, followed by a few women jogging, again with the perfect ponytails bouncing along in unison. A wide circle of guys tossed a Frisbee on a section of sand roped off for sports.

"I feel like I should be running or jumping or rolling. Or doing yoga."

"Let's find some shade instead."

We wandered along the path while cyclists and in-line skaters sliced by on the side designated for wheels, and joggers nudged past them, clearly impatient, on the pedestrian side.

"Doesn't anyone just walk?"

"They do." Salix pointed to an elderly couple strolling ahead of us, a big old dog creaking along behind them.

Trees lined the path, but all the shade had been claimed by the few people who wanted it. "Up there," she said, pointing. "Shade! I think those people are leaving."

She ran ahead to stake our claim, and by the time I caught up, she already had her violin out.

She played something classical while I took out my sketchbook and tried to do quick drawings of the people going by. Really, though, I just wanted to draw Salix. Over and over and over again. Just Salix. I chewed on the end of my pencil while I watched her. Salix played the violin with her whole body. Small sways and bows, shuffling her feet now and then, her eyes closing briefly and then opening to find me, still watching. The curve of her jaw, her slender fingers on the strings, the ruby pendant at her throat, one foot in front of the other, her strong calves, the spot where her tanned legs disappeared into her baggy shorts.

I pretended that she was the only one on the whole beach,

and that the music was just for me. I drew her, starting with the long, fluid line of her torso.

After about half an hour, she tucked her violin under her arm and sat beside me, pulling her case onto her lap and counting. "Almost thirty bucks." She grinned. "I can easily buy you a princess ice cream."

"I'm impressed. Totally impressed." The wind picked up off the ocean. I pushed the hair off my face. "You're an amazing musician. Absolutely amazing."

"Thanks." She set her violin in the case and shoved the money into her pack. "What were you drawing? Can I see?"

"Nope." I closed my sketchbook. "Sorry."

"Someday you'll show me. I know it." She stood and offered me a hand. "Let's go?"

Salix helped me up, and we kept holding hands for a second, until I started to pull away. But Salix held on. "The snack stand is over this way."

Salix bought a dark chocolate caramel almond ice cream bar for me and a dipped cone for herself. We sat on a log in the sand, not saying much. Salix put her hand on my thigh, her palm immediately hot and pulsing. I slid my hand under hers, and then we were holding hands as if it was no big deal at all. There were whitecaps on the water, and most of the swimmers had come in. Far off, the water was dappled with tiny sailboats and enormous barges. Usually I wanted to be somewhere other than where I was at any given time. On one of those boats, for example, alone and far away from the busyness and the noise and the constant decisions. But not today. This was exactly where I wanted to be. The wind on my face, the sweet taste of ice cream on my tongue, my toes dug into the sand, sitting hip to hip and holding hands with Salix, my crush, my heart racer. There was no place I would rather be, except maybe on one of those boats, sailing away, with Salix.

Pretending

Let's pretend that the story ends there. That the day at the beach will be the last image. What a beautiful image to keep. Let's imagine all the good things that came next, like love, and the baby, and the boys growing like weeds. Let's imagine my mom in Haiti, where everything was perfect and Raymond was twenty years younger and I actually liked him. Welcome to the family, Raymond.

Let's ignore the bad things. Let's ignore that all good things go wrong.

But most of all, let's pretend that my dad was back to normal. Let's pretend that he realized what an asshole he was becoming. Let's pretend that he came home every night and was happy to see his family. Let's pretend that we always knew where he was. Let's pretend that we weren't worried.

Let's pretend.

A beach. The sun. Two girls holding hands.

The end.

Heights

The boys stopped asking Claire when Dad would come home. When he did show up, it was almost always after they were in bed. He had a shower, got himself something to eat, mumbled a few words at Claire, and slept on the couch.

But mostly he just didn't come home, and I didn't want to know where he was staying.

"He's probably sleeping in the truck," Claire said.

Neither of us said where we really thought he was.

When he was home, I avoided him. I was meeting Salix. I was working on something and needed the door closed. I was taking a nap, getting changed, didn't feel well.

Claire wouldn't speak to him at all. If he was still there in the morning, he and the boys would play for a bit—gnomes, battle, castles, gnomes—and then he'd make up some reason to go.

"When will you be back, Daddy?" The boys hung off him all the way to the door.

"I'm not sure. But I'll see you soon, okay?"

Claire took to pacing. "I'm getting the baby into a good position," she said. But I knew that she was worried. About the same things I was worried about. Where was he? What was he doing? Was he even going to work? Worried about money. Worried about having the baby alone. I wasn't supposed to be with her. *He* was.

When I wasn't with Salix, I was with Claire. I gave her foot massages and made her red raspberry tea to help "tone her cervix." I kept reading the books. No matter how terrified I was at the thought of convincing Claire to go to the hospital if the time came and Dad was nowhere to be found, and no matter how much I wished that Dad would come home and actually be a dad and actually be a husband, I wasn't going to get stuck in the reality without knowing a little bit about what was going on.

I hadn't told Claire, but the deal was going to be this: If Dad didn't show up when she went into labor, we were going straight to the hospital. Even if I had to force her into the van. I would even drive her myself, if I had to. This baby was not going to be born at home if I was the only one to help besides the midwives.

Claire Glover, beloved mother and wife, died while
giving birth because she insisted on having the baby
at home, which is a terrible idea, and because her
husband was nowhere to be found and who knows if
midwives ever get to births on time, in which case—

So I was reading about vaginas and birth canals and cervixes and perineal massage and footling breech and shoulder dystocia and how a couple having sex during labor can speed things up. Not that that would be an option for Claire if her husband was a complete and utter no-show.

I was reading *Birthing from Within* one evening when Salix texted me to meet her in the park. I would never go into the park at night, and it was going to get dark soon, but I did want to see Salix. I texted her back.

Come get me?

Her reply came immediately.

I know what you're thinking, Maeve. Come anyway. There are no boogeymen. I checked. Also, I can see your building from here. I will be your watchman. Watchgirl. Whatever.

As soon as I came out of the building she shouted from the playground, from the very top of the climber, a tall pyramid of thick red rope crisscrossing down and out from a central post. It reminded me of the Eiffel Tower. She was perched at the little lookout at the top.

"What are you doing?" I peered up at her.

"Come up."

"It's pretty high."

"I saw Corbin scamper up to the top of this thing the other day, even with a broken arm. If your little brother can do it," Salix said, "so can you."

"But Owen has never climbed this thing. Not even up to the first rung."

"One foot after the other, come on." Salix bounced a little

on her rope perch, sending the whole thing shivering. "I have a prize for you when you get up here."

I wanted to go up more than I didn't want to, so, with my heart pounding, I reached with both hands and grabbed a rope. It was hard and bristly in my grasp, but I held on. I put one foot on a lower rope and pulled myself up off the ground. I would just have to do that about ten more times and then I'd be at the top. From where I was, the ground was only a short jump away, but the top was probably fifteen feet off the ground.

"How about you come down?"

"If you've never seen the view of downtown from here, then you're coming up."

I wobbled on the ropes.

"It's worth it." Salix beckoned me. "I promise. Come on!"

So I kept climbing. I made the mistake of looking down at about the halfway mark. This was not a good idea. My hands burned from clutching the rope so hard, and my feet—in flip-flops—rolled back and forth across the rope.

"Kick them off," Salix said. "It's easier in bare feet."

I slid my feet out. The flip-flops took forever to land softly on the ground.

"You're doing great!"

When I got to the top, I saw that she'd set out a little picnic on the tiny platform: cheese and crackers and cherries, a beat-up thermos covered in stickers, two plastic wineglasses with pink-flamingo stems.

"Have a seat." Salix patted the rope beside her. "It's like sitting in a hammock chair with half the rope gone."

"I c-c-can't believe that I'm up here." I arranged myself on the trembling ropes. "Corbin will be so impressed."

"Feel the fear and do it anyway, right?"

"Oversimplification, but sure."

"Look, though." She pointed. The sun was easing down behind the high-rises and tower cranes, pink and purple cotton-candy clouds strung along the horizon above the ocean.

"It's beautiful," I said. And I meant it. "It's really beautiful."

"Here." Salix filled the wineglasses from the thermos and handed me one. "A mocha for you. From Continental. The whipped cream melted, but it'll still be good." She shimmied closer. The entire rope pyramid shook. My heart took off, pounding angrily.

"Whoa." I gripped the rope with my free hand. Don't look down, Maeve. Do not look down. And then I did look down, and it was a huge mistake.

The ground rushed up with dizzying speed. I squeezed my eyes shut. When I opened my eyes, the ground had dropped away again, and I felt suspended in midair, as if there were no ropes, no pole, no Salix.

A person could die, falling from that height. I could land on my head or snap my back. Or I could break an arm. A leg. Or both. If Salix fell, she might break her wrist, and then Juilliard would be over. All because she tried to romance a neurotic girl who would never be good enough for her—who was I kidding?—and then I would forever be the girl who ruined Salix's dreams of being a professional musician. The skyline slanted to one side; then it tipped to the other.

"I have to get down." I set the flamingo glass on the ledge, but I missed and it fell off. I heard a crack when it landed a million feet below. "And you do too. Right now. Or you'll never go to Juilliard. And it will be my fault."

"What? Wait. Wait, Maeve!" Salix grabbed my wrist as I

started climbing down. "It's okay. It's really okay. We're in a kids' playground. There are cedar chips on the ground. The ropes would break your fall unless you took a swan dive off from the top. You're not drunk or stoned or stupid. You're just afraid of heights."

I nodded, my throat too dry to speak.

"Do you really want to get down? Really and truly?"

"No," I squeaked. I wanted to be on top of the world with Salix; of course I did. With cheese and crackers and tacky plastic flamingo glasses.

"It's okay to freak out. Go ahead. Freak out." Salix wasn't letting go. "Have a full-on freak-out, and then it'll all be good."

I squeezed my eyes shut. She didn't know. She just didn't know. And I didn't want her to know.

"Go through it. It won't last forever. It's like nerves before I play for an audience. Every single time I want to throw up. And I do, sometimes. One time I threw up onstage."

"You did?"

"I did. But I see the fear, and then I go through the fear, and then I get to the other side of the fear. I go through it."

I let Salix help me back up. "Don't look down. Look around. Tell me ten things that you can see from here."

"You." My heart still galloped. My knuckles ached from holding the rope so hard.

"That's one."

The streetlights popped on along the Drive.

"The streetlights. The patio at Havana's. That bus." I relaxed my grip, just a little. "A woman coming out of the corner store. The cenotaph. The bathrooms at the top of the park. A guy, his shopping cart, and he's got a dog."

"You're counting the guy as one and his shopping cart as another?" Salix counted off her fingers. "And his dog?"

"That's ten." My heart started to slow. "But if you want more, there are"—I counted—"nine hippies with drums getting ready to make a really terrible racket. And more coming across the grass."

"They should get the dying-goose man to play with them."

"We can hear the drummers from our place," I said. "Sometimes the boys come and join them. If they're still awake."

"Better now?" Salix let go of my wrist.

"A bit, yeah." I glanced at the one plastic flamingo glass still perched on the platform. "Sorry about the other flamingo."

"We can share mine." Salix handed it to me, and I took a sip. "We can get down. Now, I mean. I just didn't want you climbing down when you were freaking out."

"Smart."

The drummers started. There were about fifteen of them now, banging their djembes while a few dogs wrestled in a heap in the middle. Pot smoke wafted over, skunky and thick.

The last of the sun disappeared over the water, and darkness stretched out behind them to the east. The drummers fumbled together until they found their rhythm, and then they didn't sound so bad. Not from up there, in the dark.

"Thank you." I gave the glass back. "For getting me up here. And keeping me up here. I don't usually do things that scare me."

"Remember at Continental? When you ran off?"

"Etched forever in my mind."

"I was thinking back to that first date, which is why I invited you here."

The word *date* lifted up, available for the taking. So, with shaking hands, I took it. "Kind of a messy first date," I whispered.

"Still," Salix said softly. "This dumb idea, to bring you up here—"

"Not dumb."

"I wanted somewhere special to ask you if this was. I mean, I was going to ask you if we're, you know. If you thought maybe we could. If we are."

"If we are—?"

"If we *are*," Salix said. "If we're dating. If this is a date. If all these times have been dates."

I was so glad that I hadn't climbed down when I'd wanted to. I was glad that I'd gone through the fear. I was so glad that I'd stayed long enough to watch Salix stumble sweetly over her words in the dark. Salix, who never stumbled. Salix, who always knew the right thing to say.

"Are you going through it?" I said with a smile.

"That is exactly what I'm doing." Salix exhaled loudly. "Help me out here, would you?"

"We *are*." My cheeks suddenly burned, and my heart sped up again, but for all good reasons this time. "We are."

"I thought so." Salix smiled. "So that time at Continental was our first date."

"I'm sorry I was so weird."

"I like that you're weird."

Salix leaned forward. She was going to kiss me. This was the kiss that would push the terrible one away. I closed my eyes. Our lips were just about to meet. But then the whole web started to shake. Salix pulled away, and we looked down. Three boys were scrambling up the ropes.

"They don't even look like they're ten years old," I said. "They should be in bed."

"It's all good." Salix quickly packed everything up. She pried one of my hands off the rope and kept hold of it as she coached me down. "Put your left foot here. Exactly, yes. Now your other foot too."

"Lesbos!" One of the boys pointed. "Lesbo dykes!"

Salix glared down at them. "Watch your mouth, kid."

The boys bounced and bounced, shaking the ropes.

"You're okay, Maeve," Salix said. "Almost there."

"Faggots!"

"Wrong gender, shithead." Salix kept a hand on my back, steadying me.

We met the boys in the middle.

"You were making out up there," the smallest one accused. Another one made obnoxious kissing noises. The third wagged his tongue between his fingers. "Dirty homos!"

Suddenly I was with Ruthie, against the wall in her room. And then I was staring at Mrs. Patel slumped on the floor. Oranges rolling into the street. Beaches and bus rides and the fat lady squishing us together. Drummers and dogs barking. The broken flamingo cup. I felt my grip slipping. I teetered forward.

"Hang on." Salix jumped down.

The boys made wet smooching noises as Salix helped me from below.

"Shut up, you little shit." Salix took her hand away just long enough to yank the loudest kid off the ropes. He fell backward and landed hard on the cedar chips.

"Oh my God!" I froze. "Is he okay?"

"Don't touch me!" He sprang up. "Lesbo bitch!"

"He's fine," Salix said.

The other two boys were already at the top, and they watched silently while their friend climbed up the other side. When he was up at the top, well out of reach, he spat at us.

"Rug muncher!"

"Oh!" It was so absurd that I had to laugh as I finally stepped off the bottom rung. "Rug muncher? Seriously?"

"Come on." Salix gave the finger to the boys. She scooped up our flip-flops and her violin and pulled me away from the playground.

"Where did he even learn that?"

"I'm going to guess from a ragingly homophobic older sibling." When we got to the grass, Salix dropped the flip-flops and took my hands in hers. "That did not go the way that I'd planned. Are you okay?"

"Sure."

"Are you sure? Because we were just gay-bashed by three nasty little kids."

"I know. I'm good. Truly." But I wasn't. It wasn't about being called a lesbo or a rug muncher, though. I was angry about the boys' timing. If they'd arrived just five minutes later, Salix would've already kissed me. But they took that first kiss away. And so it was a first kiss that wasn't. It was an interrupted kiss. It was still there, but it hadn't happened. And those five minutes would never happen again. There would be another five minutes in their place—happening right now, almost finished, even—but I didn't want *those* five minutes. I wanted the other five minutes back. I wanted that kiss at the top, up there with the dappled lights of downtown spread out below. But that was gone now.

Bad Drummers

As we crossed the park, I saw Mr. Heidelman hurrying up the other path.

"That's my neighbor," I told Salix. "The musician."

He was heading straight for the drummers.

"What's he doing?" Salix squinted into the dark.

He stopped at the edge of the drum circle, his hands clasped behind his back.

"Mr. Heidelman?"

"Hello, neighbor." He swayed to the beat. "It's Miss Maeve, yes?"

"That's right," I said. "And this is Salix. She's a musician too. She plays the violin."

"My favorite instrument of all." Mr. Heidelman raised his voice over the cacophony of drums. "First chair for the Vancouver Symphony Orchestra for nearly four decades until they gave me a lovely retirement party. Which means I'm retired now, I suppose. How long have you been playing?"

"Since I was five."

"And are you very good? Or just average? It's okay to be honest. Not everyone can be gifted."

"She's brilliant," I interrupted. "She's going to go to Juilliard. Like her sister."

"I'm *applying*," Salix said. "I haven't been accepted."

"Yet," I said.

"High sights, indeed." Mr. Heidelman nodded. "I tell you what: we'll listen to these drummers for a while, and then you must come back to my place to play for me. Yes?"

"I could," Salix said. "If it's okay with Maeve."

"Wonderful," Mr. Heidelman said, and then he turned his attention to the drummers.

He started dancing, kicking up his legs and flapping his arms. He took my hands.

"Dance, Miss Maeve. Dance!"

I was a terrible dancer, and I didn't want to prove it to Salix, but then I saw her dancing too, clapping her hands and stomping like she was at a barn dance. She looked like a complete and utter goof, and I liked her even more for it.

Mr. Heidelman stopped dancing all of a sudden.

"Oh, dear." He leaned heavily on me.

"Are you okay?"

"Yes, yes." He gasped for breath. "I am not twenty anymore. Not even sixty. That is all."

I took his arm as he teetered backward. "Do you need to sit down?"

"That would be wise, I think."

The drumming slowed to a stop. Someone offered up a lawn chair. Salix helped Mr. Heidelman to sit.

"Is he okay?" someone asked.

"Should we call an ambulance?"

"No, no." Mr. Heidelman waved away the idea. "I'm okay," he gasped.

"Do you want a glass of water?" A tall man with long blond dreadlocks squatted beside Mr. Heidelman. "Wine?"

"Wine, thank you." Mr. Heidelman nodded. "A sip of wine would be very fortifying."

A girl not much older than me—with bare feet and her own baby dreads—came back a minute later with a small mason jar half filled with red wine. Mr. Heidelman took a long sip.

"You cast a spell with those drums," he said.

"Namaste." The girl brought her hands together under her chin. "Thank you."

"You looked like you were enjoying it," the guy said.

"Indeed I was." Mr. Heidelman nodded again. "But to tell you the truth, I came over here to politely ask you to stop at eleven, if you wouldn't mind. You see, I live right there." He pointed. "And an old man needs his sleep. You understand. You will help a tired old man get a good night's sleep." Mr. Heidelman downed the rest of the wine and slowly stood up. "Won't you?"

"I'm glad you're okay," the guy said.

We each took a side and helped Mr. Heidelman out of the park, where he suddenly stood a little taller and took a deep breath. "That's better. Do you think it worked?"

"That was an act?" I was bewildered.

"No, no. Not really." Mr. Heidelman shook his head. "I was winded. I did need to sit. And I did enjoy the wine. But yes, I did go over to ask them to stop at eleven. A little drama can go a long way, don't you agree?"

Mr. Heidelman unlocked his door and ushered us in. Salix went ahead, but I couldn't quite make myself take the first step inside. This was Mrs. Patel's home. And at the same time, it wasn't her home anymore at all. Glancing in, I could see the baby grand in the living room, and bookshelves lining the wall behind it.

There was no curry smell.

No TV blaring.

No Mrs. Patel.

"It's okay." Salix reached for my hand.

I stepped inside, ready for the panic to grip me, but it didn't. My eyes went straight to all the art on the wall. I started to kick off my flip-flops.

"No need to take them off," Mr. Heidelman said.

I did feel a pang of sadness then. But I wanted to know Mr. Heidelman too, and I wanted to look at all the paintings and prints and sketches on the wall. I wanted to hear him play the violin, the piano, any one of all those instruments that the movers filed in that first day we met.

Salix pulled out her violin and tuned a few strings and Mr. Heidelman put the kettle on for tea. Salix and Mr. Heidelman chatted while the kettle heated up. When the kettle whistled, it sounded just like Mrs. Patel's. I didn't feel panic or sadness as Mr. Heidelman lifted the kettle off the stove. I just missed Mrs. Patel.

I went back to the art, to clear my head.

From floor to ceiling, frames of all sizes. Watercolors, oil, pencil sketches, paintings that looked hundreds of years old, others that were very modern. I had never seen a wall so crowded with art. Another wall displayed photographs, mostly black-and-white, all of people, mostly musicians, and several of Mr. Heidelman playing in the orchestra.

Salix started to play.

Simply put, it was the most beautiful piece of music that I had ever heard. Haunting and sweet at the same time, both uncomplicated and intricately urgent.

Mr. Heidelman shuffled out of the kitchen, rubbing his hands together, his face bright with joy. "Nigel Kennedy. 'Fallen Forest.' Yes!"

Salix lifted her eyes in acknowledgment and kept playing.

For a moment I felt as if we'd slipped through a door and into another world, where everything looked the same but was covered in a fine dusting of glitter.

I stared at Salix as she played. How could she know each note by heart? How could she keep so much music tidy and organized and ready to pull out at any time? It was a kind of miracle, really.

At eleven o'clock, the drumming in the park stopped.

"You see?" Mr. Heidelman grinned. "They were happy to help an old man. And now it's time for me to go to bed."

"Thank you for the tea and cookies," I said.

"Thank you," Salix said.

"You must play for me again." He pumped her hand. "No, even better. I have an idea. You wait. It will help with Juilliard. I'll be in touch."

He said good night and shut the door.

"It'll help with Juilliard?" Salix laughed. "Is that what he just said?"

"He did."

Salix's cheeks shone red and her green eyes sparkled. "You know what?"

"What?"

"This." She slid a hand around my waist and pulled me close. She kissed me. Her lips were soft and lingered warm against mine before she pulled away. "I've wanted to do that since before those little shits showed up at the park."

"Me too." And on tippy-toe I kissed her back.

Kissing was a height.

The anticipation was the ride up, up, up, so high. To where the air was thin and there were clouds all around, and far below, everything was still going on without you, without the two of you.

And on tippy-toe I kissed her back. Again and again and again.

Dad

Salix tasted like the jasmine tea and almond cookies Mr. Heidelman had served us in china teacups with iridescent peacocks painted on the saucers. Her lips were soft. She knew what she was doing. Her hands were firm on my hips, and then on the small of my back. When we pulled apart to say good night, I could hardly believe that we were standing on concrete. Everything was so soft and pliable. The air was warm and smelled of roses. And then she was walking away, and even though I never, ever wanted her to leave, not ever, I knew that of course she had to. It was so late. And a moment had to end to become one.

The house was dark and quiet. I floated to the couch and actually swooned as I sat down. And then I was giggling, and then I was yawning, and then I was falling asleep with a smile so big that when I woke with a start a couple of hours later, my face actually hurt. It was the front door, slamming open. My dad stumbled in and flicked on the hall light, but he didn't notice me. He kicked off one shoe and then wrestled the other one off, lurching backward until he was braced against the wall, where he let out a very loud belch.

"Dad?" I sat up.

"Maevey. Maevey Gravy. Groovy Maevey Gravy."

"You're drunk."

"Sure."

"Where have you been?"

"Here and there. Sometimes here. Sometimes there."

He groped the wall until he found the switch for the living room. All of a sudden everything was illuminated in that hot, bright light that happens after the darkest dark. His face glistened with sweat. His T-shirt was soaked under each arm. His hair was flattened. There was a stain down the front of his shirt.

"Did you puke on yourself?"

"Maybe just a little." He held his thumb and finger apart about an inch.

"Where's your truck?"

"Friend."

"A friend drove? A friend has your truck?"

"She drove. She has the truck."

"Who is *she*?"

"There is no *she*," he growled. "I'm not so drunk that I don't get what you're implying. Besides, it's none of your business."

"Not my business?"

"Nope."

"Where the fuck *are* you, Dad?"

"Here, baby."

He yanked me into a hug. He reeked of vomit and booze

and sweat. I tried to pull away, and he held me tighter, the damp from his armpit wetting the back of my neck.

"You're not here." I twisted out of his grip. "You're totally gone!"

He let out a long, boozy sigh. "You want to talk existentialism?"

"No."

"Existentialism. The study of existence. That painting." He flung his arm, gesturing at the painting of us in the meadow. "Did that moment exist?"

"Why are we talking about the painting?"

"Do *you*, Maeve Glover, believe in the existence of that moment?"

"I remember it. I remember the smell of flowers everywhere. I remember we drove up there in the truck. You brought apples."

"Now, see." He wagged a finger in my face. "That's where you're wrong. I made that moment up. It never happened. It never existed. Because your mom never let me see you when you were that old."

"Because you were drunk then. Just like now."

"Sure, if you want to simplify it."

I swallowed against the lump in my throat. Tears welled up, but I was not going to cry. I pinched the bridge of my nose and squeezed my eyes shut. "This is so—"

"So what?" He opened his arms, his empty palms face up, part appeal, part surrender. "So what, Maeve?"

"The painting is a lie."

"But it's not. I made it up. *Now* it exists. And you have all those wonderful memories. That is *magic*."

It wasn't magic. He had just destroyed one of my best

memories. It was mean and cruel, and he could never take it back.

What now?

The baby was due in fifty-eight days.

The boys were killing off the kings in Gnomenville.

Claire kept pacing the house. Upstairs, downstairs, in each room, as if maybe if she looked often enough, she would find him.

But maybe on one of her trips through the house, she would walk right out the door. Because she had once before, when the twins were about a year old. He was sober when they got married, and he stayed sober until the boys were born, and then he slipped, and instead of getting back up, he kept falling and falling, until she packed the babies up and went to the Sunshine Coast and stayed with Grandma until he drove into the ditch and blacked out. When he came to, he had scared himself enough that he stopped.

"I'm going to bed," I said. "You should too."

"Great idea." He stripped off his soiled shirt and curled up on the couch and shut his eyes. "Night-night, Maeve."

I picked up his shirt, holding the stinking thing away from me with two fingers. I was going to wash it for him, help him hide this one little part. I watched him slip quickly into sleep, one hand resting on the floor, the other resting on his chest as his breathing slowed into snoring. He was ugly. He was an ugly drunk.

I dropped the shirt and went to bed, conjuring Salix's kisses, those sweet, weightless moments. I wouldn't let Dad take over. I wouldn't worry about him. Or at least I'd try not to.

. . .

When I got up the next morning, Claire was sitting cross-legged at one end of the couch, knitting. Her belly sat on her lap. It looked like the baby had grown significantly overnight.

"Did you see him?" Claire set down her knitting. "I can still smell it. Even with the doors and windows open, I can smell it." She nodded at a throw pillow tossed on the floor by the stairs. "I can even tell he used that pillow. It reeks."

"Sorry."

"Don't be." Claire picked up her knitting and started again, hooking the yarn around the needle in quick, angry motions. "It's not your fault."

But maybe it was? Maybe when I came, the balance shifted, and everything slid off-kilter.

"This is your dad's problem," Claire said to her needles. "Not yours. We've been here before. And he was here with your mother, too. And before that it was even worse. Let's hope he gets through and comes back new and improved before the baby arrives. That's the best I've got right now. I don't have the energy or inclination to kick him out, so we'll just stumble along like this for a while."

After the kisses last night, I'd pictured this morning. I would tell Claire everything—climbing the ropes, the picnic at the top, the flamingo glasses, the three boys, the drummers, tea and cookies and the peacocks on the teacups and Salix playing the violin, the kiss good night. And she would smile and gush and be so happy for me. I wasn't going to tell her about the other kisses, or about Salix's hand up my shirt. I was going to tell her everything up to that.

Instead I didn't tell her about any of it, and I didn't tell her about seeing Dad, either. What was the point? She was too distracted by the one to hear anything about the other. I kicked the pillow down the stairs and followed it. I stuffed it into the washing machine—there was the soiled shirt; he must've put it there before he left—and turned it on. I put both hands on the counter and stared at the floor. Dust, lint, a wayward gnome, a quarter, and a stub of one of the thick red pencils Dad used at work. I closed my eyes and went back to that first kiss, and then the one after that, and the one after that, and so on. I folded them into my palm like so many jasmine petals, fragrant and delicate, and I held on to them, perhaps a little too tight.

Riding a Bike

Salix arrived on her bike promptly at two o'clock that afternoon. I had completely forgotten that we'd made plans to take the boys to the spray park in Strathcona. When I answered the door, I was still in my pajamas, and I hadn't so much as washed my face or brushed my teeth. I'd been sitting up in bed, sketching and worrying about Dad, and had finally decided to text my mom about something more meaningful than how the weather was, and yes, I was taking my vitamins. I still had my phone in my hand. Send.

Dad is drinking too much again. He's messing everything up. Claire is so angry. I kissed Salix. Please advise.

"Salix! Hi!" I tucked myself behind the door as if I were naked and not just disheveled. "You're here!"

"Am I early?"

"Nope." I invited her in. "I'm not ready, that's all. Wait here for a minute."

I dashed upstairs and found the boys on the deck,

smashing handfuls of gnomes together on a piece of green felt covered with dried red paint.

"Carnage," Corbin said.

"That's all blood," Owen said.

"Okay, the war needs to pause because I'm taking you to the water park right now," I said. "Like, get your suits while I pack a snack and we're leaving right now. My friend is here and she's ready to go and I totally forgot all about it because—" I stopped myself. "Whatever. Let's go. Now!"

"Your friend?" Owen said.

"You don't have any friends," Corbin said.

"It's the girl from the ferry," I said. "The one you sold jokes to? And then the park? She brought you drinks."

"That girl is *here*?" He still sat on the floor, a pile of presumably dead gnomes in his lap.

"Is she your girlfriend now?" Owen asked.

"None of your business," I said. "Let's go. Grab your bike helmets."

"But I can't ride with a broken arm!" Corbin said.

"Shit." I thought quickly. "You'll ride in the trailer."

"That's for groceries," Corbin protested. "Or babies. I changed my mind. I can ride."

"No you can't."

"I can!"

Why had I agreed to bike there? Maybe the kisses had made me a bit stupid, because I hadn't ridden a bike since I was ten, when I fell off and broke my wrist and wisely declared never again.

Maeve Glover died suddenly today while riding a bicycle that she had no business riding. She was hit

*by a semi truck after she failed to stop at a stop sign
because she forgot how to work the brakes. Survived
by her twin brothers and the Miraculous Girlfriend,
she will be remembered as stupid in the end, despite
being a talented artist who—*

"Maeve?" Claire called from inside. "Honey? Do you want me to offer Salix some tea or something?"

"No! We're coming." I grabbed the boys' hands and pulled them inside. And then, in a whisper: "Just get ready to go. Please?"

Owen didn't want to ride his bike. He said it was too far. With too many streets to cross. And too steep on the way back.

"I'll make sure we're all safe," Salix said. "And I'll help you walk your bike up on the way home, okay?"

"I guess." Owen stuffed Hibou into his bike basket and climbed on. "If I have to."

Corbin stood beside the bike trailer, arms crossed, his blue cast dirty and covered in marker.

"I can ride with one arm!"

"Either get in the trailer," I said, "or stay home. Those are your two choices. I don't care which one you go with."

"Stupid." Corbin flopped into the trailer. "Dumb trailer."

"Going happily? Both of you?" I said. "Or not at all. Choose now."

"Going!" Corbin hollered.

"Going," Owen muttered. He did up his helmet and sighed. "Happily, I guess."

I tried to focus on the road, the stop signs, the turns, Salix to my left and so comfortable on the bike that it was nothing for her to twist and face me, chatting, or to ride with one hand. I clutched the handlebars of Claire's bike, testing the brakes every few seconds, lurching down the hill. Owen stuck close to me, doing the same, with Corbin piping up from the rear.

"Go faster!"

"You don't even know how to ride a bike right."

"You're too slow!"

"Shut up, Corbin!" I hollered.

"I don't have a little brother," Salix said, like she was making an excuse for my outburst. "Let alone two the same age." But it didn't matter, because I was embarrassed that I'd shouted at him like that.

"Sorry, Corbin."

"It doesn't matter," he said.

"It does," Salix said. "Apologize to her, man. It's the right thing to do."

"Sorry, Maeve," he groaned.

Both boys forgot they were grumpy by the time we arrived. With their helmets and clothes still on, they ran straight for the water, which shot up from the concrete and out of old hydrants and along a little culvert running along the edge, where kids could float boats and race sticks to the drain.

Salix and I found a spot on the grass in the shade and spread out a blanket. I sat cross-legged, and Salix sat with her long tanned legs stretched out in front, leaning back on her hands. After a couple of minutes she lay back with one arm folded behind her head. She pointed to the sky.

"That cloud looks like an elephant."

The boys were jumping and stomping in the little stream.

Salix reached for my hand. "Come on." She drew me down beside her.

"It doesn't look like an elephant," I said. "It looks like a velociraptor."

"It does not look like a velociraptor."

"Wings." I pointed. "Beaky head. There."

And then Owen was standing beside her, dripping and shivering and blocking the sun.

"I'm hungry."

I sat up and pulled out the snacks. Owen wrapped himself in a towel and then took a muffin and an apple into a wedge of hot sunshine by the playground.

Salix patted the blanket. "Come back?"

"Wait for it," I said.

"What?"

"Just wait," I said. And then: "See?"

Corbin sprinted toward us. He'd commandeered a water gun from somewhere—no guns allowed at our house—and was scanning the area, the gun wedged under his broken arm.

"Hostile territory!" he shouted. "Food drop required! Now, now!"

I tossed him a muffin. He caught it and kept running, circling back around to the spray park to join a group of armed boys crouched behind a wall.

"Do you want a muffin too?" I said. "Raspberry oatmeal. Claire made them. She's a really good baker."

"Thanks." Salix sat up. "She seems really nice."

"I lucked out in the stepmother department."

But Claire was more than just a stepmother. She'd parented me for almost twelve years, even if it was part-time. She was my brothers' mother. She was my dad's wife. If she left—and of course she'd take the boys with her—Dad would have nothing left here.

And it would be his fault if he ended up in a seedy room in one of the cockroach- and bedbug-infested hotels. Or a room in a shared house. And where would I stay when I came to visit? With Claire and the boys? With Dad? What a mess.

"Shit," I muttered.

"What is it?"

"Nothing." I didn't want to unload on Salix again. I didn't want Salix to think that my life was always wobbly, even if it was. I pulled out my sketchbook and searched for something to draw. A toddler in the sandbox, filling a red bucket with tiny handfuls of sand. Two old ladies sitting on a bench. Orthopedic shoes.

"Show me?" Salix said.

"No." I closed the sketchbook. "Sorry."

"Someday, though. Right?"

"Right." I picked at the grass and sprinkled some on her shirt. "Gnomenical weeds," I said. "According to Gnomantic legend, grass carries magical powers. The leaders of the Percival and Wren kingdoms have used it for centuries in their battle for domination over each other."

"I have no idea what you just said. Does that mean that you just put a spell on me?"

"Yes."

"Good," Salix said. "I don't mind. But now I'm going to stop talking about it so that I don't end up saying something really, supremely corny."

"Go ahead." I sprinkled more grass on her. "By the power of Gnomenical weed, I command you to tell me."

"Okay. How about . . ." Salix paused. "How about: Baby,

you don't need to work your magic on me, because I've been under your spell since the moment we met." She blushed. Deeply. From her neck up. "Oh, God." Salix flopped back onto the blanket.

Salix had meant it to be a joke. Only we both knew it wasn't. Not really. Not quite.

"That is corny as hell." I laughed.

"I know, right?"

"Yep."

"Yeah. Corny." I lay beside her, staring at the sky again. I reached for Salix's hand and pointed to a cloud. "That one actually looks like a stalk of corn."

"No it doesn't." Salix's hand was warm in mine. "It looks like a velociraptor."

The ride home was a lot harder, and by the time we got to the last hill, we were all pushing bikes, except Corbin, who ran ahead to open the bike locker. Once the bikes were all back where they belonged, the boys disappeared inside and Salix and I made our way up the parking garage ramp. Salix took my hand and stopped me in the alley. Up above, orchestra music drifted out of Mr. Heidelman's open windows. Cymbals clashed, flutes twittered.

"Was it weird?" Salix said. "What I said? At the park? I was trying to be funny, but—"

"What's weird is talking about Gnomenical legend," I said. I'd gone on to explain about Gnomenville at length, so much that Salix was now completely up to date with the political situation and the threats to the warring factions and the daily goings-on of innocent Percivals and Wrens caught up in the crossfire. "And by talking, I mean on and on and on and on. Sorry about that. I start rambling when I'm—"

"Nervous," Salix said. "Me too."

Her hand was hot in mine. The heat traveled up my arm and across my chest. Up to my cheeks.

"I like you, Maeve." Salix bit her lip. She looked away before adding, "A lot."

"I like you." The heat sank down, and I ached with a warm heaviness between my legs. "A lot too."

We stood there for a moment, both looking away, and then looking at each other, and then we kissed. And kissed again. And again. Until the boys sang out from the deck above, "Maeve and Salix, sitting in a tree, k-i-s-s-i-n-g!" I pulled away and looked up. Corbin and Owen and Claire all leaned over the railing, grinning down at us.

"Don't let us interrupt." Claire waved. "But I do have lemonade, and cookies."

Mr. Heidelman peered over his railing too. "I wondered what the noise was about."

"Come over, Mr. Heidelman," Claire said. "Lemonade and cookies!"

"Come up, Salix!" Corbin called down. "We'll show you Gnomenville."

"How can I resist that?" Salix said. "Now that I know so much about it." She grinned at me.

Something fell from up above. It was Hibou, landing in the rowan tree by the gate.

"Corbin!" Owen hollered. "You did that on purpose!"

"Did not!"

"Did too!"

"I can get it." Salix fished the stuffed owl out of the

branches. She put an arm across my shoulder and laughed. "That was about as unprivate as you can get."

"Welcome to my current life," I said. "All the privacy I ever had is back in Port Townsend in a little log cabin in the woods, all locked up."

My house seemed a lot farther away now: the bus ride to Seattle endless and the drive to Port Townsend impossibly long. It was as if the distance had stretched, and now it was easier to be here, in Vancouver, than to make my way back home. Maybe this was home enough for now. Maybe I didn't want to go back to Port Townsend. I hadn't checked the bus times in days. Not since that day at the park when Salix reunited me with my half of the cookie.

Five months and thirteen days, and then I'd have to say goodbye. To Salix, the new baby, Claire and the boys, and even Dad. Unless I had to say goodbye to him sooner.

That night I checked my email. There were two messages from Mom. And none from Ruthie. Just as well.

The first message from Mom was a reply to my request for advice.

> *Honey, stay out of it. Let Claire and your dad sort things out.*
>
> *Your dad has a history with alcohol, as you well know, but he's always managed to pull himself up, right? Sounds like you're having a great time with Salix. Don't worry. Send pictures!*
>
> *xoxoxo*
> *Mom*

The other email was short too. Dan had stacked our cordwood for us and would I please send him a little something in the mail as a thank-you. Maybe some maple syrup. *Love you, Maeve. Love, love, love.*

Firewood. For the winter. When I'd be back in Port Townsend. Back to getting up and starting the fire in the stove each morning, because I was always up before Mom. I'd be home in January, when the garden was finally finished, the last of the kale wilting, the ground muddy, rotten leaves and endless rain. I didn't mind the rain at all, especially in the forest. Mist shrouded the cedar trees in the morning. Sometimes I had time to sit out on the porch before the bus came and watch it lift. The rain on the tin roof, the eaves so blocked with leaves that the water poured over the edges, making a muddy little trough in the dirt. Last year Mom and I stacked some bricks at one end of the porch and put a metal fire pit on top of it so we could sit on the porch by the warmth and watch the glimmering flames.

I didn't want to think about deep, dark winter. I loved winter at home. The black sky awash with stars. The crisp air. The stillness when it snowed, which was so rare it was like magic.

Letting Go

Salix and I were at Continental one late afternoon after we'd been swimming. We were both tired, our muscles sore, when it suddenly occurred to me, as it so often did, just how much time I had left. One hundred and fifty-two days.

In the two weeks since the spray park, I'd seen my father twice. Both times in the morning. Once, he was sitting on the couch doing up his bootlaces. He was pasty and pale and hardly looked up before leaving. The other time he was throwing up into the kitchen sink.

"Good thing we have a garbage disposal," Claire said as she nudged past him to reach for the bowls.

She tried to keep things normal. She tried to make light of it. She tried not to care that he was never home, and that when he was out he was getting shit-faced. What kind of family was this baby coming into? Would he even be around when the baby came? Maeve, she said, I know you don't want to, but there really isn't anyone else I'd want. She handed me a stack of books that I'd already read. I need a backup. I just don't know about your dad right now.

I didn't know about my dad right now either. And so I read the books. Not because I wanted to. But because it's like when you take an umbrella and it doesn't rain. You have a lighter in your pocket that you never need until the one day you leave it home and it's someone's birthday and no one can find the matches. I read because by my doing so, Dad would show up and do what he was supposed to do.

Until then, it was one more thing to worry about.

"It must be nice not to worry," I said to Salix.

"I do worry," she said. "A lot."

"What things do you worry about?"

"If my mom's cancer will come back. Not getting into Juilliard. Playing in front of the Vancouver Symphony Orchestra. To name a few."

Mr. Heidelman had invited her to perform at one of their rehearsals, but she hadn't talked about it since then. I'd thought maybe it was a good-luck thing. I'd had no idea she was worrying. "You never said."

"Terrified, anxious, nauseous," Salix said, "whenever I think about it."

"That sounds familiar."

"It's not only you," Salix said. "Everybody worries." Her words were clipped, and her gaze slid toward the street. "We all have our worries. There is no corner on the market."

"No. You're right. Sorry."

So she didn't understand. And that was fine. Most people didn't. Only 3 percent of the population has an actual anxiety disorder. Worrying is different for those people. We always think things will go wrong, even if they're not likely to. We are almost always fearful and uncertain. Sure, everyone worries. But not everyone worries in the same way. Even worrying about her mother's cancer coming back could be easier for her than one panic attack for me about whether I left the stove on. That was wrong, and I knew it. But it was true. Even though her mother's cancer was so much more important than leaving an element turned on on the stove.

I could hear Nancy as if she were right beside me. I could practically smell the incense. Worrying is something everyone does differently. We all think our worries are the worst. Never compare your worries with someone else's. No one wins.

"No." Salix took my hand. "I'm sorry. There is a corner on the market, I know. I know it's harder for you. I know that it makes things hard for you." She took my other hand. "Things like life."

Someone dropped a drink and the glass smashed. Someone pulled up in a pink Vespa. We laughed at a woman in high heels walking a tangle of eight tiny poodles and carrying one draped over her shoulder like a baby. We shared a muffin. Someone Salix knew stopped to say hello, and Salix held my hand and introduced me as her girlfriend. She said the word so easily, I hardly noticed. But once I realized it, it was all I could hear.

Girlfriend. Girlfriend. Girlfriend.

Pay attention, Maeve. They'd been in junior orchestra together, Salix said as he left. And then a girl walked by, and Salix leapt to her feet.

"Maya, hey!"

It was the girl from the ferry terminal in Gibsons. The one with the clipboard and ponytail. She was wearing a cute little dress, like something out of the fifties. Robin's-egg blue, with tiny white polka dots. Her ponytail was up high, and she was wearing cat's-eye sunglasses. I was so busy noticing how cute she was and how frumpy I was and how good she would look beside Salix, I could barely say hello before she said her goodbye and continued down the street.

"Her mom just lost her job and they might have to move."

Salix was going to compare. This worry is worse than that worry. But then she didn't.

"Which is not a big deal to her. But it would be for you, am I right?"

I nodded.

"I get it. At least I think I do. It's worse for you."

"I'm not pretending."

"Why would you?"

I didn't want to talk about it anymore. I took out my sketchbook and began to draw the girl sitting against the newspaper box. She had dreads, and a big backpack with a cat sleeping on top of it. She had a sign that said BE A DEER AND SPARE SOME CHANGE. She wore a pair of fuzzy antlers, the kind you'd see in a dollar store before Christmas.

There was worry, and then there was *worry*. Ninety-seven percent of people worried just fine. They felt the range of related emotions, but they could still do life, even simulta-neously. The remaining 3 percent? We were incapacitated.

"Let me see?"

I shook my head.

"Why not?"

"Would you ask to see someone's diary?"

"No."

I closed the book. "Same thing."

"But it isn't, is it? It's a sketchbook. Pictures. Drawings. A collection of your talent, right? Like listening to me play."

My palm was warm on the worn cover, each corner so battered it was almost rounded, the spine reinforced with rainbow duct tape. Could I show her? I had never shown anyone my sketchbook. Not even Ruthie or Dan.

I slid it across the table. Salix opened it to the first page and smiled. A sketch of the fox with the limp.

"It's not in any particular order," I said. "S-s-sometimes I add things after. Glue on bits. Or color stuff. Things." I could hear my words get thick and clunky as she turned the pages. A portrait of Jessica.

"That's her?"

I nodded, unable to speak.

"Your first girlfriend." She studied the portrait and then glanced up. "Did you hear me call you my girlfriend?"

I nodded again. I wished I could say something, but I felt like I was sitting there naked at a table outside a coffee shop. Absolutely naked.

"Is that okay with you?"

Say something, Maeve. Don't just nod again.

"It's perfect," I squeaked as my heart started to pound. Oh no. The panic. The fucking panic. Salix turned the page, and then again, and then there were the dissected hearts.

"Sorry." I snatched the book back and stood, clutching it to my chest. "I can't."

"Are you going to run away again?"

"No." But I backed away from the table, as if I was.

The girl with the cat grinned up at me, antlers swaying.

"Spare change?"

"No!"

Salix dropped a dollar into the yogurt tub by the sign and took my hand and led me back to the table. She pushed my sketchbook away from her. "You're right. It is like a diary. Playing the violin is different. I won't ask to see it again."

"Okay. Th-th-thank you."

Everybody worries.

Which is why it's so hard to be someone who worries more. More often. About more things. More intensely, and with my whole body. My heart pounded, and my arms grew stiff. My fingertips prickled, which always happened just before they went numb. I stared at the street.

"Maeve?"

What's there to worry about? Don't make such a big deal about things. It'll blow over. Don't dwell on it. Shake it off. Choose to not worry.

As if it were a choice!

"Maeve." Salix packed up our things and took me by the hand. She walked me home, like I was some kind of invalid, silent and incapable beside her. When we got to my door, she said goodbye. And then: "I'm sorry."

"Why?"

"That I pushed you to let me look at it," she said. "And I'm sorry that sometimes you panic and get so anxious."

"Me?" I managed a small smile. "Never."

She pulled me into a tight hug. "It doesn't have to be so hard."

"It just is what it is. Until my parents let me take something for it."

"But right now, it doesn't have to be so hard."

She was being so sweet, but she didn't understand. It just wasn't that easy.

"If you start freaking out, call me and we'll go for a walk. Or we'll ride the night buses. We'll smoke some pot and get the giggles and eat a whole bag of chips. We'll walk up and down the alleys looking for treasure and avoiding skunks. Any of those things. All of those things. None of those things. Whatever you can think of." She pushed me away just enough that she could look into my eyes. "In fact, you don't even have to think about all the silly things." She kissed me. "I can do that too. Your girlfriend will be in charge of distractions."

"My girlfriend." I smiled. "That's a pretty good distraction right there."

Confrontation

Just after midnight, I heard the front door open and close. It was Dad, creeping home yet again. He probably was out of clean underwear, or wanted some food, or needed a shower. This was my chance. Confront him. Face it head-on. Don't let it get the best of me. A worry will cease to exist once it has been confronted, Nancy said. You kill it by facing it.

I sat in the dark for a moment, Salix's words loud in my head.

You are brave, Maeve.

What are you afraid of?

What's the worst that can happen? He gets better? He gets worse? So then it will either make a difference or it won't. You can't lose, Maeve. If you call him on his shit, he has to answer. He has to. He owes you that much. He loves you.

I could hear him moving up there, the floor creaking quietly. Maybe he wasn't fall-down drunk; maybe this would go a lot better than I hoped. Or maybe I should call Salix and tell her to meet me at the park with a big bag of chips. No. No. I needed to stop running the other way. If there was anything I could do to get Dad back on track, it was my responsibility to do it, fear or no fear. I still had to do it. For Claire. For the boys. For me.

I stopped at the top of the stairs, out of sight.

He was sitting on the edge of the couch. He'd pulled the coffee table to his knees and was leaning over it. The light from the one lamp on cast him in a warm, orange glow.

What's the worst that can happen?

Never mind anything that came before, because then he tucked his head down and snorted a line of cocaine through a rolled-up dollar bill.

And this wasn't even the worst thing. I could see it all unfold from here. The family, undone. My dad, unemployed and drunk and high and living on the street. Maybe we'd never see him again. Maybe this was the end of everything.

"Dad," I whispered.

"Maeve. Shit! I didn't see you. . . ." He wiped his nose with the back of his hand. "It's not what you think—"

"What are you *doing*?"

I should've stayed downstairs. There was no point in confronting it head-on. This was worse than not knowing. This was worse than worrying. I wanted to take it back. I wanted to take the trip downstairs in reverse, undoing it along the way, and then I wanted to run in the opposite direction. Running away was better than this.

"What is that?"

I knew what it was. But I wanted him to say it. Admit it. Or dare to deny it. I wanted to hear him say something, give me some kind of explanation that would make sense. But he wasn't saying anything at all. His hands were folded in his lap, and he just stared at me, his face in shadows.

"Dad?"

"It's not what you think."

"It is."

"Maeve, it's not—"

"It is! I'm not stupid."

He shook his head. "It isn't . . . I just . . . it's been . . ."

There was nothing he could say and he knew it.

"Fine." I stepped into the light.

"What are you going to do?"

"What are *you* going to do?"

He lifted his shoulders, and after a long moment he let them drop. That made me angrier than all his other bullshit heaped together into a great big stinking pile.

A shrug. It turned out to be the one thing that made the difference between all my hopeful coasting and pretending and shutting it all out, for better or for worse.

I headed for the stairs.

"Maeve." He stood. "Maeve, stop. Don't—"

"Don't *what*?" I spun. "Don't tell her? She already knows you're a fucking drunk, Dad."

I started to cry. I stood halfway up the stairs, gripping the railing.

"Don't tell her. Please."

"And then what?" I was sobbing now. "And then I'm

251

holding your secret? And then it's okay? It's not okay! We all thought it was bad. And now it's even *worse*."

"Let me fix it. I can fix it, Maeve. I've fixed it before."

"Fuck you."

"Maeve—"

"Fuck you!" I ran up the stairs.

Claire was sleeping on her side in a cocoon of pillows. Owen was asleep beside her with Hibou wedged under his chin. I wanted to scream, and I wanted to whisper. I wanted to tell her, and I didn't want to tell her. I wanted to be right there, and I wanted to evaporate. Sure, everyone worries.

I put a hand on Claire's shoulder.

"Claire?"

She opened her eyes. "Maeve? What is it?"

"Dad's downstairs. You need to come."

She looked at me in the dark and silently said everything.

"Before he leaves again." I pulled away the pillows and helped her out of bed.

She lumbered down the stairs ahead of me, tying her robe over her belly.

Dad was already at the door, shoving his feet into his shoes.

"Where are you going?" Claire said.

"I need some fresh air."

"Tell her." I took Claire's hand. "Tell her!"

"I wasn't—"

"You were!"

"Were what?" Claire's grip on my hand tightened. "What's going on, Billy?"

He stared at his feet. One shoe on. One shoe off. He was not going to say it.

"You have to tell her!" I shouted.

"The boys—"

"What?" I said. "You're worried that you'll wake them up? That's what you're worried about? Because I'll go wake them up right now and you can explain yourself. How about that?"

"Maeve thinks—" He shook his head. Kicked off the one shoe. "Maeve thinks she saw me snort a line of coke. But I—"

"Tell the truth, Billy." Claire pulled away from me and turned on all the lights, one switch at a time, until the room was ablaze with light. She marched up to him and jabbed his chest. "I can handle the truth, but don't you dare throw your daughter under the bus. Don't you dare."

Dad looked past Claire, at me. His mouth was set in a straight line. His eyes danced from me to Claire, from me to Claire. He was trying to stand still, but he couldn't. He kept shuffling his feet back and forth.

"Get out," Claire growled.

"I can handle it. It was just one line. Strictly recreational."

"That's what you're saying to your teenage daughter?" Claire scoffed. "Seriously? And the drinking? You're going to tell her that getting fall-down drunk is perfectly fine too? Really, Billy? This is where you're at? Why don't you offer her some? Hey, it's no different than a glass of wine at Thanksgiving, right? Here, give it to me." She held out her hand. "We'll all do some together. It'll be fun."

Dad opened his mouth and then shut it. He ran his hands over his stubble. "There's nothing I can say right now, is there?"

"You can say that you're sorry. You can say that you're going to stop. You can say that you're going to get help. That's what the hell you can say." Claire's voice rose into a shout. "And if you can't think of that on your own, then you can get the hell out!" She barged past him and flung open the door. "Get out! Go! And don't come back until you're ready to be the father and husband we need around here. Go play with the drunks and cokeheads. Go!" She kicked his shoes out onto the step and then stood back and waited, arms folded.

"Claire, please." He sounded defeated. "I can explain."

"Get out." Her voice was barely a whisper now. "I swear to God, Billy. Get out."

He stepped outside and picked up his shoes. He looked so pathetic at that moment, clutching his shoes to his chest, his socks slumped at his ankles.

"Please—"

Mr. Heidelman's door opened. He stepped out in his pajamas and pushed his glasses up his nose.

"Is everything okay?"

"It's fine," Dad said. "Everything is fine, Mr. Heidelman. Thank you."

"Really?" Claire shook her head. "Really, Billy? Enjoy the fucking gutter." She slammed the door.

Call me, Salix had said. We'll do all those silly things. But I did not want to do silly things. I wanted to be pissed off and scared and awash in panic and anxiety. The situation called for it. A midnight bus ride or spending ten dollars in quarters on the Pac-Man machine at the gas station was not going to work. Not at all.

I got the broom and hit the painting of Dad and me in the meadow over and over until it clattered to the floor, and then I wrestled it onto the balcony and tossed it over the edge. It landed on top of the garbage bins in the alley, which was exactly where it belonged.

Saying the Hard Stuff Out Loud

I dreamt of Carol Epperly jumping in front of the train. The train speeding along, the blue sky and green forest a rushing blur, and then Carol stepping onto the tracks, and the screeching wheels.

Was Dad supposed to be Carol? Or was he the train?

The entrails on the track. The train screeching, sparks like fireworks. The passengers with their hands pressed to their mouths, horrified. What happened? Someone jumped in front of the train. But did she jump? Maybe she just stepped onto the tracks. As if she was supposed to be there all along. At that moment. Exactly right.

Then it *was* Dad jumping in front of the train.

And then I was trying to stuff him into my suitcase. But he bulged out the sides and it wouldn't close. I dragged it to the bus anyway. To the train. I was going home. I was already home. The fox on the porch. The muddy forest. Carol Epperly. Mrs. Patel, slumped on the floor.

When I woke up and went upstairs, the first thing I saw was Dad's shoes, neatly placed beside the jumble of the rest. He was home, which made no sense after what had happened the night before.

The boys came down together, deep in discussion. The Percival king was missing.

"Where did he go?"

To the bar. To some street corner. To some slut somewhere. To some dark alley. To the coffee table and a rolled-up dollar bill.

"Can you help us find him?" Corbin asked.

"Did the Wrens capture the Percival's king, Corbin?"

"Owen says I put him down my cast, but he wouldn't even fit. I didn't take him."

"He's really missing?" I asked. "He's actually lost?"

The boys nodded.

"The king is lost?" I almost laughed.

Perfect. The king was missing. Spilling out the edges of the suitcase. Stepping in front of the train. Just a little wooden gnome that could fit in the palm of my hand, but as big as Dad.

"We'll find him." But I wasn't sure.

We looked for King Percival. On the deck, over the railing—the painting was already gone, and I didn't care one little bit—behind the couch, under the cupboards in the kitchen, even in the washing machine. No king. After about an hour, Owen flopped onto his back in the middle of the living-room floor and wailed.

"He's gone!"

"He's somewhere." Corbin sat beside his brother. "We'll find him."

"He's dead," Owen said with a sigh. "The king is dead."

"He's *not*." I bristled. The boys had no idea that they were talking about one thing and also talking about another. "We'll find him," I insisted. "I promise."

Billy Glover died shoeless and suddenly on Tuesday from a cocaine overdose, following a fight with his wife and daughter, who were just trying to get him to do the right thing—

"Let's go ask Mom if she'll take us to Alice Lake." Corbin patted Owen's arm. "Would that make you feel better?"

"King Percival is not at the lake." Owen sniffled. "He was just here yesterday."

"We'll go swimming," Corbin said. "I'll even let you push me off the dock."

"I don't want to go until we find King Percival."

"We looked everywhere," I said. "Maybe if you go to the lake, you'll remember where you left him."

"Come on." Corbin bounced up. "Let's go ask Mom."

Corbin pulled Owen to his feet.

"Ugh," Owen said.

"I don't know if you should." I glanced up the stairs. "She might still be sleeping. Dad must've come in really late, and he—"

He was still up there, when he should be at work.

Was he sleeping on the floor? Had Claire let him sleep in the bed with her?

The boys were already halfway up the stairs, and then they were disappearing into their parents' room, and I heard their happy squeals.

"Daddy!" The boys' laughter cut into the quiet. "You're home, you're home!"

Low, rumbled murmurs from Dad.

Not so low murmurs from Claire.

More laughing.

I reached for my phone and texted Salix:

I sincerely hope that you are doing absolutely nothing today.

Now I was ready for distraction.

More laughing, and then the boys leapt down the stairs, hollering.

"The beach! The beach! We're going to the beach!"

They streaked across the living room and down the other stairs to get their swimsuits. They were back up in less than a minute, digging through the closet for the beach toys.

"Maybe King Percival is in the lake," Corbin said.

"He's not in the lake," I said. But then I realized that he was pretending. "Or he could be, I suppose."

"He might be," Owen said. "The Wrens might've sent assassins in the middle of the night. He could be in grave danger. It might even be too late."

Claire came down first, her robe loosely tied across her belly. She padded barefoot into the kitchen and put the kettle on the stove.

"Boys? You two go hang out on the deck for a little bit, okay? I'll let you know when we're ready to go." They marched outside in their flippers and masks and snorkels. She put a hand on my shoulder. "Billy is coming down in a moment to join us, so we can talk."

I didn't want to talk. I wanted to listen. I wanted to hear what the plan was, and how things were going to get better. I wanted Claire and Dad to recite a list of all the reasons why everything was going to be all right.

Claire made coffee and offered me some. I shook my head. Everything already tasted sour. Coffee would make it worse. She poured a cup for herself and one for Dad. She brought them to the living room and placed them on the table, right where Dad had snorted cocaine the night before. I stared at the spot until it was blurry and my eyes stung.

The shower turned off upstairs, and a few moments later Dad came down dressed in cargo shorts and an old Railway Kings T-shirt. He sat beside Claire on the couch and put an arm around her.

"Sit, Maeve." Claire patted the couch on her other side. Instead I sat in the big orange easy chair across from them.

"Go ahead, Billy."

"First of all, I am so sorry, Maeve." His voice cracked. "It was cocaine, and it was shitty of me to pretend that it wasn't."

Shitty of him? Like being late to pick me up at the bus? Like not being there when Mrs. Patel died? Was that the kind of shitty we were talking about?

"Thank you, I guess."

"I've been a total asshole ever since you got here, and I'm sorry."

"Okay."

"It was bad before, too." Claire leaned forward over her big belly and reached out. I let her take my hand. "We should've told you. But I hoped it would get better. Your dad said it would. And we wanted you here. We didn't want you to be all alone in Port Townsend."

Dad parked his elbows on his knees and rubbed his forehead with the palms of his hands.

"Billy," Claire said.

"I'm not sure what happened." He pulled his hands down his face and groaned. "But I'm going to make it better."

"Look at her," Claire said. "Look at your daughter when you're talking to her."

He lifted his eyes.

"I fucked up, Maeve. I really did."

He stared at me until I looked away. No one said anything for what felt like ten minutes, but it was probably only seconds.

"So now what?" I finally said.

"It's over." My dad rubbed his face, harder. I could hear his stubble scratch.

My skin became ice. "You mean you're breaking up?"

"No!" Dad looked up.

"Not for now." Claire and Dad shared a look. "Remember before?" Claire said. "We got through it, right?"

The months I hadn't heard from him. Or Claire. The months where Vancouver hadn't even existed, and Dad and Claire hadn't either, as if just by drifting away from each other, they'd made everything disappear around them, including me. As if remembering that was any reassurance.

"We're better together."

"Believe it or not," Dad said with a laugh.

"I don't know if I do," I said with a catch in my throat. "Cocaine? Are you doing heroin, too?"

"Of course not."

"But it's not far-fetched, right? Go back a few years, there it is."

"Decades, now."

"Your drummer dying wasn't enough to keep you away from this shit?"

"It's not heroin."

"Fine. It's not heroin. Why do you do this, Dad?" I was angry, my fists balled. I wanted to hit him. Pummel his chest and slap his face and kick him and kick him until he was covered in bruises and got it. Until he understood what he was throwing away. "Why do you always fuck it up?"

"I wish I knew." He was kneeling in front of me now and pulling me to him. I let him hug me. He held tight. He smelled of mint toothpaste, citrus shampoo, and lavender soap. Clean and fresh and scrubbed and fragrant. As if being clean would make it easier for me to believe him.

He was no king. He had no crown. No castle. No knights. He had no robes, no carriages, no queen, no princes or princesses. He'd never been a king, and so I was the stupid one, for ever having thought that he was.

"Maeve," he said quietly. "Where's the painting?"

"What painting?" I raised my eyes and stared at him. "The one that didn't ever exist in the first place?"

"Maeve." Claire reached for me, but I twisted away. "Where is it?"

I said nothing.

"Where is it?" Claire's voice grew stern. "Tell us where it

is. It's not yours. It belongs to us. You had no right to take it down."

"It's okay, Claire." Dad looked sad then, and I was glad for it. For a moment, and then I was sad too, and I started to cry.

NA or AA every day at first, and then twice a week.

Dinner at home on his days off.

Check in with his sponsor every day.

No going out with his friends until after the baby was born, at least.

Claire would be in charge of the money. She would give him an allowance.

He would answer his phone. He would answer his texts.

No assholery would be permitted.

He wasn't going in to work that day, which was so rare that the boys didn't quite know what that meant. They sat on his knee, perplexed as he and Claire fumbled through an age-appropriate explanation about what was going on. Thank goodness they didn't go for their share-absolutely-everything approach to parenting on this one. The boys didn't have much to say at first. They looked at each other and grinned.

"Does that mean—" Owen said.

"That you can take us to the lake?"

We were all so tired, Claire, Dad, and me. Going to the lake was the last thing I wanted to do. Especially with him.

"Sure," Dad said. "If it's okay with your mom."

"Okay." Claire sighed. "The fresh air will do us all good."

"I'm not going," I said.

"Maeve, please." Dad reached for me, but I turned away and went back downstairs.

When they were ready to go, Dad asked me to help him pack up the van in the alley, which I knew was his way to get me alone and try to convince me to go with them.

"Please come?" he said, handing me a beach chair.

"No thanks."

"Like Claire said, the fresh air will do us all good."

"I'm not getting into that van and playing the Happy Family Game."

"We are a happy family."

I threw another beach chair into the back of the van and said nothing.

"I've hardly seen you since you arrived."

I stared at him.

"Okay, okay." He lifted the wagon into the back. "Please come?"

"No."

"You're mad about everything. I get that. This isn't your mess."

"It *is* my mess. You're going to ruin *my* family. Claire and the boys and the baby are *my* family too. If you don't fix things, you're going to ruin everything."

"I hope not."

"That's it?" A delivery truck rumbled down the alley. "You *hope* not?"

"Yes." He rested his hand on the door of the trunk. He

stared at the wagon and the towels and the bag full of plastic buckets and shovels. It was all so colorful, and dirty. The towels were clean but stained. The cooler was full of fresh food, but it was scratched and the lid was held on with duct tape. The plastic wagon was sun-bleached and cracked in more places than I could count. Everything was okay, and everything was not okay. "Yeah. I hope not. And that's all I've got to offer right now, Maeve. Take it or leave it, kid." He slammed the door closed. "I'm sorry, and I'm sorry, and I'm sorry. Take it or leave it."

A Girl in My Bed

After they left and while I was still standing in the alley, my phone buzzed.

Absolutely nothing.

For a moment it made no sense. But then, as the crows shrieked overhead and someone hollered up the street, I remembered.

Come over?

We sat on my bed and I told her.

"I saw my dad do a line of coke last night, right in front of me."

"In front of you?"

"He didn't know that I was watching."

"That's awful, Maeve." She put an arm around me. "Did you tell him that you saw? Did you tell Claire?"

I told her the rest, and when I was done, I felt numb, but

just for a moment, and then there was a terrible pounding in my head and I started to bawl.

"It's okay." Salix pulled me to her and I soaked her shirt.

"He's such a liar! And a total failure as a dad. We need him and he's messing up so badly and all he can say is that he'll *try*."

"What can I do?" Salix pulled away. "Can I make you a cup of tea? Want to go for a walk?"

"I just want to stop worrying so much! I can't even do anything, so what's the point?"

"You told me that you can't really help it, right?" She wiped my tears with her shirt.

I nodded.

"So worry. Just go ahead and worry. Worry as hard as you can, and then keep worrying."

"That sounds awful."

"But if you can't stop worrying, you have to figure out how to worry and keep living, right? We need to find you a really, really big box."

"What for?"

"Not a box. A backpack."

"What?"

"For you to put your worries in, so that you can take them with you, and when you figure out how to not worry so much, you can get rid of them one at a time. And then the backpack will get lighter and lighter until you'll be so light you'll float right off the ground."

I kissed her then, because there were no words for how much I liked her in that moment. Loved her, maybe.

"What can we do right now that will help?"

"Let me draw you." I grabbed my things and sat at one end of the bed.

She sat at the other end of the bed, legs crossed. "Will you let me see it?"

I glanced up.

"When you're finished? Just that page?"

I rubbed out a line that didn't belong. "I don't know."

"Okay."

"What if he can't do it?" Another wave of sickening worry came over me. "What if he can't keep it together, and so it literally falls apart? What if the baby never even knows him?"

"Let's stop talking about it." Salix reached for me. My sketchbook and pencils fell to the floor. She kept leaning forward until I could feel her breath on my cheeks. "Let's stop talking about hard stuff and do something that feels good instead. I'm in charge of the distraction department, remember?"

Salix's lips on mine, her tongue sliding between them. She pushed me onto my back and slid her hands up my shirt until she was peeling it off.

My heart raced. My hands shook as I reached for her.

"You know porn?" The words just came out, and now I had to go with them, no matter how badly I wished that I'd never said them. Dumb. Dumb. Dumb.

"Sure," she murmured into my neck.

"You know the girl-on-girl stuff?"

"Maeve?" She pulled away.

"I've seen it," I said. "You know, little bits of it, on the internet."

"Okay." Salix drew out the word, hanging it up at the end. "And?"

"The straight stuff is all dicks and balls and vaginas and tits and butts and mouths and humping. And the girl-on-girl stuff is so *fake*. It's not real. That's not what girls do, you know? The girls in porn are automatons." I did my best robot voice. "I-lick-you-you-kiss-me-pinch-my-nipple-arch-your-back-bend-over-moan-moan-sigh."

"It's okay," Salix said.

"Porn?"

"I mean it's okay if you don't know what to do." She took my hand. "I don't know what to do either."

"You don't?"

"Not really." She kissed my hand. My wrist. The soft crease of my arm.

A man and a woman. We all knew that. A man and a man, easy to figure out. I even knew that Dan liked to be on the bottom, and what that meant. But the mechanics of two girls? Two real girls? Not two porn robots? No one had told me. No one talked about it at school. There was no health class about this, two girls in bed together.

Salix took her shirt off too, and then we were getting naked, and then we *were* naked, and I wasn't thinking about anything other than the weight of Salix on top of me, and the blood rushing to all the right places, and Salix's tongue on my nipple and her hand between my legs and the electric buzz of the two of us together. This. Us. Together. This was the only thing. The one and only thing.

Avoidance

I didn't want to see any of them.

Not Claire.

Not the boys.

Definitely not Dad.

I didn't want to know if he was doing well, or if he was sliding.

I didn't want to see him succeed, and I didn't want to see him fail.

I didn't want to hear from Mom about anything that she needed me to do for the house.

I didn't want to hear from her about Raymond. *Things are so good between us*, she'd written. *He treats me so well, Maeve. I imagine good things.*

I didn't want to sign for the package that was the birth pool. I didn't want to be there when the midwife checked the heartbeat and laughed with the boys, who would argue over who was going to cut the cord.

I wanted to be with Salix. All the time.

She wasn't messy. She wasn't fucked up. She was a good thing. And she had nothing to do with the mess at home.

"Do you think Raymond will come home with her?" she said.

"Look up." I took her hand and pulled her into the park. "Look up."

A murder of crows across the sky, coming from the north at an angle.

Hundreds and hundreds of them, going home.

Give your father a chance, Claire had said when she'd seen me the day before, already on my way out. He's doing great so far.

Maybe he was. Maybe he wasn't. Maybe it would last. Maybe it wouldn't. I didn't want to sit in the murky unknown. I wanted to stand on concrete. I wanted to stand on concrete and hold hands with Salix and look up at the sky, at the crows heading surely home.

What Happened
with Ruthie

It was Salix who picked up the letter from Ruthie. The mail was behind the door when we came from the park for lunch one day. Dad was at work. Claire and the boys were out at a bird sanctuary more than an hour away. We had the place to ourselves for at least half the day.

"Hydro, bank, and something for you," she said as she came up the stairs.

A postcard from my mom, I assumed. But it was an envelope, with a return address of ASRA, University of Alaska, Fairbanks. ASRA, which stood for Alaska Summer Research Academy. I recognized Ruthie's writing right away. My stomach clutched into a knot.

"Who's it from?"

"A girl."

"A *girl*." Salix held me from behind and looked over my shoulder. "Why are your hands shaking?"

"I told you about Jessica."

"This is from her? I thought she lived in California."

"She does. This isn't from her."

Inside was one sheet of paper, a row of little Tardises marching along the bottom.

Dear Maeve,

I was going to email you back, but we don't have internet in the field, and it was down when we went into the main campus, which is a four-hour drive. So I'm writing you a letter. How weird is that? Not that weird, I guess. If you're a geek.

I'm so sorry to hear about Mrs. Patel. I know that she was a very good friend. And I'm so sorry that you were the one to find her. I can't imagine.

Is your dad better now? Claire? The boys? The baby? The baby isn't due for a while, I know. But all that before-birth stuff. It's okay?

I hate writing letters. Especially this one.

You know, I didn't know what to say to you ever since that day, but now I do.

I'm sorry for what I did.

Really sorry.

Your friend,
Ruthie.

ps. I have a girlfriend. She can name all the Doctors in order, along with who played them and the dates. She told me that I should've apologized by now. She's right. I was violent. I should never have put my hands on you like that. And I'm sorry that I was weird about you and Jessica. I shouldn't

*have kissed you. And I should've stopped when you
said no.*

    I'm so sorry.

pps. Q. What do you call an "e" that runs away?
    A. An escapee!

"It's from Ruthie." I handed the letter to Salix. "My best
friend. Or, she used to be."

After she read it, she looked up, confused and concerned.
So I told her.

Things ended when Jessica moved back to California not
even a month after she arrived. I love you, she said. I love
you, I said. Come see me! I will! Two weeks later she emailed
me to say that it was over and that she'd found a new girlfriend, and she hoped that I would find the right person and
fall in love. What we had, Maeve, was a two-sided crush, you
know? But I didn't know, and without thinking, I forwarded
it to Ruthie. My feelings were hurt, and I wanted someone
to know. But it was also kind of funny, too.

Her reply was so fast, it was hard to believe she'd had
time to compose it. An invitation to make hexaflexagons was
exactly how someone like Ruthie smoothed things over. So
I went, because I missed Ruthie. I wanted things to go back
to normal. As I walked up her front steps, I knew what I was
going to say. Now we have BJ—Before Jessica. Not *blow job*,
Ruthie. It's not funny. And AJ—After Jessica. She was just a
blip in our timeline, that's all.

Ruthie's mother answered the door and ushered me down to the basement. I tried not to think back to all the papier-mâché and broken glass on the floor, but it was hard not to. There was Ruthie, standing at the bottom now, smiling. She handed me a pair of scissors.

"I have a template."

"A template?"

"For the hexaflexagons," Ruthie said. "I need to make one for each person in my class. Final project." I followed her into her bedroom. *Doctor Who* was playing on her computer.

"Eleventh, right?"

"Tenth." She muted it and sat at her desk beside a bowl of barbecue chips and a couple of cans of root beer—two of my favorite things. She opened the drawer and pulled out a pack of red licorice. Also a favorite.

She gracelessly ripped open the package. "Want one?"

"No thanks." I sat on the edge of the bed. What was she doing? Were we going to talk about Jessica? Or maybe we were going to pretend that she never happened?

"I've numbered the triangles," Ruthie said through a mouthful of licorice. "That way we can do a pattern on each one that will come together when it's folded."

"Ruthie?"

"Or we can leave them plain." She rolled up another piece of licorice and stuffed it in her mouth. "And they can color them after. I was going to bring a box of markers."

"We're not going to talk about it?"

Ruthie's expression was blank. She chewed and chewed. She held out the package of licorice. "Want one?"

So we were not going to talk about it.

I took a piece and nibbled on it. "Thanks."

We cut strips of paper—not talking at all—and Ruthie demonstrated how to fold them and glue them, and how to work the hexaflexagon so that it showed one surface, then another, then a third. Ruthie's fingers seemed unusually nimble.

When we'd made enough, she put them in an envelope and stood up.

"You should probably go now."

"I could stay," I said. "We could watch a movie or something?"

Ruthie patted her thighs, something she did when she was particularly nervous. "I can't."

"Okay." Confused, I picked up my bag. Ruthie was still patting her thighs, and then all of a sudden she was coming at me.

"Ruthie—"

She pushed me against the wall with such force that one of her science-fair trophies toppled off the shelf above and landed on the bed. "Ruthie, stop!" I put up my hands, but Ruthie leaned in, and then I was pressing up against Ruthie's breasts through her shirt and they were enormous and squishy and Ruthie's face was in mine and her mouth was open and wet and she smelled of barbecue chips and licorice and she was kissing me with such ferocity that I could not breathe.

And I couldn't speak, because Ruthie's mouth was on mine and she was sliding her face back and forth, as if that were kissing, but it wasn't. It wasn't at all. I tried to push her away, but Ruthie planted her hands on either side of my shoulders and kept slobbering on me until I finally ducked down under her arm and was free.

"What the hell are you doing?" I clutched my bag to my chest.

Ruthie sank to the floor. "You picked her."

"It wasn't about picking!"

"You were supposed to pick me."

"I didn't *pick* anyone!" I could hardly speak. I was breathless, and shocked, and had no idea what to say. I backed away. "I never liked you that way. *Never.*"

"Of course you didn't." Ruthie put her head in her hands and started to sob.

Part of me wanted to kneel beside her and put my arms around her and tell her it was okay. But then I felt bile rising in my throat and I ran up the stairs instead, stopping short when I saw Ruthie's mom at the kitchen counter, chopping vegetables, as if everything were absolutely normal.

"All done, dear?"

I could only nod, and then I rushed out the front door and down the steps and onto the sidewalk. I stood still for a moment, totally stunned. And then I ran, and I kept running, all the way across town to my mom's office, where I sat on the curb by the car and waited, my breath hot in my chest, my pulse bounding. When I saw Mom walking across the parking lot, I started to cry. "What is it, baby? What happened at Ruthie's? Are you okay? Are you hurt?"

I was fine. I was fine, right? Everything was fine?

I didn't tell my mom.

I didn't tell Dan.

I didn't tell Dad, or Claire.

I didn't tell anyone. Until I told Salix.

. . .

"What she did to you was sexual assault." Salix's jaw tensed. "Damn right she should be apologizing. Just because she's a girl doesn't mean she can get away with forcing herself on you."

"You know, after it happened, I didn't know what to think. I thought maybe it was my fault. I asked myself, What if it was a guy? And I knew the answer: I'd tell. But I was confused. And I still am. I felt sorry for her."

"Would you feel sorry for your assailant if it was a guy?"

"Assailant? That's a bit harsh."

"What she did was harsh. Just because she's a girl doesn't make it any less harsh."

"But she's not just a girl," I said. "She's Ruthie. She's my weird and socially tragic and totally harmless best friend. She was confused. She was trying. She thought that because Jessica was gone and we both—"

"There's no excuse." Salix's expression was grim. "Are you going to write her back?"

"Of course." I didn't even hesitate. Of course I'd write her back. Ruthie was the gigantic ogre that had forced me against the wall, but she was also my oldest friend, and I wasn't willing to break up with her.

"I hope she behaves better with her new girlfriend."

"It's good that she told her, right?"

Salix nodded. "That part is a very good thing."

"If I thought for one second that Ruthie was dangerous, I wouldn't write her back. I trust her." I pulled Salix to the couch and sat in her lap. I draped my arms around her neck and kissed her. "I have good instincts. I knew you were a good thing. A very good thing."

Girlfriends and Parents

It took a couple of days to write Ruthie back—eight long pages about everything that had happened since that afternoon. I walked up to the post office and mailed the letter, and as I came out of the post office, there was Dad.

"I followed you."

"Drunk, junkie, *and* stalker?"

"Ouch." He put his arm around me. "Walk with me."

"To where?"

"The Legion," he said. "For a meeting."

"I suppose that's a good thing."

"I'm looking forward to this one." He dropped his arm. "The one I go to on the way home from work is so boring. Boring stories. Boring people. Everyone is so *tense*. And so *boring*. Promise me that you'll never be boring, Maeve."

"I'd rather be boring than a drunk."

"Fair enough."

We walked south, joining the early-evening bustle on the sidewalk. The restaurant patios were full of people and pitchers of sangria and plates of sweet potato fries. The shops were open later during the summer, so doors were open and people browsed and music leaked out onto the street.

"I've kept my word," Dad said. "I've gone to a meeting every single day."

"Good for you."

We walked along in silence for a while, and then he took my hand.

"Where's the painting, Maeve?"

I wished that I knew. I wished that I could bring it back. I wished that I had left it on the wall.

"I threw it in the alley." My voice caught. "Someone took it. I'm sorry."

"Okay." He nodded and nodded. "Thanks for telling me."

"It was mean. What you said about it."

"It was. I'm sorry too."

I was supposed to meet Salix in front of the liquor store where she was busking. That was at the end of the next block. First of all, I wasn't sure that I wanted to lead Dad right to the front door of a building full of alcohol. Secondly, I wasn't sure that I wanted him to meet Salix. Salix was sparkling and clean and all the good things. Dad was messed up and dark and several bad things in a row.

We were nearly there, but we could still cross the street. The intersection was steps away.

No. I did not want him anywhere near the liquor store. No. I did not want him to meet Salix. Not at all. Maybe never. He wasn't welcome to be part of the story yet.

"Let's cross here, Dad."

"We don't need to. I can resist the liquor store, Maeve. I'm more of a bar guy anyway." And then he stood still. "Hear that?"

Salix. She was playing "Clocks" again. The song she'd been playing that first time I saw her at the bus station.

"The light's red. Let's go."

"She's amazing."

"Yeah, she is." I tugged his arm. "We're going to miss the light."

"I've seen her around, busking." I could see him thinking, linking the various parts. He grinned. "That's her, isn't it?"

"Who?"

"That's the girl. *The* girl." He was already walking away. "Come on, introduce me."

"I don't—" I didn't want this to be happening. I didn't want him to ruin it. I didn't want the two of them to collide like this. If they met, I wouldn't be able to have them *un*meet, ever.

"Dad!"

He spun back, a big smile on his face, handsome and bright-eyed. "What?"

So this was how it was going to go.

"Okay. Wait for me."

Salix was playing with her back to us.

"Don't." Dad stopped me from getting her attention. "I just want to listen for a minute."

He closed his eyes and listened until she finished the song

and set her violin down to get a drink of water. Salix noticed me then.

"Hey," she said.

"Hey." We smiled at each other for a long moment, and then I remembered to introduce them. "Salix, this is my dad. Billy Glover."

"Pleased to meet you, sir."

"Call me Billy." Dad tossed a handful of coins into her case. "You're very talented, sweetheart."

"So are you," Salix said. "I'm a big fan of the Railway Kings."

"That was a million and a half years ago, but thank you."

"Can I walk with you?" Salix put her violin away. "Where are you going?"

I glanced at Dad.

"A meeting," he offered. "I'm sure you've heard all the gory details."

I didn't deny it. I didn't say anything. Salix took my hand.

"Come on." Dad sighed. "I don't want to be late."

The sidewalk in front of the Legion was crowded with smokers standing in knots of two or three, waiting until the last minute to go in. Dad lit a cigarette and inhaled deeply, standing off to the side with us, observing the crowd just about to go in. It was a typical East Van mix: punks with chains and scowls, hipsters with carefully crafted facial hair, old men and women with walkers and stoops and wrinkles, a little group that looked like they'd just come from an office downtown, and another group that looked like they were all longshoremen. The sidewalk started clearing out.

"I hate this shit," Dad said. He dropped his cigarette and

ground it underfoot. The baby was due in four weeks, and I couldn't have cared less if he never quit smoking. If it was going to help him stay clean and sober, I'd buy him cigarettes myself. "It was nice to meet you, Salix. I wish I'd met you sooner. And I'm sorry for that."

Performance Anxiety

A couple of days later, Salix and I met Mr. Heidelman outside the Vancouver Symphony Orchestra building. He led us through a back door and along several hallways, until we ended up in the theater, where the entire orchestra was rehearsing a Mozart concerto, which I would not have known if Mr. Heidelman had not told me what it was. When it ended, the conductor waved Salix onto the stage.

"This is it," she whispered. "I might vomit. If I do, can we just pretend that it never happened?"

"Climb up to the top and don't drop the flamingo wineglass. All the way to the top. You can see the city lights from up there. You can do it. And the view will be worth it."

"Don't drop the flamingo glass," Salix said. "Got it."

"Kick off your flip-flops," I said. "It'll make it easier to climb."

"Done." She glanced down at her boots, polished to a shine.

She put her hand on mine. She was trembling.

I squeezed her hand. "Tell me ten things you can see from here."

"A scuffed-up floor." She looked up. "Exit signs. An empty theater. The stage. Lights. Musicians. The conductor." She took a long, slow breath. "My violin. My hand. You."

"Better now?" I let go of her hand.

"A bit, yeah." She kissed me on the cheek. "Thank you."

Salix followed Mr. Heidelman up the stairs and into the spotlight.

"Good morning, everyone," he said. "May I introduce you to a fine young violinist, Salix Bradley."

The conductor was a large man, balding, with a bushy gray beard, red-framed glasses perched at the end of his nose. "What are you going to play for us, my dear?"

"I'm going to play the first movement and ..." Salix paused. I could see her swallow, and then swallow again. She glanced around. "The first movement."

My insides ached for her. Vicarious nerves.

She took a breath and gave her head a little shake. "The first movement and the cadenza of Beethoven's Concerto in D Major, opus sixty-one." She lifted her violin and readied herself to play.

I wouldn't even have been able to get up there. I wouldn't even have been able to climb the steps. My legs would have been too weak. And if I had made it to the stage, I would have just curled up into a ball and trembled until someone carried me off. It was a miracle to me that Salix could be up there. And it was a surprise to see her be nervous. She just was not that person to me. She was strong and brave. But there she was, scared of something.

I gripped the chair, my stomach churning. She looked so small standing still on that gigantic stage, with the rows and rows and rows of musicians staring at her, and the bright, hot lights suspended way up above, glaring down.

Salix stood, frozen. It felt like an hour passed, even though it could only have been seconds before she lowered her violin.

"You can do it," I whispered. "You can do it."

Salix looked in my direction. The stage lights were so bright that she couldn't actually see me. But maybe she didn't need to. Her shoulders rose. She took a deep breath in. Just when I thought I might have to run to the bathroom to vomit, she set her violin under her chin and turned back to the orchestra.

"And then I'm going to play an original composition of mine," Salix said.

"Whenever you're ready." The conductor smiled.

Salix put the bow to the strings and made a note, and then another. Then she stopped.

"Sorry." Salix gave her head another little shake. "Nerves."

"A matter of course. Take your time."

Salix adjusted her violin and let out a long breath. Then she closed her eyes. I was hardly able to breathe.

Salix began to play.

The music was much larger than I had ever heard from her before. The acoustics of the theater lifted the notes up and out until the sound nearly filled the space. I had heard Salix practice this piece for weeks now, but it was as if I was hearing it for the first time. Every note danced in perfect form, and even I knew that she was playing it flawlessly.

The musicians listened intently. There were about a hundred of them, and they all held their instruments in their laps, but not at ease, more as if they had to stop from playing along with her.

When she finished, the silence wasn't quiet at all. The musicians murmured among themselves, and behind me Mr. Heidelman let out a low whistle.

The conductor gave a little twirl of his wrist. Continue.

"I wrote this for my girlfriend, Maeve, who sometimes lets fear get the best of her. It's called 'Fear Itself.'"

I let out my breath, not knowing that I'd been holding it. She hadn't told me that she was writing something for me. At first the notes were long and mournful and almost made me want to cry. And then the tempo quickened, and the song fell open and spread out, and for a moment I didn't like it at all. Not because it was bad, but because it wasn't as beautiful as the beginning, and I couldn't tell where it was going. The notes were so many raindrops, falling. But then Salix closed her eyes and swayed, and collected the song into something calm and beautiful, and it was a warm, glowing orb, something I could imagine holding in my hand.

Finished, she lowered her violin and bowed. The orchestra members leapt to their feet, clapping and cheering and whistling, all of them. I sat there for a moment, stunned. But then I leapt to my feet too, clapping so hard that my palms stung.

"Brava!" Mr. Heidelman shouted. And then we were both yelling. "Brava, Salix! Brava!"

Birth

Claire took Owen to get his cast taken off the next morning. He wanted to go swimming without it to celebrate. I had the bright idea to use the wagon to bring all the beach stuff down to the van, rather than carry armload after armload. Even with Salix helping, it was a task that felt like it went on forever: towels and flippers and masks, beach balls and inflatable dolphins, umbrellas, chairs, buckets, shovels, sunscreen, hats. And then all the food. While Salix and I packed the van, Claire was gathering sandwiches and carrots and berries and muffins and piling it all into the cooler.

I had an idea that I hadn't told anyone about yet. Seeing Salix in front of that orchestra had inspired me. She had felt all the hard feelings, but she had done the hard thing anyway. She just *did* it. She was prepared to handle whatever happened. Or maybe not prepared, but at least willing to do it and hope for the best. Feel the fear. Do it anyway. So when everyone else was buckled in and Claire was about to wedge herself behind the steering wheel, I put my hand on the door.

"I'll drive."

"You'll what?" Claire said.

"I'll drive. If that's okay with you?"

"Of course!"

"We're all going to die!" Corbin screamed from the backseat.

"Save our souls!" Owen said.

"Enough." Claire handed me the keys and went around to the passenger side. She put her swollen bare feet up on the dash and pulled her skirt up to her hips. "Hallelujah. Let's go."

"You can do it, Maeve," Salix said.

I steered the van out of the garage and down the alley to the street, where I had to suddenly stomp on the brakes to avoid hitting a cyclist who was zooming down the hill on the sidewalk.

"Holy shit!" Corbin hollered. "You almost hit that guy!"

"Language," Claire said. "She didn't hit him. You're doing fine, Maeve."

"He's supposed to be on the road! Not the sidewalk." I gripped the wheel, my breath caught in my throat. And then I undid my seat belt and got out of the van. Sure, feel the fear and do it anyway. Theoretically. But in real life? "I changed my mind. Someone else drive."

But no one else got out. I leaned in. Four sets of eyes gazed back at me.

"Get back in and drive us to the lake, Maeve." Claire

patted the seat. "Everyone makes mistakes. Next time don't forget that there is a sidewalk at the end of the alley."

"I almost killed him."

"But you didn't," Salix said. "A near miss is a miss. They happen all the time. Let's go."

Owen stuck Hibou up to the window and made her wave with a stubby wing. "Hibou will drive if you want."

"She'd probably be better at it than me." But all the same, I got back in.

"I'll drive," Corbin said.

"You can have a turn in the parking lot at the lake," Claire said. "If it's not too busy."

Claire directed me to the upper parking lot, which was about half full.

"This'll do." Claire slid her swollen feet back into her flip-flops and heaved herself out of the van. "I want to go for a swim first, but then the boys and I can come back for a drive."

"Yes!" Corbin said.

"Not me," Owen said. "It's not legal."

"Up to you. Maybe Hibou will want to give it a try." Claire slung her purse over her shoulder and headed for the trail, a pronounced waddle in her step. "You guys bring the wagon with everything. I'm going to dunk my gigantic puffy self in some nice cool water."

Salix and I swam to the middle of the lake and floated on our backs, watching the clouds move slowly across the bright blue sky. When we finally came out of the water, Claire laid out sandwiches and cherries and carrot sticks and cheese and chips and salsa.

"I am so hungry," she said as she filled her plate. "And can you pour me some iced tea from the thermos?"

I poured her a cup, which she downed in one go. And then I filled it up again.

"Thank you." She belched. "Heartburn." She sat in a chair, flopped her head back, and groaned, her belly gleaming in the sunlight. "I just want to be naked and floating."

"The floating you can do," I said. "But your favorite lifeguard is here and I doubt he'd let you take off your bikini."

"Is he?" Claire twisted in her seat to look at the lifeguard tower. "The one with the stick up his ass and a thing for young girls in bikinis?"

The lifeguard turned his head in our direction, as if he could hear us talking about him. Claire waved, and he waved back, which made us all laugh.

When the boys were hungry enough to get out of the water, Claire told Corbin that if he wanted to go drive the van, he'd better be quick about it. "I don't think we'll stay much longer. My back really hurts."

"Can I sit in the driver's seat just by myself this time?"

"No. You sit on my lap."

"I can't sit on your lap."

"Fine, we can push the seat back and you can stand between my knees. But no pedals. I'm in charge of those. Help me up, Corbin." He gave her a hand. "I want to take a nap. In a real bed." She reached for her sarong and knotted it under her belly. "Owen? Last chance."

Owen shook his head miserably.

"Another time." Claire kissed the top of his head.

"We can go for one last swim," I told him. "You and me."

When we got out of the water to help Salix pack up, Corbin came running across the sand. "Maeve! Maeve! Help!"

The lifeguard hopped down from his perch, shielding his eyes from the sun. "What's the matter?"

"The baby!" Corbin shouted.

"What?"

"The baby!" Corbin skidded to a stop. "Mom's having the baby right now!"

The lifeguard jogged over. "What's going on?"

"My mom is having a baby in the parking lot," Corbin said.

"I'll get the first-aid kit," the lifeguard said, very quietly. "And the sat phone."

"You can call 911 on that?" I screamed as he jogged away. He turned back for a moment and gave me a thumbs-up.

"Claire cannot have the baby here." I shook my head. "Not in a parking lot." No. This was not happening. Not happening. Not happening!

"It is happening!" Corbin hollered. "She said so!"

Had I said that out loud? What do we do? We stood in a loose circle, every single one of us with our hands dangling at our sides. Every single one of us wide-eyed and staring at each other. It was *not* happening. Get her to the hospital.

How long did we all stand around, dumbfounded, while Claire was all by herself at the van?

"We have to go." No one moved. "We have to get her to the hospital!"

"She can't have a baby in the van!" Owen wailed. "She's supposed to be at home."

"She hates hospitals," Corbin said.

"It doesn't matter. She's going." I pushed Owen toward our jumble of beach stuff. "Owen, just throw everything into the wagon. Salix, you help Owen. Corbin, you come with me."

Salix stood by the table, not moving.

"Salix!"

"Yes?" She glanced around, blinking. "Yes. Got it. We'll meet you at the van."

Think, Maeve. Don't feel. Just get her to the hospital. That's all you have to worry about. The ambulance will come and they'll take her. She'll be fine. The baby will be fine.

I grabbed Corbin's hand and we ran across the beach and down the trail. The lifeguard followed behind, bellowing about how he'd only had five minutes on emergency child-birth in his advanced first aid course.

That was more than I'd had.

I found Claire leaning into the back of the van, swaying and moaning. She shrugged me off when I touched her.

"Claire? What's happening?"

"Baby."

"No." No, no, no, no. There had to be a way to stop this. Not yet, baby. Not right here. Not now. Not with me. Not without Dad. Not without the midwives, or a doctor, or a paramedic. Or a firefighter! Even a police officer. Where was the ambulance? Where was everybody?

"You can't have the baby here, Claire," I said. "I'll help you into the backseat. Owen and Salix will be here in a minute. We'll drive you to the hospital in Squamish if the ambulance isn't here by then."

"No."

"No?"

"This baby is coming *now*."

The lifeguard set his first-aid kit down beside the van and stood back, arms folded. "Shit."

"Baby." Claire rocked her hips. "Mmm. Hmm. *Baby*."

"Okay, hold on. We have to get you to the hospital. Hey!" The lifeguard pretended not to hear. "Hey! Help me get her into the van." I took her arms, but Claire shook me off again.

"Don't! Don't touch me." She braced herself against the van and groaned, this time a low, primal rumble. "Not going. Staying here."

None of the many first-aid classes I had taken had covered what to do when a woman was in labor, not for even five minutes in between splints and burns.

Think about the childbirth books. Stages of labor. Fetal stations. Think about everything that I read about when I thought Dad would be a no-show. What did the midwife say last week?

Baby is nice and low, Claire. Baby is all set.

Trust the mother if she says it's too late to get to the hospital. Make the mother as comfortable as possible. If a birth is happening quickly, that usually means all is well, unless the baby is preterm—

"Is it too early?" The baby was due in three weeks, right? "Are we in trouble? Is the baby in trouble?"

Push away the worst thoughts. Push away the worst ones. Push them away.

Claire shook her head.

"But three weeks is too early!"

"Now. Now, now, now, now."

"Okay. Okay." I spun in a circle, stunned. I'd read too much and not enough. I could not do this. But I had to. It was happening with or without me, and I wasn't about to abandon Claire.

The lifeguard sat on the curb now, staring at Claire, his face pale.

Finally, something stuck out. *When the urge to push begins, birth is imminent.*

"Are you feeling pushy?"

"Yes." Claire looked up and focused on me with clear, wide eyes. "This baby is coming right now, Maeve."

"I'm sure the ambulance is almost here. Just hold on. Okay? The hospital is only ten minutes away."

"Now. Here."

"You can't make it to the hospital? Really? Just try. Please? Just wait?"

"No." Claire groaned again. "The first-aid kit—"

"The lifeguard brought his."

Claire shook her head. "Find ours."

"You put it back in?"

She nodded.

I leaned past Claire and dug around in the back. A sleeping bag, a soccer ball, several pieces of Lego, a set of tire chains. And the first-aid kit. I swept everything else out of the back.

"Corbin, spread out the sleeping bag."

I could hear the rumble of the wagon approaching, and Salix's voice. "We're here!"

"Bring me the towels!"

The lifeguard kept staring.

"Do something!" I shouted at him. "Find out what's taking so long! We need an ambulance *now*."

"No ambulance," Claire growled. She sucked in a huge breath and let out a loud, low bellow. My stomach twisted into a hard knot. Knots. What if there's one in the cord? Or if it's wrapped around the baby's neck? What if it rips? What if something goes wrong? What if this baby ends up dead?

The Glover family is devastated to announce that their baby died at birth, after being born in the back of a filthy van—

Stop it, stop it, stop it! Do this one thing. Don't think of anything else but this one thing. And then the next one thing. One thing at a time. Feel it. Fear it. Get it done.

"Yes, ambulance!" I helped her into the back of the van. Claire rolled onto her knees, wrestled off her bikini bottom, and started rocking back and forth.

"What can I do?" Salix said.

"I don't know!" I covered my face with my hands. "I don't know. I just don't know."

The boys sat on a rock at the edge of the parking lot, their arms around their knees, wide-eyed and silent.

"I do know one thing. Everything is going to be okay, boys." I tried to smile. I even gave them a stupid thumbs-up. "Mom is going to be fine. And so is the baby. I promise." But even as I said it, I didn't believe it.

"Oooooooooh," Claire moaned through loose lips. "Ooooooooooh."

I draped her sarong across her back, trying to cover her, but she yanked it off.

"Breathe." Because that's what they always say, right? "Breathe, Claire."

"The first-aid kit."

Salix opened the red bag, and a little wooden gnome toppled out.

"King Percival!" Owen dashed over to scoop up the gnome.

"Birth kit," Claire gasped.

Sure enough, there was a package labeled BABY. I unrolled it: gloves, scissors, a clamp for the cord, a little rubber bulb for suctioning, a couple of disposable pads, folded in fours. Salix shook one open and handed it to me.

"Thanks." I glanced up.

"Are you okay?"

I didn't answer. I didn't know if I was. Or if I wasn't.

Catch the baby. Catch the baby. Just make sure that the baby doesn't end up sliding past me and out of the van and onto the dirt, ripping away from Claire, and cracking its head open. No dead babies. No dead mothers. Easy does it.

"What can I do?"

"Keep an eye on the boys."

Claire screamed. I could hear Salix tell someone passing by that it was all under control.

"No it's not!" I hollered. "Where is the ambulance?"

Everything was out of control.

Claire squatted, her legs spread. Her thighs were wet with blood. I didn't want to look any closer, but I had to. I had to catch the baby. No one else was going to help. There was only me.

"What can I do?" I said. "What do you need?"

"Head." Claire reached between her legs. "The head is crowning."

"Do you want to be on your back instead?"

"No!" Claire turned a bit so she could prop herself up on the backseat, facing the front. "Catch the baby, Maeve."

She let loose one deep, long groan.

I forced myself to keep my eyes on the dark shape that was emerging through the blood and the ooze.

"Is it a boy or a girl?" Corbin shouted from the rock.

"Salix, hand me the gloves!"

Claire growled. She put her hand against the bulge and gave a long, controlled push. The baby's head was out.

"Oh!" I dropped the gloves, stunned. And then I reached forward as she bore down again. One shoulder appeared, then the other, and then the baby's whole body slid right into my hands. A brand new baby *in my hands*.

"Baby!" Claire rolled onto her back then and reached

for the baby. "Hello, baby! Oh, hi there!" She let out a laugh. "A girl! A baby girl!"

"A *girl*," I whispered. And then I laughed too. "A girl!"

"A girl!" The boys leapt off the rock and came running. "A girl! A girl! A girl!"

The baby made tiny fists and let out a little wail.

"Oh, give her to me!" Claire held her against her chest while I found another pair of gloves and wrestled the little plastic clamp onto the cord.

"I want to cut it!" Corbin yelled. We were out of gloves, so I took mine off carefully, and he wore them as he sawed at it with the scissors from the kit, the too-big glove fingers flopping back and forth. "That is so gross," he said when the cord was severed.

I wrapped the baby in the cleanest towel, and then there were sirens. An ambulance and a fire truck careened into the parking lot, screeching to a stop beside us. Two paramedics and four firefighters grabbed oxygen tanks and jump kits and blankets and hurried to the van, where Claire had already put the baby to her breast.

"I'll take one of those blankets, please." Exhausted, Claire grinned weakly at the men. They all gawked at her, until one of the paramedics snapped to and tucked a blanket around her and the baby, then retrieved a tiny knit cap from the ambulance and snugged it on the baby's head.

"Hello there," he said to the baby. "You made a dramatic entrance, didn't you?"

After we saw Claire and the baby off in the ambulance, we put everything back into the van and tossed the bloody towels into the garbage bins. Then we made our way to the hospital in Squamish. I couldn't drive, so Salix did. I was too stunned. I was too elated. I was too exhausted. I was too shaky. The boys bounced in their seats, shouting at the top of their lungs, and I didn't even mind.

"Baby! Baby! Baby!"

I stared at my shaking hands.

"That just happened." Salix put her hand over mine. "It really did. You were amazing. You are amazing."

"Everything is amazing," I said under the chanting coming from the backseat. It didn't matter if Salix heard or not. Either way, it was absolutely true.

By the time we got to the hospital, Claire had already called Dad.

"What did he say?"

"He kept shouting what I was saying to the guys on set. 'In the parking lot! A girl! Stupid lifeguard! Maeve was brilliant! Everyone's fine!' And laughing and laughing. And then he was crying so hard that I told him he had to calm down before he drove up here."

"Look at her." I touched her soft, downy forehead. "You surprised me, little one."

"Want to hold her while I have a shower?"

"Definitely."

Claire placed the baby in my arms, and then she kissed me on the cheek. "Thank you."

"You're the one who had a baby."

"You did so much. You helped so much. You were so strong. I knew that you had everything under control, and that made it so much easier to just let it happen. I'm so thankful. I love you, Maeve."

"I love you too, Claire."

The boys stood on either side of me as Claire walked gingerly toward the shower.

"Can I hold her?"

"No, me first!"

"Both of you will have to wait," I murmured. "I'm not letting her go." I could hardly hear the boys arguing as I gazed at the baby. "Look at you." She was fast asleep, her little lips puckered and rosy. She was here and she was safe and the emergency was over. Perfect fingers. Perfect eyelashes. Pink cheeks. Tiny button nose. Claire's chin.

Salix took a picture of me and the baby, and I sent it to Mr. Heidelman, and Ruthie, and Mom in Haiti.

Hello, baby!

There was too much to say, about the beach and the parking lot and the back of the van and the slippery new baby in my hands and the ambulance, but I just sent those two words. The rest could wait. For now I just wanted to hold my tiny new sister and marvel at how it had all turned out just fine.

When Claire got out of the shower, she went to sign the discharge papers, against the doctor's orders. A minute later we heard Dad running down the hall.

"Claire? Where are you?"

When he found the room, he dropped to his knees at Claire's side.

"Unbelievable." He lifted the baby out of her arms. He nuzzled her head and breathed her in, his eyes closed. "Hello, sweet thing. Hello, baby girl." Tears streamed down his face.

"I'm so sorry that I missed your entrance, but wow! You know how to put on a show!" He laughed and laughed, and then he rose up to kiss Claire hard on the lips. "She's *beautiful*. And perfect. And so are you." He kissed Claire again and then handed the baby back to her. "Okay, everybody. Let's take this spectacular baby home."

Night Swimming

Of course they named her Alice. Claire joked that they should call her Alice Lake, but they named her Alice December instead. This was after some discussion, because now Claire wondered if she'd had her dates wrong. Maybe she'd conceived in November? Or maybe Alice was just a bit early. She wasn't too small, though, no matter how Claire calculated the weeks, and so they went with Alice December after all.

When they got home, the midwives were waiting on the front step. Beside them, propped against the wall, was Dad's painting of us in the meadow.

We all stood and stared at it. All lined up: the boys and Claire, Dad with the baby in his arms, Salix, and me.

"But how . . . ?" I touched it. Except for a scratch along the bottom and a crack at one corner of the frame, it was fine.

"Let's have a good look at your beautiful baby," one of the midwives said.

When Dad just stood there, Claire took Alice and ushered the boys inside, and Salix, too.

"Was it you?" I asked.

He shook his head.

Mr. Heidelman's door opened, and he leaned out with a great big smile on his face. "Congratulations!" He saw us staring at the painting. "I brought it up from the alley. I thought you might be ready to have it back now. My restoration guy will come, my treat. Go. Go now and be with your baby. I've ordered pizza. It will arrive in ten minutes."

Inside, the midwives clucked and murmured and fawned over Alice and Claire, and me too. "What you did was amazing! Maybe you'll become a midwife."

"Not a chance."

"Well, you should be very proud of catching your baby sister."

That part was for sure.

And it was amazing.

When Dad brought the painting in, he hung it right back up, damage and all.

"I'm not sure that I want it repaired," he said.

"Me neither," I said.

After supper, Salix and the boys and I went down to unpack the van. Owen scrambled over the seats, obviously looking for something.

"What's the matter?"

"I can't find Hibou," Owen wailed. "She's gone!"

"She's not gone. We'll find her." Where had I last seen the owl? "Hang on, hang on. We'll find her." I rooted through the bag of damp swimsuits. Salix emptied the bag of buckets and shovels onto the ground.

"Did you take her inside?"

"No!"

"Where did you last have her?"

"By the van. When Alice was born. I think."

"That's right." Salix nodded. "You had it when we were sitting on the big rock."

"Hibou is a *girl*."

"Let's go check inside," I said. "Just in case you took her in."

"I didn't."

"Let's go check anyway."

Hibou was not inside. We looked in every likely place, and a whole bunch of unlikely places too. Like the fridge.

"Why would she be in there?" I held open the door while he checked the shelves.

"I got the milk out for supper!" He sank to the floor and covered his face with his hands. "Oh, no. I remember. I put her down when I picked up King Percival."

"By the rock?" I said.

"Yes!" Owen wailed. "I have to go get her." He leapt up and ran for the door.

"Owen?"

"Owen!" Claire gave Alice to Dad. "You can't walk all the way to the lake, honey."

"I'm going to get Hibou." He opened the door.

"I bet she'll end up in the lost and found," Salix offered. "You can get her the next time you're up there."

"I have to get her now," Owen said. "I'll hitchhike."

"No, you won't," Dad said.

"Mom hitchhiked across the country when *she* was a kid."

"I was sixteen!" Claire protested. "You are not hitchhiking to Alice Lake."

"I have to go get her!"

"Here." Dad deftly shifted Alice into the crook of his arm. He dug the van keys out of his pocket and gave them to me. "Do you mind?"

"Right now?"

"Sure, why not?"

"I delivered your baby in the back of a van in a parking lot in the middle of nowhere and now you're going to send me back up there to get a stuffed *owl*?"

"Please go get her?" Owen clamped his arms around my waist. "Please, please, please?"

I glanced at Salix. "You don't mind driving?"

"I'm in," she said. "I'm so wired right now I probably won't sleep for the next three days."

By the time we got to Alice Lake, the gate was locked. Salix parked the van and climbed over. I had a flashlight, but I didn't want to turn it on. We walked along, holding hands under just a sliver of moon and the dark all around, the trees towering black against the sky. I only turned on the flashlight to find the right rock, and Hibou behind it, just where Owen said she would be.

. . .

On the way home, we drove with the windows open. The wind was warm on our faces and smelled like summer—blackberries and dry grass.

Marvelous. Causing wonder, admiration, or astonishment—surprising, extraordinary. Yes to all of those things. And I didn't mean just Alice, even though her birth was marvelous, in every single possible way. I meant *me*. It was marvelous that *I* had done it. *I* was astonished and surprised. It was extraordinary for anyone, but especially for me. Maeve Glover was not someone who could deliver a baby in a parking lot, but she'd done it anyway. I admired myself for it. I was astonished at what I could do. And I wondered what else I could do. Maybe I would always wear the heavy boots of anxiety and the prickly coat of worry, but maybe—even still—I could just be a person who belongs in the world, even if it's hard.

"I want to show you something." Salix pulled off at Porteau Cove and parked the van beside the beach. "Come on."

I got out and stared up at the starry sky, and the glassy, calm waters. "It's beautiful."

"That's not what I wanted to show you." She took my hand and led me to the water. "Wait here."

She picked up a stick and swished it through the water, and the most magical thing happened: a million filaments of light sparked up from under the surface.

"What is that?" I trailed my hand through the streaks of light.

"Bioluminescence." Salix knelt beside me. She explained about the phytoplankton lighting up as the water was agitated. "Scientists don't really know why they do it. They have some guesses. But mostly it's a mystery."

"It's amazing."

"I'll show you something even more amazing."

"I'm not sure I can handle any more amazement today."

"Trust me." She took my hand and pulled me up. She eased my shirt over my head and let it drop to the sand, and then she moved closer, her hands cupping my breasts. She circled my nipple with her tongue, and I thought I might spark into a million filaments of light too. I kissed her and put my hands under her shirt. Her skin was warm and soft, and I could hardly breathe as I tugged the shirt over her head. Without a word, the two of us stripped off the rest of our clothes until we were standing naked in the slim moonlight at the edge of the water.

"Ten things we can see from here," she said. "The trees and the water."

"The highway way up there," I said. "Headlights passing. The train tracks."

"That island. A boat. The pier." She smiled. "You."

I lifted her hand and kissed it. "You."

"That's ten. Come on." Salix led me in. The cold lapped my feet and I gasped, my body still hot from Salix's touch. "Look down." The water around our ankles glowed. "Watch." She took a few steps deeper, leaving a sparkling wake behind her, and then she dove in.

She was swimming in tendrils of light. I dove in too, and swam out to her, and it never occurred to me—not once—that I'd always been too afraid to swim in the ocean before. I swished my arms and kicked, churning eddies of light all around me. Salix came up behind me and grabbed me and held me, her body pressed against mine. And then I took her hand and we slipped under the water together. I opened my eyes and saw a sea of sparkling stars, and Salix, nearly glowing. The salt stung my eyes, but I kept them open. I didn't want to look away from all the glimmer against the black.

I wanted to lift the threads of light out of the cold, dark water. I wanted to lock them into a tiny bottle and hold it in the palm of my hand forever. But I couldn't, and so I held the day instead. This one day. This one shimmering day when everything changed, and everything stayed the same.

Acknowledgments

Thank you to Christianne's Lyceum, where my teenage beta readers critiqued an early draft with their usual thoroughness, sharp criticism, and brilliant observations. Those smarty-pants are Aliya Samad, Seemi Ghazi, Henry Richardson, Lynda Prince, Johanna Killas, Marie-France LeRoi, Jamie Fannin, Pippa Rowcliffe, Koshi Hayward, Wendy Sage-Hayward, Katianne Hayward, Brooklyn Higgs, and Darlene Higgs. A special thank-you to the leader of all smarty-pants (even if she only wears dresses), Christianne Hayward, who continues to bring up future authors and writers and thinkers at her Lyceum programs while at the same time supporting all the grown-up artists and writers and thinkers. She is the creative mother to a legion of us. Check out her magic at christiannehayward.com.

Thank you to all the hands that passed me and my manuscript gently around until it landed with Emily Brown at Foundry, who sold the rights in such a spectacular way that a rainbow danced above my head for weeks. Thank you to the delightful Jess Regel at Foundry for all that she does for me and for the larger world of bibliophiles and the writers who enable them. I am thrilled that you are my agent, Jess. Truly.

Thank you to Kelly Delaney at Knopf, who loved Maeve and her story so much that she wanted to bring it out into the world. And with a splash! Kelly is an ace editor who knows exactly what's going on in the literary universe. I trust her implicitly, which is such a relief.

Thank you to my children, Esmé and Hawk, who don't mind me wearing earplugs while they wrestle, or jump from the top bunk, or howl at each other while I write.

Never, ever lastly, an infinity of gratitude for my partner, Jack. Simply put, and because she doesn't like a long ramble, she holds the world together for me and keeps me on it.

NEW FROM
CARRIE MAC

Red Twilight

JUNE 26

I am cradling Pete's head in my lap, sitting by the tent flap, looking out. Wildfires are closing in from the west and the south, with smoke so thick it's like a bank of fog across the whole sky, turning the sun, which is just about to slip behind the mountain, into a blood-orange ball. In this strange twilight, everything looks like it's been washed in thin blue shadows. Even Pete. He looked so red in the daylight, because of the fever, but also because of the orange nylon of the tent he has not been out of since yesterday. The air in here smells like sour milk and the rankest body odor you can imagine. Not Pete's regular body odor, which I once described to him as skunk cabbage and cinnamon stew, with a dollop of sour cream past its best-by date on top. Call me weird, but I never minded it. But this is different. Not quite like how Gigi smelled with the lung cancer chewing her up from the inside out, but similar. Dangerously sour. Uniquely foul. Scary, if a smell can actually make you afraid.

I close my eyes and will something beautiful to take over, something to make this moment simple and quiet and dim and safe. Gigi, her hair in rollers, sitting on the back porch in her sateen dressing gown with the peacocks on it, painting her nails while I shuck a bowl of Dad's peas, sweet and plump. The sun just about setting, and Gigi telling me why she thinks Robert Redford is the man she should've married. My mom playing the piano inside. Pete climbing that slant of rock a few days ago, and me, with my bare feet on the hot dirt, looking up at him and the blue sky beyond. That was the last time we saw blue sky. He let go with his right hand and reached up. I wish I'd taken a picture of that one moment, when he looked like he was about to scoop up a handful of sky and drink it. I don't need more pictures of the two of us, like the ones we did take. I need pictures of him. Just Pete.

It's almost dark enough to use my headlamp, but I'm not going to waste the battery. Outside the flap, I watch the moon rising so slowly.

"It looks like a werewolf movie just before the transformation," I say. "What's that one Gigi loved?" I know what it is, but I hope he'll say it. Or say anything. He hasn't said a word for too many hours to think about. I give him what feels like the longest time to think of it and say it, but he doesn't. *"American Werewolf in London,"* I say. "That's the one."

He nods, a tiny smile on his lips.

"She was definitely not a movie snob," I say with a little

laugh. "Remember when she took us to see *Children of the Corn* that Halloween? How old were we? Way too young. That scene right at the beginning in Hanzer's Coffee Shop, when the kids poison the coffee and then murder all the adults? They stick that one guy's hand in the meat slicer? We were only eleven."

He shakes his head and barely lifts both hands, fingers splayed.

"Ten?" Right. Just a few months after his mom died. "Way too soon, right?"

He nods.

"She knew it," I say. "Or else she wouldn't have told us not to tell the dads."

I wish we were actually having a conversation about Gigi's obsession with Hollywood, and not here wondering if the fires are going to close in on us. Like this tent, which is closing in on us.

We bought this tent after almost a year of walking dogs, when we were fourteen. It weighs only as much as three blocks of butter, but we can sit up in it and play cards and drink cheap powdered hot chocolate we buy in bulk at Thrifty Mart. It's a very, very tight fit, especially considering that Pete grew three inches after we bought it. Gigi said that he grew three inches the *day* after we bought it, but the truth is that we bought it on Black Friday, and then we didn't use it un- til spring break, so I guess no one should've been surprised, considering Pete was as tall as his dad by the time we were thirteen. That's when Gigi put a mark above all the others on the doorway where my dad has been tracking our heights. She used permanent marker and wrote the date of his sixteenth birthday. Her prediction, she said. She was absolutely right.

Right now this tent feels like a coffin.

We have to get out.

"*American Werewolf in London* was a bad one to bring up," I say. "Sorry." Best friends backpacking, attacked by a pack of wolves. One is mauled to death, one becomes a werewolf.

"You be the werewolf," Pete murmurs.

"Pete!" I hold his cheeks in my hands. "Hi!"

He opens his eye just for a few seconds, and I really get to see him, because otherwise he doesn't look like himself. His forehead is slick with sweat, and his puffy cheeks are red and shiny with oil. I can't look at his nose, or lips, or ears, which are black at the tips and getting worse. Look at his necklace instead, Annie. An instant of panic sends my fingers to find the matching one around my neck. It's still there, thankfully. If I lose mine, or he loses his, things will only get worse. This is very hard to imagine. We need all the serendipity, magic, and luck we can muster. God too, if it's a believing sort of day. I touch his necklace with one hand and mine with the other.

I believe in the talismans that I keep in a bulging Altoids tin, so many tiny pieces of the planet that Pete and I have found. I believe that if Pete has them, everything might end up better than if he didn't have them. Not to say that I think they will fix this. I just know that they won't make it any worse. I shake out his filthy, sweat-soaked sleeping bag, which I should've laid out on a rock to air, and move aside mine too. I don't see the tin.

Pete lifts a hand to show me that he has it, bulging with luck and good fortune and all things wishes-come-true. There is so much good luck in there that I am absolutely certain something, something, *something* good is going to happen. A plane overhead. A fire crew within earshot of the whistle I sound as often as I think to. Enough rest and water and PowerGels that Pete gets strong enough to walk out of here, or I develop the superhuman strength that moms get when they have to lift a car off their child with their own bare hands. I need that strength, to carry Pete out of here on my own.

"Show me," Pete says as he hands me the tin.

I pull off the elastic band that keeps it from popping open because it's so full. That's how much good luck is in there.

Inside, on top, a small, clear, perfectly faceted crystal. I hold it up to the light. It seems impossible that it came out of the earth, and we found it just days ago, when nothing was wrong yet. When we were digging in the dirt like two little kids, putting our treasures into plastic beach buckets.

"Where did you get that?" he says.

"You know, Pete."

"Tell me, though." His words are thick and slow. "Each one. Story."

We've been through the tin twice.

The last time was only an hour ago, when the sun was still up but slanting toward the end of the day.

Pete's wearing his favorite shirt, soft and thin, dark blue with a silver unicorn leaping over a silver mountain, with a silver moon overhead. It is caked in vomit, though, and so wet with sweat that I could wring it out. His body is trying to fix this, and for days I had absolute faith that it would, but now I'm restless with dread. I can't leave him, and I can't stay. If I go, he'll be alone. If I stay, there will be no help. I have rocks spelling "SOS" by the creek, in the clearing. I was sure that one of the water bombers would've seen it by now. That was my Big Plan, and it hasn't worked. Neither did setting signal fires. A triangle of three, which means "help." But no surprise that one more little fire gets ignored when half the state is on fire.

Right now I'll take him outside. He can get some fresh air—smoky, yes, but better than the heady air in the tent. He can feel the breeze on his wet face, let his sweaty and impossibly swollen, red body feel the world outside this tent, even if it's burning to the ground out there. And maybe I can think just a little bit better.

"Let's go outside," I say. "Get some air. Do us both good."

He nods.

"I hate it in here," he whispers in a slur. "Like a coffin."

"Let's get you out, then." I close up the tin without the band and give it back to him. "Hold that for a sec."

He nods again, fingers tightening around it.

"I'm going to slide you," I say. "Fast or slow?"

"Fast."

"Good choice." I ease his head off my lap and onto the makeshift pillow of clothes folded into his hoodie. I shift him over so he's centered on the sleeping mat. He's lying on his thin quick-dry towel, and I am so grateful that we decided to bring those; otherwise, he'd be sticking to the foam because it's been too hot even to lie on the sleeping bag since late morning. He grunts a little, but I keep working. I clear the things away from the door of the tent. Our headlamps, the pot and pocket stove, the Uno cards we haven't touched for a couple of days.

"Outside will help so much, Pete. I saw a few bats last night. And an owl. You can really hear them in this valley. Maybe we'll even hear some wolves, which would be awesome, so long as they stay way the hell away from us. Maybe coyotes instead. Yeah, that'd be better. Just little scrawny coyotes yipping."

He grunts.

"Hang on," I say as I take hold of the foot of his sleeping bag. I shimmy him down to the vestibule as gently as I can. This is not fresh air at all, but it's better than being in the tent. I stand up, my muscles aching from having sat on the hard ground for so long, my legs so wobbly that I have to take an extra few seconds to get solid footing before I use my feet to clear a path through the pebbles and pinecones and sticks. Don't stop, Annie. This is *doing* something. I turn back to the tent and see that Pete is moving.

"Stay still, dumb-ass," I say. "Give me a sec. I'm going to pull you all the way out, but not over a bunch of rocks."

But then I realize that he's having a seizure. Not a huge one like you see in movies, but as if someone turned the dial down on one like that. Without thinking, I reach in and grab the foam mat and yank him out in one incredible pull. Three steps and he's clear of the tent. He is a foot taller and fifty pounds heavier than me, but he feels as light as a little kid. I grab his shoulder and far knee and pull him onto his side, like the home nurse showed me to do with Gigi when she started to have trouble swallowing but was still eating mashed everything.

"Stop it, Pete." I hold him from tipping right over, his entire body stiff and shaking, his legs kicking at nothing, his eyes wide open and staring at me without seeing me at all. "Stop it."

I should've been counting.

"Stop it, Pete! Stop it! Stop it! Stop it!"

How long has this been happening? What about when I wasn't looking? Is this it? Is he dying? Right now?

I lift my eyes up and whisper to the god that I don't believe in but wish I did.

"Please make him okay. Please, *please* make him better. Please tell me what to do."

When he is finally still, he doesn't say anything. He just breathes, shallow and fast. I squat beside him and watch him for a long time, waiting for another seizure. When my knees buckle, I lie down beside him, my head on my arm, the cool dirt and pebbles under me. He's better now. I can close my eyes for just a second, like an amen.

I am sure that I don't sleep, but it is dusk when I open my eyes, and so much cooler. I know I must've dozed off, my arms around him. Something is different on the horizon, along the ridge of low-slung mountains to the west, where the sun is just disappearing. It's like it's actually touching down on the forest, because there is a gossamer thread of rippling orange flames, the air above it giving up and melting into a watery wash of heat.

Pete is asleep. This is good.

The little tin full of good luck and good fortune and hope and beautiful things and tiny treasures lies open on the ground, the talismans scattered on the dirt.

I lean forward, about to let go of Pete to collect all the shiny bits of hope from the hot, dry forest floor, where they are lost under pine needles and debris. I squint, and realize that I can see only some of them in the hazy moonlight. If I want to go get them, I have to let go of Pete. I can't do that.

My talismans are still good luck, I tell myself. Even if they are scattered on the dirt in the wilderness. They are my good luck, and so I get to say that they can still be good luck if they're lost.

But I don't really believe that they are lucky anymore, because this has been the unluckiest time of all.

This might even be the way that we actually die, with no

one left behind to write the tragic event in the Notebook of Doom. When we get home, I will write ten pages about this. At least.

For now, I don't want Pete to wake and see how close the wildfire is, so I grab the mat this time and pull him back into the tent. That will be more comfortable.

He opens his eyes but quickly closes them again.

"Do you know what day it is, Pete?"

"Wednesday."

"Correct," I say. "What grade did I get in biology?"

"Trick question." He's speaking so quietly that I have to be nearly cheek to cheek to hear him. "You failed. Not just biology. The whole year."

"Who is the president?"

"Annie," Pete says. "Why are you asking this stuff?"

"You had a seizure. Aren't you supposed to ask questions like that?"

"A seizure?" Pete struggles to sit up. "That's crazy."

"Exactly." I help him take a drink from the pot of water.

"I feel a bit better now."

"Maybe it was your fever breaking."

"Maybe." He starts to roll onto his knees. "I'm going to go take a leak."

"No!" I grab his arm. "Just use this." I hand him the bag. "I'll go out. You're not strong enough yet."

I leave him inside and go out by myself. I stand right in front of the tent in case he tries to look out. He cannot see what I'm seeing. The flames are taller now, wicking along the tops of trees just across the valley. The moon is red. The smoke is thick and drifting our way.

This is a terrible place to be.

We have to get out of here.